Praise for *Forever Hold Your Peace*

"With plentiful laughs on one side of the aisle and long-standing, multi-generational drama on the other—this is one wedding you won't want to miss. RSVP YES."
**—Steven Rowley, bestselling
author of *The Guncle* and *The Celebrants***

"Full of surprises and bursting with love, *Forever Hold Your Peace* is a wildly fun mashup of romance and family drama with one resounding message: love conquers all."
—Taylor Hahn, author of *The Lifestyle*

"An unexpected delight, a love story two generations in the making with characters that you cheer for from the first page. [This is] the book that will restore your faith in the staying power of true love."
—Annabel Monaghan, author of *Nora Goes Off Script*

"Liz & Lisa are at the top of their game with *Forever Hold Your Peace*—A LOT of heart with just the right amount of snark! You're gonna love it!"
—Julie Slavinsky, Warwick's

"Brimming with sparkling wit and a lively cast of characters, *Forever Hold Your Peace* is at its heart a romance about a second-chance friendship and a once-in-a-lifetime love twenty-five years in the making."
**—Ashley Poston, *New York Times* bestselling
author of *The Dead Romantics***

"You'll want to shout I DO! to this layered and hilarious walk down the aisle."
**—Allison Winn Scotch, *New York Times* bestselling
author of *The Rewind***

"*Forever Hold Your Peace* is exactly what you want in a novel: a great love story, family drama and lots of humour and insight. It made me laugh, tear up and smile at the end. Add this to your TBR immediately!"
**—Catherine McKenzie, *USA Today* bestselling
author of *Forgotten* and *Hidden***

FOREVER HOLD YOUR PEACE

Also by Liz Fenton & Lisa Steinke

How to Save a Life

The Two Lila Bennetts

Girls' Night Out

The Good Widow

The Year We Turned Forty

The Status of All Things

Your Perfect Life

FOREVER HOLD YOUR PEACE

A Novel

LIZ FENTON AND LISA STEINKE

alcove
press

Copyright © 2023 by Liz Fenton and Lisa Steinke

Published in the United States by Alcove Press, an imprint of The Quick Brown Fox & Company LLC.

Alcove Press and its logo are trademarks of The Quick Brown Fox & Company LLC.

Library of Congress Catalog-in-Publication data available upon request.

ISBN (trade paperback): 978-1-63910-352-2
ISBN (ebook): 978-1-63910-353-9

Cover design by Heather VenHuizen

Printed in the United States.

www.alcovepress.com

Alcove Press
34 West 27th St., 10th Floor
New York, NY 10001

First Edition: July 2023

10 9 8 7 6 5 4 3 2 1

To our fellow authors: we're all in this together.

CHAPTER ONE

It was official, Olivia decided. The Amalfi Coast was the most romantic place in the world. Every Instagram story she'd watched before arriving hadn't been exaggerated. She now understood that the experience of being immersed in the beauty of the towns speckling the coastline of Southern Italy made you desperate to share. To try to convey that the tomatoes in the quiet fishing village of Praiano were more vibrant than anywhere else, their plump juices sweeter. That the red wine in the mountaintop town of Ravello was smoother. The locals in the coast's namesake town of Amalfi did smile wider. And here, in the picture-perfect cliffside city of Positano, love felt deeper. So deep that it became a part of your soul.

She never wanted to leave.

Olivia couldn't see Zach's hazel eyes behind his dark aviator sunglasses, but she was sure they were slightly narrowed as he focused on navigating the boat through the crowded Positano harbor. She hadn't known him long, but she'd already memorized so many of his expressions. The way his eyebrows dipped when he concentrated, how he chewed the inside of his cheek when he told her about his childhood, the teasing smile that played on his full lips when he was about to kiss her.

But he still surprised her with a new detail about himself every day. Like when they'd boarded the sleek sky-blue motorboat earlier and Zach announced with pride that *he* would be her captain for the day. The words had tumbled out quickly as he'd explained they were riding in a nineteen-foot pleasure craft, a Cayman 585 open boat with a Yamaha 40/70 engine. There was so much she didn't yet know about him. Those unknowns could fill the biggest tome in her mom's bookstore back home.

Olivia knew there was only so much to learn about a man in six weeks. That you could spend nearly all that time exploring his body and mind in one of the most romantic cities in the world and still not know everything. Olivia could draw a map to every freckle on his taut chest. She could trace the small birthmark on his shoulder. But she'd had no idea he had a boating license.

They were now past the harbor and he pushed the throttle, accelerating their speed. He drew Olivia to him with one hand, his other lightly gripping the steering wheel. She rested her cheek on his shoulder as the warm summer wind kicked up, and they headed out to sea. She liked that there was still so much to discover about Zach, that she was slowly turning his pages, absorbing who he was. There would be time to learn if he replaced the trash bag in the garbage can after taking it out.

At twenty-four, Olivia was in love for the first time. They could figure out the rest later.

Zach brought the boat to a stop. His forearms flexed as he expertly dropped anchor next to the Li Galli Islands between Positano and Capri. Olivia's breath still caught every time she stared at the vibrant blue-green hues of the Tyrrhenian Sea. She took in the rocky coastline of the largest island, a half-hidden castle-like villa peeking out from behind the lush trees. Olivia had searched it up—finding pictures of celebrities like LeBron James and Beyoncé and Jay-Z renting out the private compound. She imagined them sipping espresso as they watched the yachts glide by.

Olivia was so caught up in her thoughts she didn't hear Zach slide up beside her. He ran his hand over her stomach before pulling her in for a kiss. Olivia's heart turned upside down as she tasted the sea salt on his lips.

"What do you think of the view?" he asked.

"It's insane," Olivia said. "I can't believe I'm here." She paused, pulling his aviators down to look at him, her heart catching. "With you. Can we stay forever?"

Zach's eyes flickered, and Olivia worried she'd said too much, too soon. They'd discussed the future, that they'd intended to continue their relationship when they went back to the States, but hadn't said the word *forever*. Hadn't talked about marriage. But Olivia knew what she wanted—to never wake up without him by her side again.

Zach felt so perfect *for her* that she'd only told her younger sister, Chloe, about him. She hadn't wanted to jinx it. She'd called Chlo after the first week, excitedly trying to explain how getting to know Zach was like one of those paper fortune tellers they'd folded up and played as kids. They would write on each flap something positive or negative that could happen to them in the future. One of them would place their thumbs and index fingers inside the origami shape and ask the other for a number. They would count together and open the flap to reveal the answer: *a million dollars, bankrupt, beat up chevy or a corvette, four kids, two-story house,* or *single for life*. With Zach, no matter what flap was opened, it revealed something more special than the last. She'd marveled to Chloe that she didn't know how it was possible that this stranger could land in her orbit one day, and the next, she couldn't remember her life without him.

Chlo had giggled. "He must be huge."

Countless times, Olivia and Zach had lain in the tiny bed in her rented flat, their limbs intertwined and their skin slick with sweat from their body heat as they talked about what life together would be like back home. There was no air conditioning in her Positano apartment, but they didn't care. Both silently sacrificed coolness for closeness. She hoped they'd always want to be touching. That he'd never stop resting his hand on her forearm while they sat at their favorite café sharing a chocolate croissant and two Americanos. That he'd always grab her hand and guide her across the street—whether it be the narrow roads of Positano, where they had to dodge the mopeds flying by, or the wide tree-lined boulevards in Pasadena where he lived.

They'd said *I love you* for the first time within days of meeting while on a romantic hike. They'd mapped out the best route from Zach's house (which he owned!) in Pasadena to Olivia's studio apartment in West Hollywood. They'd debated which one of them would attempt to recreate the lemon linguine they'd noshed on at Da Vincenzo. Which of each other's friends they would love instantly, and which would take some time to warm to. But the discussions hovered inches above marriage, like a helicopter trying to find the best place to land.

"Did I say too much?" Olivia stammered, wanting to pull her words back inside her. She would wait as long as it took to be his wife. There was no rush. "I'm caught up in the moment . . . it's so beautiful here . . ." She trailed off as a large cabin cruiser of tourists blew past, forcing their boat to roll in its wake. Olivia grabbed the back of the passenger seat to steady both her body and her emotions.

When she turned back to face Zach, he was balancing on one knee. Or trying to. The boat had other ideas. He was clutching the edge of a small table with one hand, sweat trickling down his face as he held himself in place. In his other hand was a small box, nestling a simple silver ring with a small diamond. It was perfect. Olivia gasped.

"It wasn't too much," Zach said. "I don't ever want to spend another day without you, Olivia. Whether it's here or Los Angeles or even North Dakota, I don't care, as long as we're together."

"We'll have to reevaluate things if this relationship moves to Fargo. I don't do snow." Olivia laughed and pulled him up to face her and ran her shaking hand through his hair. "Ask me." She smiled.

"So assertive. One of the many things I love about you." Zach put his lips to her ear, his warm breath sending a lightning bolt to Olivia's toes, and whispered, "Olivia Abbott, will you marry me?"

"Of course," she whispered back, before bringing her lips to his. So this was what it felt like when someone's heart burst with joy? As an avid reader, she'd read descriptions of love in novels, but found them cliché. Heart pounding? Butterflies? She hadn't understood. Until now. Now she *was* every single love cliché. And she couldn't be happier about it.

"She said yes!" Zach yelled to a man and a woman in a small speedboat. When they looked confused, he repeated it in Italian. "*Lei ha detto si!*"

They cheered.

"How did you know how to say that?" Olivia asked. Zach's Italian was rudimentary at best. He basically charmed his way through most conversations. It was Olivia who did most of the talking to the locals, but she was still far from fluent.

"I looked it up and practiced," Zach said. "I wanted to be able to say it in every language so the whole world could know!"

Olivia laughed. "French?"

"*Elle a dit oui!*" he blurted in a horrible French accent.

"German?"

"*Sie sagte ja!*" he said, his syllables hard.

"You put a lot of thought into this," Olivia teased, tracing his abs beneath his white linen shirt. Speaking foreign languages was a major turn-on, but more than that, she was touched by the care he'd taken in preparation of this proposal. "I'm impressed."

"Then let me impress you some more," Zach said, pulling her into him and wrapping his arms around her. "*Ti amo.*"

"*Ti amo,*" Olivia echoed, and let herself melt into the moment. Let herself feel all the things those fictional characters in her novels had been feeling for years.

* * *

Two hours later, Olivia nervously entered the password on her phone. She remembered this feeling when she arrived at the Naples airport two months before. It seemed a lifetime ago when her Italian consisted of only *per favore* and *grazie*. When she'd needed to use the Google translator app to ask for help finding the bus to Positano. Had it only been eight weeks since she'd dragged her luggage up the steep stone stairs in search of her apartment? She'd prayed she was following the map correctly, that she hadn't ascended *one hundred and eleven* stairs only to learn she was lost. And yes, she had counted them.

The now familiar steps that no longer made her calves burn when she walked them were so narrow that Olivia couldn't extend her arms without hitting the ancient buildings on either side, and only a sliver of the June sunlight could squeeze its way through. When she emerged at the top, sticky with sweat and heavy from the weight of twenty-one hours without sleep, she'd been ready to call her mom and announce that she'd made a huge mistake. That she had been a fool not to learn Italian first. That she had been too out of shape to trek these stairs every day—they were much steeper and more treacherous than they looked on TikTok, by the way. Cursing under her breath, wishing she'd known the Italian word for *fuck*, she'd turned back in the direction from which she'd come and gasped.

The view. It had taken her breath away. The sea that hugged the rocky shoreline was a brilliant sapphire blue—the water so clear she could practically see the mackerel and sea bass that she knew swam below its surface. The yachts that bobbed in the bay seemed tiny, reminding her of the ones that she'd captained in her mom's claw-foot bathtub as a child. The picturesque houses that were inconceivably perched on the vertical cliffside were painted in vibrant shades of red, pink, and yellow. The gorgeous California coastline, where she'd built sandcastles as a toddler, lain out with her friends as a tween, and leaned against a lifeguard stand in her senior class photos, simply could not compete. She'd said later that it was the view that changed her life, because it convinced her to give Positano one more day.

And now, Olivia hoped that her mom's reaction to her news would pleasantly surprise her the way the view still did. But what she couldn't possibly know was her mom's response was the last thing she should be worried about.

* * *

June Abbott fumbled for her cell phone, knocking over a tumbler of water that sent her cat, Meowsers, darting from the room. She was disoriented, straddling sleep and consciousness, as she searched her overcrowded bedside table. She turned on the lamp and pushed aside a stack of half-read novels with her reading glasses perched precariously on top. She located the charging cord and followed it to her phone hanging off the side of the nightstand. She squinted at the screen. Why would Olivia be calling in the middle of the night?

June's heart started to pound as she imagined worst-case scenarios that were more likely to be the plots of her favorite thrillers than to happen in her real life. Her daughter had been kidnapped, and the call was about the ransom request for her safe return. Or Olivia was dangling from one of the many cliffs she perched next to while posing for Instagram. Or her firstborn was lost at sea—an innocent day trip to Capri gone awry. June frantically pressed all the wrong parts of her iPhone until she finally got it right and her daughter's face filled the screen.

"Hi!" Olivia said, her sea-glass-blue eyes shining, her blonde hair piled on top of her head in a messy bun. Her smile faded halfway when she noticed her mom's strained expression. "Everything's fine! I'm okay!"

June's exhale of relief was audible.

"I wasn't kidnapped by Italian pirates roaming the Tyrrhenian sea."

June rolled her eyes. "I wasn't thinking *that*." She put her hand over her chest, her heartbeat so rapid she might have just sprinted. Except she didn't sprint. Ever.

"Uh-huh. I got the hiking boots you sent. I'm sure they were a million dollars to ship!" Olivia twisted her mouth. "Based on the most recent series of scream emojis you left on my Insta, I'm guessing you want me to wear them so I don't slip off a cliff while I'm posing for photos?" Olivia smirked. "So subtle, Mom."

June shrugged. "Can't hurt."

"My high-tops are fine—they will save me." Olivia smiled.

"Will they?" June asked, remembering the image of Olivia leaning back on a rock with her chin tilted toward the sun, her eyes closed (closed!), the ocean appearing to be thousands of feet below.

Olivia sighed, and June knew what she was thinking, because she'd said it many times since she'd arrived in Italy. Why send your young adult daughter on vacation alone to a foreign country if all you were going to do was worry?

She had a point.

But still, the worry always seemed to win.

"So, if everything's okay, why are you calling in the middle of the night?" June asked, her alarm bells still ringing. It was three AM in California. Did good news ever come at three AM? "Miss me so much you can't sleep?" June hoped as she stared at herself in the little box on her screen. Her forehead wrinkles were like deep rivers running under her blonde hairline. She should cut bangs. And the bags under her own sea-glass-blue eyes were heavy and dark. She flipped off the lamp.

"Mom! I can barely see you now."

Reluctantly, June turned the light back on and vowed not to look at herself. But it was impossible. Her middle-of-the-night face was screaming that she needed Botox—maybe fillers? She'd told herself (and her daughters) that it was okay to age. But with every new line that showed up, she found herself warming to the idea of doing *something*. A little pop of poison between her eyebrows wouldn't hurt, right? she thought as she stared at Olivia, who could have been her twenty-three-year-old self's twin.

"I did miss you, yes, but also—" Olivia waved her left hand.

June squinted at her daughter's fingers moving back and forth. There was a diamond ring on the important one.

June's mouth fell open. She'd figured the call might be about something man related, but a fiancé? No, that couldn't be what this was. Olivia wasn't dating anyone. If she was, June would know. A week or so after Olivia arrived in Italy, once she'd picked up a few more Italian words and found the confidence to go out for a glass of wine alone, she'd had a fling with a local—a short but well-built waiter whose name escaped June now. Verenzio? Vindonio?

"Is that—"

A coy smile clung to Olivia's lips.

June kept her face still, but her stomach roiled. Maybe, just maybe, it was a gift Olivia had given herself.

"It is! I'm engaged!"

June couldn't find her voice and grabbed for the tumbler of water, remembering that it was on the floor. How was her daughter engaged? She didn't have a boyfriend.

"I know what you're thinking," Olivia said. "You didn't even know I was dating someone."

June moved her head up and down robotically. She wanted to dig into that. To ask why Olivia hadn't mentioned him. But she didn't trust herself to say it without sounding judgmental and, if she was being honest, hurt. She had naïvely believed Olivia told her everything. That they were *that* mother and daughter. She'd bragged about it to her book club while drinking sauvignon blanc!

Was Olivia pregnant? Is that why she hadn't mentioned him? No, she couldn't be. After Olivia told June about the one-night stand with the waiter, June had immediately shipped off a Costco-size package of condoms. Another not-so-subtle gesture.

Was this the part where Olivia revealed that the condom had broken, and her fiancé was the Italian waiter? That she and Vincenzo—that was his name—would raise the baby on the Amalfi Coast? June fought her rising panic as she imagined seeing her daughter and future grandchild once a year. She made her voice sound as neutral as possible. "I am a little surprised." June's throat constricted as she eyed the puddle of water on the floor that Meowsers was now licking.

"I know. I am too."

"Oh?"

"We'd discussed the future, but not marriage." Olivia looked at her ring. "I hoped he wanted all the same things I did. But I didn't think he'd ask this soon. But I'm so happy he did!"

June rolled the word *we'd* over in her mind. Her daughter was now one half of a *we*. Her stomach rolled again at the thought of Olivia sharing her life with someone else. She wanted her daughter to be happy. To find someone. But June had figured she'd have plenty of time to get used to the idea while Olivia narrowed down her choices to the right man. This felt sudden. And very unlike her daughter.

"We'd said *I love you*—pretty early on, in fact, I told him first!" Olivia giggled and watched her mom's face for a response.

June pushed a sound out of her throat that she hoped was in the ballpark of a laugh.

"He said he'd never wanted to spend another day without me. And I felt the same way. I've never felt like this before. I don't think I've been in love before now. I thought I had. Remember Jason?" she scoffed.

June half nodded as she struggled to conjure an image of Jason. It was years ago, and the relationship hadn't lasted long, but June remembered a head of thick black hair and that he had a tall, lanky frame.

"Now I know what love is supposed to feel like." Olivia grinned. "He just asked me—a couple of hours ago. On a boat! That he drove! I had no idea he could do that."

June bit her lip. *Boats are one of about a thousand things you probably don't know about him.*

"It was so romantic, Mom. Like right out of one of the romance novels you and I love."

June agreed. She and Olivia talked multiple times a week. Her daughter constantly updated her on her life. June wondered again why Olivia had left out the most important thing of all.

"Then he called out, 'She said yes!' To everyone we saw. In multiple languages. It was so cute." Olivia's eyes sparkled. "I can't wait for you to meet him."

June smiled brightly but felt dizzy. Her daughter's words had come at her fast, with shallow breaths in between, reminding June of when Olivia was a child. When the twangy music from the ice cream truck would ring through the neighborhood and an eight-year-old Olivia would fling open the front door, eyes wild, and say, in one long run-on statement, *MomtheicecreamtruckishereIneedyourwalletthurryfastbeforeImissit.*

"Mom?" Olivia said, looking intently at June.

June looked away, wishing they weren't on FaceTime so she could hide. Her feelings. Her face. All of it.

"I know it's a lot of information, but I'm happy," Olivia said. "Oh, and I didn't tell you the best part. He lives in Pasadena! Insane coincidence, right?"

June exhaled. Pasadena wasn't far from where June lived in Long Beach. Only a jaunt up the 710 freeway to the 110. June finally made her mouth work. "What are the odds of that?" What *were* the chances that two people who met in a tiny seaside village in Italy lived only thirty miles apart in California? One in a thousand? A million? Had they been fated to meet?

Olivia mimicked June's thought. "It's like we are meant to be."

June thought of her ex-husband, William—Olivia's dad. Their argument over Olivia's college graduation gift came crashing back. It had been June who'd pushed for Positano, who'd said that the cost she and William would incur would be worth it. That it would be good for Olivia to have an adventure. Their daughter had worked as a tutor through college, not because she had to pay for her tuition but because she wanted to build her savings. She'd made the dean's list every semester. She'd graduated early with honors, only to immediately throw herself into studying for the LSAT. She'd passed and been accepted to UCLA School of Law, where she was enrolled this fall.

June prayed that was still the plan.

June couldn't remember Olivia taking a real break in the last four years and had felt the Amalfi Coast would be the perfect reprieve for her daughter. But William had pushed back, countering that Olivia was practical, like him. She'd want money. She'd prefer the option of how to spend it—if she chose to spend it at all. Maybe she'd invest! He'd accused June of trying to live vicariously through Olivia. Because June had never taken the trip to Italy she'd always talked about. June had bitten back at that. But inside, she knew her ex-husband wasn't entirely wrong.

June had won the argument in the end—like she did most times with William. But she wondered now if she had prevailed. What would William say to June when he found out that their level-headed daughter was engaged to a man she'd known for five minutes? A man Olivia had met because June wouldn't relent about wanting Olivia to immerse herself in a different culture? To experience luxurious beaches! To marvel at the charming harbors! When June had been perusing guidebooks on Naples and the Amalfi Coast, she'd imagined the way the Mediterranean sun would feel against her own cheeks. But now she could see that her selfish motives might have led to this three AM FaceTime.

Of course William would blame her for this. She was already blaming herself.

And what if Olivia really was pregnant? June was *not* ready to be a grandmother!

Not that June could have asked at this moment. Or bring up Olivia's father. Olivia was too happy. Her smile was so wide, the rest of her face disappeared behind it. June recognized that ear-to-ear grin. When your happiness couldn't be contained. It exploded out of your eyes, your face, your walk. June had felt that way about a man once too. Not William. Someone before him.

"What's his name?" June asked.

"Zachary. Well, Zach. I call him Z most of the time."

Z.

"What's he like?" June asked, as her mind drifted. She wondered what had changed for Olivia. She'd viewed her oldest daughter as a staunch feminist who wore her ten-year life and career plan around like a medal of honor. A plan that Olivia had always been quick to remind June had zero room for marriage until *after* she was gainfully employed as a lawyer. Was Italy to blame? Had Olivia been hypnotized by the romantic Amalfi Coast? What had June recently read? That it was one of the top honeymoon destinations in the world?

"He's . . ." Olivia paused, a deep blush spread across her cheeks. "He's so great. He's kind. And smart. He's so well read that he makes me look like I hardly ever pick up a book. You'll love this—he's finished over half of the one hundred classics you should read before you die! Including, wait for it, *Moby-Dick*! I was like, my mom challenged me to read that, and after seventy-five pages of harpoons and whale blubber, I felt like my soul had been sucked out of me and I gave up. And you know what he said?"

June shook her head.

"But it's based on a true story!"

I said that to you too, a million times.

"You said that to me!" Olivia echoed June's thought.

"I did." *But did he make it through* Infinite Jest? June thought. Then tried to shake her internal dig away. As a bookstore owner, June should have been happy to hear this part about her future son-in-law. But she couldn't get there. Not quite yet.

Olivia pressed on, seemingly oblivious. "And he's funny—like witty funny. There's so much to love. You're going to adore him. And not only because he's so adorable!" Olivia giggled.

June twisted her lips into a smile. "Of course. Yes. When you get back, we'll—"

June stopped. A handsome man with dark hair that curled around the ends, a long nose, and green eyes sat down next to

Olivia. June hadn't thought she was going to meet him *right now*. She sat up straighter and pulled her duvet over her loose top.

"It's so nice to meet you. V has told me so much about you," he said. His incredibly white teeth made June squint.

V?

V and Z?

Will their future kids be named W, X and Y?

Zach—*Z*—was still talking. "As Olivia said, I'm a bibliophile. I can't wait to see your bookstore. Well, the inside, anyway; Olivia showed me the exterior online. I'm impressed you're an entrepreneur."

Oh, he's good. Using the word bibliophile.

Zach was talking with his hands, the leather bracelet wrapped around his wrist swinging as he spoke. "But you just met me, literally seconds ago, so maybe I should tell you a little bit more about myself before I crash your workplace?" He laughed awkwardly, and Olivia squeezed his bicep. He studied June's face, searching for what, she didn't know. Acceptance? Scrutiny?

June was doing her best to keep her face neutral, but William always told her she would make a terrible poker player.

"Thank you," June managed.

"I'm sure you're shocked. I'm a perfect stranger who's now going to be your son-in-law!" He looked at Olivia as if he still couldn't believe it was true.

That makes two of us, June thought.

"You must have questions. I know my parents will, for Olivia. Ask me anything!" He thumped his chest and flashed a smile, again revealing two rows of bone-white teeth. "I'm an open book—which I'm sure you appreciate." He laughed at his own pun.

Do you tip well? Do you want kids? Who did you vote for in the last election? June knew she couldn't ask these things. But had Olivia?

Olivia leaned against his shoulder. The two of them were sitting so close together that June wasn't sure where Olivia ended and Zach began.

"Mom?"

June knew that voice. Olivia was pleading with her to ask him something.

"Sorry, I'm taking it all in."

"I get it," Zach placated her.

But he didn't get it. There was no way he could *get* what June was feeling. June could barely comprehend it herself.

June forced her mind to stop spinning and focused. "I always love a good story of how couples met."

His entire face brightened. "I was taking pictures—I'm a photographer—and there she was—"

Olivia jumped in. "Like with an actual camera, Mom. Not an iPhone. He's been the one taking my Insta pics. The secret is out—he's the reason my feed is the bomb now."

June sighed quietly as she absorbed his career, feeling like that was the real bomb. Photographer. How were they going to afford to live in Southern California? Olivia still had three more years of school before she would be able to make a living.

As if Zach had read her mind, he added, "That's not what I do to pay the bills. I take pictures for fun. I'm in real estate, Mrs. Abbott."

"Mrs. Abbott," Olivia groaned. "That sounds so old-school. You can call her June, right, Mom?"

Or J?

June nodded again, because she didn't know what else to do. Was this how things worked now? Out with the old school, in with the new? You meet your daughter's fiancé on FaceTime while wearing a ratty Depeche Mode T-shirt and he calls you by your first name?

Thankfully, Zach didn't call her June when he continued. She wasn't ready for that. She wasn't ready for any of this. "I was reloading my film—there's this spot where I love to take pictures on Via Arienzo. You have an amazing vantage point of the beach, the port, and the west side of Positano. And I looked up, and there she was. The most beautiful woman I'd ever seen." He smiled at her. "They say it's impossible to meet someone without a dating app these days, but we've beaten the odds!"

"I deleted my profiles the first day I met him!" Olivia told June. "I had a feeling."

June had never been on a dating app, although Olivia had encouraged it many times. But June wasn't interested in dating. She liked her easy, predictable life that would only be disrupted by a man. But June had listened patiently as Olivia walked her through it. Tinder was for one-night stands. Hinge was for relationships. Olivia had shown June her profiles—giving her a tutorial on how they worked. June couldn't remember it all now, but it had involved a lot of swiping, liking, and matching. It seemed like a lot of work.

"Anyway, I walked up to her and said hi."

Olivia picked up the story. "He scared the shit out of me. I was looking at something on my phone and didn't see him. I dropped everything I was holding—the phone, my bag, my coffee. He was, like, a total stalker!"

"I wasn't *that* close," he interjected.

"I could see the sweat on your forehead!" she said, her eyes twinkling. "I was sure he was a creeper at first. I saw the camera and thought he'd been taking pictures of *me*. I asked him to show me—to prove he hadn't!"

"And then my charm and good looks won you over." He laughed.

"Whatever." She pushed him lightly.

"For what it's worth, you're way more beautiful than anything I photographed in the Amalfi Coast."

"Isn't he so sweet? And that's how he really talks!"

June felt like she was watching a little old couple being interviewed in *When Harry Met Sally*. She had to admit, it was cute. But it also felt like a dream. Her daughter couldn't be engaged to a man she's known for . . . ?

"When did you meet?" June asked casually.

Olivia and Zach shared a look.

Zach answered. "Six weeks ago."

"Almost seven," Olivia added, as if that would help.

June weighed her next words carefully. She realized that asking them if this was some terrible TikTok prank that Gen Zers were playing on their parents wouldn't go over well. She also didn't want to make the same mistake her mom did when she told her she was engaged the first time. June could still remember the heavy weight of her mom's disapproval as she drove from her childhood home back to her campus apartment. She didn't want to make Olivia feel like that. Ever. Plus, he'd read *Moby-Dick*. He couldn't be that bad. June struggled to find something to say, but she was coming up blank.

"Mom, you must be exhausted. We should let you go. I'll call you tomorrow, okay?" Olivia said, the smile that had lit up her face gone. June's heart hurt. She couldn't let her daughter hang up feeling badly.

She struggled to find something positive to say. "I'm happy for you both, sincerely. I'm a little surprised. That's all. It was nice to meet you, Zach," June said, and found that she meant it. She only wanted the best partner for Olivia, and if this amateur photographer/real estate agent was him, then she would work hard to embrace him. "Call me tomorrow," June added, hoping her daughter understood that's when she would feel comfortable saying more. And asking the complicated questions. Like, *Why did you keep this man a secret?*

Because in June's experience, secrets only led to disaster.

CHAPTER TWO

The next day, Olivia leaned against the railing on the narrow terrace of her studio apartment. It was perched above a delicatessen—the smell of freshly baked baguettes from the morning lingered in the air. Olivia released the breath she'd been clutching for dear life since she'd talked to her mom for the second time. When June called her back earlier, she'd had a lot of questions—many she hadn't felt comfortable asking in front of Zach. Olivia had done her best to explain why she'd agreed to marry a man she'd only known for a few weeks. After not spending any time with him in the "real world." But no matter what she said, it felt like her mom didn't get it. Didn't get *her*. June's skepticism had felt like a straw, sucking out every ounce of Olivia's excitement.

How did she put into words how her heart had opened in a way it never had before? That in the hundreds of hours they'd talked, she'd told him things she'd only shared with her sister Chloe, who was her best friend. That she fell more in love with him each evening that they spent lounging on the patios of restaurants clinging to the cliffsides while drinking tangy Aperol spritzes and devouring spaghetti alla Nerano and lemon risotto with ricotta—the colorful plates they were served on as beautiful as the dishes themselves. Night after night they ordered heaping scoops of pistachio gelato (their favorite flavor) and took long walks through the winding streets. Then they'd fall into one of their beds, their hands on fire as they touched every inch of each other's bodies.

They filled their days playing a game they called *Open the Retro Paper Guidebook Olivia's Mom Gave Her and Do Whatever It Says on That Page*. It was against the rules to Google anything. As they walked the gorgeous gardens of Villa Cimbrone in Ravello and devoured tiramisu while drinking carafes of house wine, Z told her about growing up as an only child and how he'd invented an imaginary friend that he hung out with for the better part of one summer. When they'd taken a ferry to Ischia and swam in Sorgeto, one of its many hot springs, Olivia giggled as Zach willingly smeared green age-defying mud all over his body. Olivia had confessed that she and her sister had secretly schemed for her parents to get back together after their split, Chloe going so far as to try to fake a ruptured appendix. It felt cathartic to laugh while explaining how they'd Googled the symptoms, not thinking through the fact that their father, an anesthesiologist, would see right through the ruse.

When they'd hiked the Path of the Gods, a five-mile clifftop trail with bird's-eye views of the Amalfi coastline so stunning that the pictures Zach took couldn't capture its essence, Z had confided that photography was his true passion. It was one of the reasons he'd chosen to travel to Italy—so many beautiful and inspiring subjects! He'd gone into real estate because he hadn't wanted to let his dad down. Since Zach was a boy, his father had told him they'd be business partners when Zach grew up. One of Zach's first words had been *commission* (though it came out more like *mish-un*).

Zach had confessed that his dad meant well—he was never forceful or demanding in his dream that they one day work together—but Zach also couldn't remember a moment when he'd been given a choice in the matter. He'd often walk into his dad's office and study the endless real estate awards he'd won, displayed on every wall and shelf. Zach would feel a pit in his stomach, wondering if he could ever find the same success. Or if he wanted to.

Later, after Zach had his license, his fear of disappointing his father would make him physically sick and he'd often throw up before their open houses. Once his dad overheard him and knocked on the bathroom door of one of the estates they were selling, asking if he was okay. Zach thought, *I could tell him right now that this isn't my passion, that I want to find a way to make photography a career,* but he lied and said it was food poisoning instead. Olivia felt for Zach. She could relate because it had been her father's idea for her to go into law, but in her case, she was also passionate about it. She hoped Zach would one day find his voice and follow his own dreams.

Olivia didn't know if Zach put his dirty clothes in the hamper or if he called his grandparents on their birthdays (two of her mom's questions), but she knew he was kind to the staff at every restaurant, that he had different smiles depending on what was amusing him, and that he didn't talk in complete sentences before his first cup of coffee in the morning. She couldn't explain how her heart had melted when she met the calico named Bart that Zach had befriended. The cat could be found on the stone wall outside his owner's shoe shop. Zach would give him pieces of prosciutto in exchange for a few scratches behind the ear.

Zach opened the door.

"Yeah, man, I can't wait for you to hang out with her back home."

Zach was talking to Logan, his best friend from high school. He flipped the phone around. "Say hi to my future wife!"

"Hi, Olivia! Congratulations. I can't believe Zach's going to be a married man!" Logan said, his eyes widening.

"You know what they say. It's like a domino effect. You could be next," Zach said.

"No way, man, I'm going to be a bachelor for life!"

Olivia laughed.

Zach talked about Logan so much that Olivia felt like she already knew him. They'd also FaceTimed after a few drinks last week—Olivia, a little buzzed on prosecco, had quizzed Logan about what high school with Zach had been like. There had been a lot of laughs as Logan recounted the story of Zach jumping off the Santa Monica bridge naked on dare night and hinted there might be video evidence. It had only been noon back home, and Olivia respected the way Logan had calmly put in his AirPods so that his entire office didn't have to listen to their antics but kept talking to them for another thirty minutes in hushed tones. They'd called Chloe right after, Olivia wanting to share her best friend too.

She thought of her conversation with her mom again and felt a pit in her stomach. Logan was cheering them on. Chloe was excited. Why couldn't her mom be happy for her too? Trust her that she knew what she was doing?

Zach glanced at Olivia and twisted his mouth. He could tell she was upset. "Dude, let me call you back," he said, ending the call. "Hey," he said gently and wrapped his arms around her. She rested her head against his chest and her body curved into his, like they were two connected pieces in a puzzle. "So how bad was it? Scale of one to ten?"

Olivia looked up at him and traced her finger over the stubble on his jawbone as her mom's questions swirled inside her.

"Twelve," she sighed.

Zach sat down and pulled her onto his lap. "If it helps, Logan is excited. He's already planning the bachelor party. I'm told it will be in Vegas."

Olivia offered a thin smile.

"And don't forget how excited Chloe is," Zach added. When they'd called Chloe to tell her, she'd screamed in delight from her room in the house she shared with their mom. Had June heard?

"I want my mom to be too," Olivia said quietly.

"Why don't you think she is? What did she say?"

"Well, we didn't discuss wedding venues, if that tells you anything." She took a breath. "It was more like, where will you live? Does he have medical insurance? What's his religion?"

"Religion. Wow. She wasn't messing around."

"That's nothing. You want to know the best one?"

"Have I ever been convicted of a crime?"

"No!" She jabbed him with her elbow. "But you haven't, right?" Olivia snorted but also held a breath. She couldn't imagine it—he was so gentle—but what if he hadn't always been this way? Or could there be a trigger in the real world that made him different? Her mom had instilled enough doubt through her pointed questions and thinly veiled jokes—like how could Olivia be sure Zach was *the one* when she had known him less time than it took to complete one of those beach-body-ready workout programs?

"Would it change how you feel about me? If I had?" Zach waited a beat. "Because I wasn't sure how to tell you this, but I did some hard time for murder a few years back, but I'm innocent, I swear! I was framed!" He grinned.

Olivia elbowed him again. "Would you stop?" She blew out a breath. "My favorite one was—am I pregnant?"

"Brutal," he said. "Wait. You're not, right?"

Olivia gave him a sideways look. "Come on."

She didn't tell him the hardest-hitting question of all. The one that had made her mom's voice crack when she'd asked it. The one that made Olivia's heart ache. *Why didn't you tell me about him?*

She didn't know how to answer. She typically told her mom everything. She always had. Her mom had shipped her condoms, so clearly there were no topics that were off-limits. Maybe deep down she hadn't been ready to share him because she knew what she'd have to face from her mom once she did. The judgment. The questions. The skepticism. Not that she blamed her mom for feeling these things. When her parents gave her the Italy trip as a graduation present, they'd probably been thinking she'd bring home lemon-scented candles and soft leather handbags.

Not a fiancé.

That was the joke Chlo made earlier. Olivia smiled at the memory.

Zach interrupted her thoughts. "I don't blame her for the pregnancy question. She's trying to make sense of this. And she's worried about you. I am a convicted murderer and all." He smiled softly.

Olivia glanced at her ring, still shocked by the sight of it. She'd never thought she'd be engaged this young. Her plan had been to wait—in fact, she'd reiterated that to her parents last fall when she found out she'd been accepted at UCLA. She intended to pass the bar and get a job as a junior associate *and then* think about getting serious with someone.

But Zach had changed all that. How many nights had they sat out here, staring at the starry sky? Zach taking her hand in his, their fingers tracing yet another constellation, his love of the solar system never getting old.

"What about your dad? Have you told him yet?" Zach asked gently.

"I'm going to have Chloe do it."

Zach arched an eyebrow. "Do you think that's a good idea?"

Olivia sighed. "Maybe not, but I don't want to have another conversation like the one I had. My mom is the *easy* one."

"Trust your gut," Zach said simply. "Do you think your dad will be pissed that I didn't ask for your hand?"

"I think we've bucked every tradition on this engagement. It will be better this way. He can have some space to process it all. He'll be okay as long as I'm happy. And start law school."

"Of course you're going to law school! I only asked you to marry me so I could have a lawyer in the family," Zach deadpanned.

Olivia punched Zach playfully. "If you ever leave me, I'll take everything. Don't forget that."

Zach leaned down to kiss her. "If I was ever so stupid as to leave you, I'd deserve it. So Chloe's okay with telling him?"

Olivia laughed. "She can't wait. Chloe loves the drama." She checked the time. "She's going to call him today. I'll know more later."

Zach crossed his fingers dramatically.

"Did Logan agree with you that you should wait to tell your mom and dad until we get back?" Olivia asked. She had initially been surprised that Zach wanted to wait. He had practically told everyone in Positano at this point. Tommaso, the man who owned the bakery below her apartment; Donna, the woman who worked at their favorite gelato place; and more strangers on the street than she could count. He'd argued that telling his parents the news in person was the best way. That his mom was well meaning but could be a little *high-strung* and *slightly overbearing*. And that his dad was laid-back and chronically upbeat, but would immediately want to discuss what it meant for the real estate business they ran together. After her mom's reaction, Olivia now understood that Zach was being smart. That no matter how easygoing the parent, dropping a bomb like this produced shrapnel.

"He did agree. And don't worry. I know when I meet your dad and mom in person, they'll both fall in love with me hard and fast. Like you did," he teased, then brushed a strand of hair away from her eye. "And you're sure you're okay waiting to post on your socials?"

After the proposal, when Zach and Olivia started talking about who they'd call first, Zach had asked her if she could wait, not wanting his mom to find out that way. "My mom follows my accounts like a hawk," he'd said and run his finger along the sensitive part of her arm, tickling her.

"She's on more than Insta and Facebook?" Olivia asked, thinking those were the only two platforms most parents were on, if any. Her mom had zero social media. Olivia had to screenshot her Insta posts to share them with her.

"She has them all!"

"Even Snapchat?"

"Yep."

"Huh."

"My mom says she's on all of it because of her job, but I think it's to stalk me." Zach laughed, but Olivia wasn't sure he was joking. His mom sounded like a lot. She hoped she wasn't.

"Speaking of hard and fast . . ." Zach's lips brushed against her ear now. "We could skip dinner and stay in."

"We could." She kissed him, then pulled back. "But we'd miss the pizza. That mozzarella. Those fresh tomatoes. The basil . . ."

"Are you choosing pizza over *me*?" he said in an Italian accent.

"No, of course not. Well maybe a little . . ." Olivia laughed. "But I promise you some action after dinner. You'll be my dessert," she giggled, thankful they'd moved off the topic of moms and dads and quick engagements.

"That was so cheugy. That sounds like a line from one of your romance novels," he teased.

"First of all, you are cheugy for even saying *cheugy*, which is so out now. And number two, those authors are way better at sexy dialogue than I am. Obvs."

As they walked out the door into the warm night and headed down the brick-paved street toward the restaurant, Zach grabbed Olivia's hand, careful to dodge the stream of fast-moving cars that could barely fit on the narrow road. She tilted her chin toward the sky, letting the stars dazzle her once more. It was in this moment, as Zach kissed her forehead and pointed to a cluster of stars he called Capricornus, that she fell in love with him all over again.

* * *

Nine time zones over, June brewed a pot of the overpriced organic shade-grown coffee that promised to reduce the bloat she'd felt since entering her late forties. She wanted to blame the chemical-laced beans she'd drunk for years for the unyielding bulge in her gut but had a feeling it was more complicated than that. She was unwilling to give up the glass or two of pinot grigio she sipped each night as she listened to waves hit the beach a few blocks away, so she held tight to the belief that the coffee company and their beans sourced from a shady mountain in Colombia would eventually solve her gastrointestinal issue.

June finished pouring the dark liquid into two Yetis and settled into the black wicker love seat on her front porch with her friend Fiona, who had been waiting patiently for the engagement scoop. June had bought the outdoor sofa at the boutique down the street from the small bookstore All Booked Up that she owned on Second Street, the touristy enclave of Long Beach. It burst with lively open-air restaurants, colorful candy shops, and dive bars that satisfied both the families and university students who lived side by side in the adjacent neighborhood. Belmont Shore held many juxtapositions—it was quaint but also modern. It was both quiet and loud. Small yet big. And in these contrasts, June had married and divorced and raised her two daughters. It was, for better or worse, her forever home.

Fiona took a sip and smiled. "You always have the good stuff. Now," she said, leaning in. "Tell me everything."

June played back her second conversation with Olivia as Fiona listened, interjecting with a few thoughtful questions but mostly letting June talk. She'd met Fiona years ago when she'd first opened her bookstore. Fiona had strode in with golden hair that reminded June of a palomino. Fiona ended up spearheading All Booked Up's first official book club, and their shared love for losing themselves in stories had made them fast friends. The first time June walked into Fiona's living room and saw a dog-eared copy of *The Devil Wears Prada* on the coffee table, she knew this was a woman she could connect with. They'd bonded over their shock at the *Gone Girl* twist and celebrated the ensuing popularity of the unreliable narrator. They'd secretly confided that they'd love to have a few drinks with Joe from *You*, even though he was a serial killer. June could always count on Fiona thinking the book was better than the movie. In short, Fiona was the first real friend she'd made in a long time. So of course she was her first call after Olivia's bombshell.

"I came on strong," June admitted.

"Like your coffee," Fiona quipped.

June cringed. "Stronger! I asked a lot of questions . . . and *maybe* made some passive-aggressive remarks disguised as jokes?"

Fiona considered this. "Interesting. You hate to make people uncomfortable. Especially the girls. Do you think it's because of how your mom reacted to your first engagement?"

Leave it to Fiona to hit the nail right on the head. She owned the adorable flower shop three doors down from the bookstore, but June had always thought she'd make a great therapist.

"Maybe," June said.

"You are not your mother, June. But be careful. The more you push back, the more you'll push her away."

June knew she was right. She had tried to be objective, to separate her past from Olivia's present. To shake off thoughts of her own mother, Eileen, and her reaction to June's first engagement. But it had proved nearly impossible. With every word June spoke to Olivia, her mother's voice became more pronounced in hers.

Chloe poked her head out the front door. "Hey, Fi! I put aside the new Blake Crouch for you."

"That's so sweet, thank you. I'm excited to read it."

At twenty-one years old, Chloe was taking classes part-time at Long Beach State and working at the bookstore. June's ex-husband, William, had been prodding June to force Chloe to produce a five-year plan, but June secretly enjoyed having her youngest daughter living and working with her.

"So, your sister is engaged!" Fiona said, glancing sideways at June.

Chloe clapped, her blue eyes bursting with excitement, her sandy-brown ponytail swinging. "It's so romantic!"

"It is romantic," June echoed. And she meant it. She hadn't forgotten how in love she'd been when she got engaged the first time. The intoxication of having an unwritten but exciting future.

Chloe continued, "Where do you think they'll get married? I hope it's on the beach. Or maybe Las Vegas? Or will they return to the scene of the crime, so to speak?"

"I think they have plenty of time to figure it out." June laughed softly.

"I'm pretty sure Olivia wants to start planning right away. Get married sooner than later," Chloe said.

"What?" June asked. Fiona put her hand on June's arm so she wouldn't say more.

"Did Olivia tell you she wants a quick engagement?" June asked. She'd expected it would be at least a year before they got married. Give them some time to get to know each other. Give June some time to get used to the idea. "She didn't mention that to me."

Chloe delivered her signature smirk to June. "She was a little busy dealing with your cross-examination. Where did you get some of those insane questions? Overbearing parents dot com? 'Do your religious beliefs line up'? Really? We don't go to church. And I can't believe you asked if she was pregnant. Doesn't that violate some law?"

June exhaled and looked at Fiona, who was grinning. Not a mother herself, Fiona always told June how much she loved watching her with her daughters—especially when they were sparring. "What? Am I going to be canceled now?" June had been worried that she'd come on too strong with Olivia, and now she had confirmation.

"No. But I think you pissed her off," Chloe said.

June winced. This was bad. When the girls said that, it meant they'd had it with June or William. Why hadn't she left the bad-cop role to their father like she usually did? "Is she okay? Should I call her back?"

"Chill. She's fine. She's in love. Even *you* can't ruin that," Chloe said sharply.

"Chloe!" Fiona shot her a look. "Tell your mom you're only teasing."

"Mom, I'm messing with you," Chloe said obediently. "But seriously, relax, okay?"

Of her two daughters, Chloe was the one with the harsher tongue, often causing arguments when her tone or intent was misunderstood. She was also the far more rebellious of the two—Olivia had been the more cautious child. Had anyone asked June, she'd have bet her life savings that it would be Chloe, not Olivia, who threw a wrench into the spokes of her carefully planned future.

"I'll try not to ruin everything," June replied evenly.

Chloe ignored her mom's comment, leaving June to wonder what else Olivia had said. "So, Olivia low-key needs a favor from us. To tell Dad. Hold on while I get him on FaceTime."

Fiona stood up quickly. "I think that's my cue to grab another cup of coffee," she said before disappearing inside the house. Chloe plopped down next to June.

June shook her head. This favor was anything but *low-key*. "What? No way. She should tell him herself."

"To be fair, Mom, she's a little scared now after your reaction."

June was momentarily stung. But she couldn't argue. She had only her stupid list of premarital counseling questions to blame for this.

Her ex-husband's face appeared on Chloe's screen. June moved her lips into the shape of a smile and tucked a piece of her blonde hair behind her ear.

"What's up?" William asked, his voice brisk but warm. "Everything okay? You haven't FaceTimed me with your mom since you backed your car into that skate ramp." A smile ran around his lips as he spoke. William loved to give his youngest a hard time. He and Olivia often butted heads because they were so much alike, but he and Chloe always had an easy rhythm between them.

Chloe shrugged. "How long until you stop bringing that up? It was dusk. They shouldn't have left it in the middle of the road."

"So you've said," William retorted as he ran his hand through his thick sandy hair. June spotted the twinkle in his gray eyes.

"Anyway," Chloe said, drawing out the word dramatically. "We have some major tea on Olivia."

William's eyes narrowed. "Tea? Olivia drinks coffee. Or should I say *espresso*, now that she's living the Italian life."

Chloe laughed. "Dad! It means—"

34

"I'm kidding. I know what it means. The surgical interns told me. So, spill that tea!" William said, a playful look crossing his face. Proud of himself that he knew his daughter's lingo.

June cringed, knowing William wouldn't be feeling playful after hearing the news. She worried his feelings would be hurt. Not that he was sensitive, but it was his firstborn daughter getting married. It was hard enough that Olivia had kept Zach a secret from June; June would have curled into a permanent fetal position if Olivia hadn't told her about the engagement directly. She needed to say something before Chloe did. "It's good news!" June let that sentiment roll off her tongue, trying it on. *Was* it good news? It could be. But it could also lead to disaster, like June's first engagement that destroyed not one but two relationships. Three if she counted the one with her mom, which had never quite recovered.

June rubbed her bare ring finger, remembering her mom's biting words when she showed off her gold band: "Where's the diamond?" Her mother had grabbed June's hand and twisted the ring, as if the gem would suddenly appear.

June swallowed hard so she wouldn't cry. "It's all he could afford!" she hissed. June had fought to cling to her happiness, but her mom's scrutiny was like a worm on a mission, finding its crevice, working its way into June's mind, becoming all she could think about.

"Olivia is engaged!" Chloe chirped, pulling June from her thoughts.

June saw a flicker of confusion cross her ex-husband's face. He made eye contact with June, and she gave him a reassuring smile—one that she hoped conveyed, *We will get through this together.* They'd been less-than-stellar spouses but made great exes. Go figure.

June studied William's passive expression as Chloe excitedly narrated the romantic proposal and marveled at how William could sit there without interjecting one *What?* or *How?* or *It's too soon!* But he'd always been that way—able to control his emotions to the point that it sometimes drove June mad. "React!" she would yell in the middle of almost every argument. His lack of emotional response made June feel like she was fighting with herself. And maybe she was. But she'd learned to read his eyes, the tilt of his head, the clenching of his jaw. And it might have been a decade since their divorce, but she still knew this man. He was concerned. And he would be sure to tell Olivia all about it when she did get brave enough to face him.

William looked at June. "What do you think of all this?"

June took a breath. "She seems very happy."

"You know that's not what I'm asking."

"I think she's an adult, and we have to let her make her own choices, good or bad." June thought of her own mother again. This was her chance to fulfill the promise she had made to her younger self about her future children. She would protect her kids, but she wouldn't prevent them from being happy. She wouldn't interrogate every choice they made. Or ruin the excitement behind their new adventures. She'd be happy for them, trust them. Even if their decisions didn't make sense to her. If only she'd realized how complicated that might be. It had been an easy vow to make after a heated argument with her mother when she was only twenty-three.

"This isn't about graduation," June had asserted when her mom insisted she'd be throwing her degree away. "Or the type of ring he gave me. It could be three carats and it wouldn't make a difference. You hate him. You always have."

June's mom's expression softened. "I don't hate him."

June huffed. "Why can't you support me—for once?" Her eyes filled with tears, and she looked away before her mom could see.

Her mom clasped the strand of pearls around her neck as if they were a life raft. "Look around!" She waved her pencil-thin arm. "Even after your dad died, I gave you everything—kept this roof over your head." She made a face. "I've given it all to you." She stopped to take another long, exasperated breath. "But I can't give you this. One day, when you have your own children, you'll understand." Her voice was shaking. "You'll want to protect them."

"Hold on," William said, and June refocused on the here and now. He pulled his phone back, and his screen went black for a few seconds. "I'm sorry. There's an emergency C-section coming into the OR, and I need to get downstairs to administer the spinal block. Continue this discussion later?"

June wasn't sure which one of them he was referring to, but she answered anyway. They needed to talk about this—privately. "Yes. Call me later."

His square disappeared without a good-bye, which didn't faze Chloe or June. When William was at the hospital, it was hard to compete with the patients he was trusted to anesthetize. June had eventually given up trying.

"He seemed to take that well," Chloe said. June murmured a noncommittal response. She knew her ex-husband. He would have a lot to say about this when they talked one-on-one.

June changed the subject. "What does Grandma think about Olivia getting married? Have you spoken to her? Olivia said she texted her and hasn't heard back." Eileen was surprisingly savvy with technology. June worried her mother's nonresponse could mean only one thing.

"You want me to feel her out about it, don't you? See if she approves?" Chloe frowned. "Why don't you want to call her yourself? She's definitely not ghosting her. She probably hasn't responded yet because of the time change. It's still early."

"Regardless. It's better if you call. It's complicated," June said.

"Isn't that interesting? A child who doesn't want to face a parent." Chloe raised her eyebrows.

"Touché," June said, picking at a loose thread in the couch's cushion. "So, will you?" What June couldn't say to Chloe was that Olivia's announcement would be the catalyst for a conversation she and her mother were careful to avoid.

"I got you. But Grandma will be happy for Olivia."

June felt a pang. She needed to do a better job of staying in touch with her mom. She told herself she didn't call more because she was busy running the bookstore, but the truth was she avoided picking up the phone because every conversation they did have seemed off a beat, like they were listening to two different versions of the same song. They'd fallen out of sync the night June stormed from her house over two decades before and had never found their rhythm again. "I hope you're right," June said, before signing off to swim in the sea of regrets from that night.

CHAPTER THREE

Zach turned off Orange Grove Boulevard and on to Waverly Drive and tugged at the collar of his pale-blue shirt. It felt like it was cutting into his larynx, making it hard to breathe. He undid the top button and drew a deep, harsh breath, as if he'd reached the surface after being underwater. He hadn't told Olivia how nervous he was to introduce her to his mom. Correction: he hadn't mentioned he was nervous at all. Because that would mean he'd have to explain his relationship with his mother. That he had a hard time telling her no—almost always deciding the battle wasn't big enough. That she was tough to please, never thinking any woman he'd dated was right for him. That she liked to spend *a lot* of time with Zach. He was her only child and she'd never remarried, so she leaned on him a lot. He loved her, but he was feeling the pull to separate from her. And he knew that pull was Olivia.

Logan had told Zach he could tell Olivia was different from the others, that she'd understand. Zach wanted to believe he was right. But every day since they'd returned to the States a week ago, he'd told himself it would be the one when he'd tell Olivia everything. But as soon as he got up the nerve, he would remember past girlfriends who had accused him of being a mamma's boy when they'd seen how much his mom's opinion mattered to him. Especially her opinions about *them*. They'd put him in the middle—forced him to make a choice. They'd never won that fight. But Logan was right; they also hadn't been Olivia. Zach would go to bat for her if it came to it. But he prayed that it wouldn't. That his mom would see that Olivia was different from the others. And that Olivia, who was also close with her mom, would understand the tight bond he had with his.

He took another deep breath as he thought of something else he hadn't told Olivia. Something he probably never could. Not even Logan knew.

"Are you okay?" Olivia asked. "You're breathing pretty hard over there."

Zach met Olivia's bright-blue eyes and felt like she could see inside of him. He wanted to tell her everything, but he couldn't. Now wasn't the right time—not that there ever would be a right time.

"I'm fine," he lied.

"Okay," she said. He could tell she didn't believe him, but he was thankful she let it go.

"Here we are," he said as he pulled the car to a stop in front of his mom's house.

"Wow, this house is sick. Now I'm really nervous," Olivia said as she stepped out of the car. She tugged at the hem of her floral dress—one he'd never seen before. And since they'd returned from Italy, all of the clothes she'd brought with her had been hanging in his closet. The dress was nice, but it didn't look like *her*. This morning she'd kept changing her outfit, she and Chloe on FaceTime as she modeled the different ensembles—finally settling on the one Olivia had once worn to a sorority tea. They had called it a "mom pleaser." Zach hated that he was relieved she'd worn the dress. That his mom would be pleased.

Zach had changed his flight home from Positano to come back with Olivia. The astronomical change fee had been worth every penny. When they landed at LAX, Logan picked them up in his truck. It made Zach smile to watch Olivia stand on her tiptoes and Logan bend down so they could hug. He hadn't told her how tall Logan was—nearly six foot seven. He liked that he knew Logan would be another person who'd look out for Olivia, that she could call him at any hour if she needed something and he would be there. They'd swung by Olivia's place to grab some of her things and went on to Zach's, where they'd slept ever since. She'd already called her landlord and given notice. They'd gone to her place over the weekend and packed the rest of her items.

Zach had gotten to see a whole new side of his future wife (the words still sounded odd to say) as they packed her apartment. Her bookshelves were overflowing with tomes. He found a worn copy of *Summer Sisters* by Judy Blume and noticed she'd annotated it. They filled two boxes with journals alone. Zach read a few lines from a poem written in a diary labeled *Seventh Grade*, which described rivers of tears streaming down her face because Jake Boranski had broken her heart. "I will hunt him down for hurting you!" Zach teased. Olivia snatched the journal away and swatted him playfully, ordering him to get back to work.

Her dresser was covered in framed pictures of her family—many of them her with her mom and her sister. But there were also photos of her grandmother, aunts, uncles, and pets she'd had over the years. He picked up a photo of Olivia and her dad. She couldn't have been more than twelve, her teeth wrapped in braces as she grinned proudly, holding an award that Olivia explained was for a debate contest she'd won. Her dad was smiling at her, not the camera. Zach was nervous to meet the man he knew was a fierce protector of his daughter but also excited to get to know him, because every family member he met would help him learn more about what made Olivia *Olivia*.

He loved seeing her in his house. *Their* house. He'd tried to put it into words, telling her she was like the perfect soft leather couch he'd never known he needed.

"I'm a couch? What the fuck?" she'd said, wrinkling her button nose.

"That came out wrong," he said.

"Ya think?" she'd laughed.

He tried again, telling her how he smiled when he saw her car keys in the dish on the kitchen counter, her pink electric toothbrush resting on his sink, her shampoo in the shower. But mostly he loved that she was there, fitting not just into his house but into his world like she was always supposed to be there.

They'd had Logan over for dinner almost immediately, Zach attempting to recreate their favorite pasta dish but failing miserably, Logan making a joke that he'd had better linguini at the Olive Garden. They'd all laughed as they drank Chianti and pretended it tasted as good as the bottles they'd had in Italy, trading stories until nearly two AM, Logan crashing in the guest room, the three of them picking up right where they left off the next morning over breakfast.

Now Olivia grabbed the box that held the gorgeous blue-and-yellow porcelain serving platter they'd picked out for his mom in Ravello. Pasqual, the owner of the shop, had promised it was something all moms would love. Zach hoped he was right. He needed a win today.

Zach took Olivia's hand and found it damp with sweat. He bent down to kiss the top of her head. "She's going to love you," he predicted. As he guided Olivia up the path to the front door, his heartbeat was in his throat. He put his hand on his neck, his Adam's apple pulsing. This engagement was the first decision he hadn't asked his mom's opinion about—*before he made it*—and it wasn't lost on him that it was the most important. A part of Zach knew it was because he didn't want his mom to get inside his head—to find something about Olivia he hadn't seen and then couldn't unsee. She had a way of doing that. With everything.

The door opened as they approached.

"Zachary!" his mom cried, her arms outstretched as she waited for him to walk into them. She looked beautiful, as always. Her dark-brown hair, with its blunt bangs and a sharp cut that barely grazed her shoulders, had been styled the same way for as long as he could remember. She was dressed in her weekend wear—crisp white pants, high heels, and a light cashmere sweater. He'd explained to her that it would be okay if she wore workout clothes on the weekends like every other woman her age, but she'd given him a look like he'd asked her to eat that cheese that came out of a spray can.

He hugged his mom, pulling away quickly and stepping to the side. "Mom, this is Olivia. And Olivia, this is my mom, Amy."

His mom gave Olivia a once-over. "So, *she* is the surprise you mentioned on the phone. And now I'm realizing the reason you hardly posted on your socials?" Amy laughed lightly. "I thought maybe you had brought me a present from Italy?"

"Well, we have that too!" Zach laughed, but it came out more like a squeak. He pointed at the box Olivia was holding. Olivia flicked her eyes at him in confusion.

He had only told Olivia that the engagement would be a surprise to his mom, not that she would be too. He had planned to tell his mom the whole story many times over the past week, but when they'd talked last night, she'd kept going on about how much she'd missed him while he was gone and how excited she was to get back to their weekly dinners and movie nights, and he hadn't been able to find the right way to tell her. "Yes! Surprise. This is Olivia." He put his arm around her. "I met her in Italy. But she lives here in California too. And she is so special and sweet and kind that I wanted to wait to tell you about her in person! So here she is!" He was rambling. Blood rushed to his cheeks.

Another look of surprise flashed across Olivia's face. He knew he'd have a lot of explaining to do later.

"Oh, please," Olivia said. "I'm not that special. I'm just me. I can barely walk in these shoes—I tripped on the way up here. I have sweat rings under my armpits, although that's probably TMI!" Olivia laughed, and to his relief, his mom did too.

He let out the breath he'd been holding. Maybe Olivia's warm and easy personality would win his mom over.

"It's very nice to meet you," Olivia said. "And here is your *other* surprise." She held out the gift.

"So many surprises. If you tell me you're pregnant next, I might pass out." Amy smirked, but Zach could see the strain on her face.

Olivia laughed, not realizing his mom wasn't joking. "Nothing in here except coffee." Olivia patted her stomach. "I was too nervous to eat this morning."

Amy arched an eyebrow at Zach, as if to say, *So nice you gave HER a heads-up about meeting ME.*

He flashed a huge grin at his mom, hoping it would help, but she didn't return it. "Should we go inside?" Zach asked, already thinking about the stiff drink he was going to pour himself.

"Yes, of course. Sorry. Follow me."

They trailed his mom across the wide-plank pine floor, through the all-white living room and into the all-white kitchen. Amy set the box on the counter. "May I open this now?"

"Please!" Olivia said.

Amy lifted the package, bouncing it lightly in the air. "Too heavy to be a *future grandma* T-shirt!"

Olivia giggled and shook her head. "God no. I'm starting law school in a couple of weeks—no time for any of that!"

Amy's eyes brightened. "A lawyer? Tell me more."

Olivia told Amy about the classes she was enrolled in at UCLA as Amy tore the paper off the box and Zach beelined for the bar and. "Drinks?" he asked as he grabbed some ice from the freezer and put it into a glass. He reached for the bourbon and poured himself a double.

"Please," his mom and Olivia said in unison.

"Rosé?" Amy asked.

Olivia nodded heartily. "My fave."

Amy pulled the platter from the box and traced her finger over the hand-painted lemons. "It's beautiful. Thank you."

Zach handed her and Olivia a glass of rosé.

He held up his bourbon and thought of a toast that would make his mom happy. "To being home."

Amy smiled at that. "Should we go out back and talk? It's such a nice day."

His mom set the platter on the counter as they followed her to the backyard. Zach wondered if she'd display it the way the shop owner had said most people did. Or if it would end up in the back of some cabinet.

"Your home is gorgeous," Olivia said as they sat down.

His mom's phone pinged, and she swiftly picked it up. "Sorry—work," she said, then fired off a text. Her phone was like an appendage. She made Zach look like he was never on his. And that was saying a lot. As the director of communications and marketing for the Pasadena Rose Parade, her job since Zach was in elementary school, Amy had been tasked with making it shine for years. There was always some PR nightmare she had to fix. Whether it was an unseasonable cold snap threatening the blooms or a rose princess being cringey on social media, she made it go away.

Now the iPad was making a noise, and she grabbed it off the counter. She let out a breath as she read a message. "Hold on," she said, and whipped a stylus out of her pocket. She tapped hard a few times and smiled. "Okay. There. That should do it." One more ping filled the room. "That's the DoorDash," she laughed. "It should be here in fifteen. Your favorite, Zach," she said, and looked pointedly to Olivia, as if she were supposed to guess. "Sushi! From Sushi Roku! I hope you eat sushi, Olivia?"

"Yes. I love it."

"Oh, good." Amy seemed relieved. "Tell me how you guys met."

Amy's phone sprang to life once more. "Sorry, it's work again. The Rose Parade is only five months away, and . . ." She talked as she typed. "We found out about a proposed float from a company that, let's say, does not support women." She gave Olivia a knowing look. "At all. It could have been a huge

46

problem had I not caught it when I did. Crisis number one hundred and fifty-three avoided," she said with a little twist to her lips.

"Zach told me about your job. It sounds—" Olivia started but was interrupted by the chime of one of Amy's devices.

"Sorry, let me tell my assistant, Alyssa, I'm with my son." Amy typed quickly and then flipped her phone over on the table to signal she was done answering it. "Okay, you two, you really have my undivided attention now," Amy said, scooching forward on the couch. "Tell me everything! And don't leave anything out. I think there have been enough surprises for one day. And you've had an entire week since you got home—plenty of time to perfect your meet-cute story!" Her eyes bored into Zach's, and his face heated up again as he tried to figure out how to say they were engaged, and why he'd waited so long to tell her.

CHAPTER FOUR

Through the window, Amy's heart clenched as she watched Zach open Olivia's door and help her into the car. She was torn by their engagement news. Her only son, who was never impulsive about anything, had picked up a fiancée in Positano as easily as a tan. Amy was happy he was happy—it was obvious from the moment he stood awkwardly on the front porch with Olivia that he had fallen hard—but this felt rushed, unvetted. Reckless. This was the rest of his life.

Amy liked Olivia—which was both surprising and annoying. It would have been much easier for her to talk her son out of this if she couldn't stand the woman. Which had been the case with Zach's previous girlfriends, who'd all tried too hard. Treating Amy like a nut they wanted to crack. One of them had gone so far as to invite Amy to get a mani-pedi. She'd politely declined. What would have been next? A sleepover? Another had sent an edible arrangement. Amy squished her nose as she remembered the poor mango and pineapple trapped beneath the cellophane. Zach had obviously warned them she was tough.

But they'd misread her, thinking *I only want what's best for my son* equaled *You can buy my affection through 1-800-Flowers.*

Amy wasn't trying to be hard. She wanted Zach to get married. And she'd always known he would likely marry young. When it came to love, he was a lot like his father—a man-size puppy dog with a huge heart that he wore on his sleeve. But did it need to be right now?

First impression of Olivia: easygoing, smart as a whip, and incredibly likable. And Amy didn't like most people. Amy knew there would be no fruit baskets or girls' day invitations coming her way from Olivia, and this pleased her. The platter was lovely and distant, the way she liked it. Ironically, she could picture herself shopping with Olivia in Old Town Pasadena. It was obvious the girl had good taste.

But a wedding?

No, no, no, no, *and no.*

Amy cradled her nearly empty goblet of rosé. She knew all too well how marrying someone you hardly knew could blow up in your face. But she realized her own circumstances had been different from Zach's. That she'd been pregnant (and after cornering Zach in the kitchen earlier, she'd been reassured Olivia was not) and Zach's father, Troy, had proposed because he was trying to make them a family. And Amy had said yes because she was scared out of her mind and didn't want to raise a child alone.

She pulled a box out of the hall closet. An artful label reading *Photos* had been affixed to the front; her assistant had ordered it after Amy binge-watched that home organizing show on Netflix. Amy sifted through the stacks until she found what she was looking for: the few pictures she had from her wedding day. She'd recently had her hair cut at one of those places where you walked in and put your name on a list—she couldn't imagine that now. The stylist had talked her into "The Rachel," Jennifer Aniston's hairstyle, which every girl apparently wanted at the time. Amy had been too nauseous from her first trimester to care. The truth was, she hadn't known what she wanted—not when it came to the hair or to getting married.

Did Zach know what he wanted? Did Olivia? Or were they caught up in the idea of love?

It seemed like Zach had been on a perpetual search for *the one* since he'd been old enough to date. Had her divorce pushed him in that direction? He'd only been two years old, so he didn't remember the marriage. But maybe he'd still wanted to prove he could succeed at love when Amy and Troy clearly could not.

She balanced the box of photos on her lap and FaceTimed her ex-husband.

While her phone rang, she pulled out another picture. She was standing next to Troy after the ceremony, the fabric of her slip dress straining against her bump, perspiration dotting both of their foreheads. Troy had removed his jacket and wrapped his arm around her shoulder. He was grinning without showing any teeth and his eyes were bulging—from fear or excitement, she couldn't be sure. Amy was also smiling, but it didn't reach her eyes. She looked a little sad, her hand resting on baby Zach, whom she'd learned was the size of an heirloom tomato.

"I was wondering how long it would take you to call," Troy said in place of a hello.

"You already know? Oh my god. Did he tell you first?"

"Relax," Troy said, a smile spreading over his face. "They came by the office *after* they left your house. I had a client here to sign some papers, so it was quick. We're planning to have dinner later this week. Nice girl, don't you think?"

"Nice girl? That's your takeaway?" Amy raised her eyebrow.

"One of them, yes."

"Why are you so damn easygoing all the time?" She both loved and couldn't stand Troy's eternal optimism. But in a weaker moment, she might have admitted to him that as she got older, she sometimes wished she had less of a skeptical edge and more blind hope. That she could turn off the internal motor in her head that questioned everything. She held up a photo. "Look what I found."

Troy leaned forward. "Is that from the day we got married? Look at us. We're babies."

"We're the same age as Olivia here!"

"Wow. Really?"

"Yes. Really," she said, and showed him another picture. She and Troy were standing in front of the judge, their hands clasped together for dear life as they said *I do*. "We both look petrified."

"Because we were, Amy."

Amy balked. "You never said that to me."

"Of course I didn't! I was trying to be a man. Be tough. But I was out of my mind with worry. How was I going to pay the bills? How was I going to be a dad?" He ran a hand over his chin. "You never said you were scared either."

It was true. She'd never told Troy what she was thinking that morning—that the courthouse wasn't where she was supposed to be on that sweltering day in June. She should have been xeroxing press releases in the air-conditioned building of one of the summer public relations internships to which she'd been accepted.

She studied the ill-fitting suit Troy wore, the back of his hair so long it was dusting the collar of his jacket. She remembered how annoyed she'd been that he hadn't gone in for a trim like he'd promised he would.

"I know. I guess I was trying to protect you or me or the baby or all three of us, I don't know." Amy sighed.

"We did the best we could at the time, Aim."

"But in hindsight, we didn't need to get married, right? We could have made it work as coparents?"

"I don't know, maybe. But for the record, I'm glad we tried. It was the right thing to do."

"Do you think Zach is doing the right thing? Tell me you aren't a little caught off guard by this."

Troy considered her question. "Did I think Zach was going to come back from his trip engaged? No, I didn't." Troy chewed his lip. "But who am I to judge how much time Zach needs before he knows he's met his wife? Maybe they're meant to be." There was a flash in Troy's eyes that evaporated almost immediately. Amy assumed it was derived from his penchant for romance. It was why he'd insisted they try to make it work when Amy got pregnant. God bless that man, he really loved a happy ending. Amy had felt a sense of failure when she couldn't give him his. But life wasn't a movie. Accidentally getting pregnant and then getting married when you hardly knew each other typically only worked in those cutesy Netflix films Amy secretly watched.

"I cannot believe he proposed over there. Why couldn't he have waited until they got back home? Date for a while in the real world? They only live thirty minutes apart!" Amy drained the last of her wine. She knew her question didn't have an answer. She'd never been to the Amalfi Coast but knew from the deep internet dive she'd done one night when she was missing Zach how intoxicating the area could be—they probably pumped pheromones into the air over there. "This is all hitting a little close to home, don't you think? It reminds me of us—I mean, minus the baby part. At least they aren't pregnant. I asked."

"Of course you did." Troy smiled. "I think it's pretty simple. They're in love."

Amy frowned. "But love's not enough, is it? What if they end up like us?"

"We had the baby, and then we had to create the love to go along with it. They have the love up front. So I give them a fighting chance. I think you forget what it's like to be young like that—to have the entire world ahead of you." Troy took one hand away from the phone and ran it through his dark-blond hair. "Of course they believe they're going to make it. Life hasn't thrown them any curve balls yet."

"And when that happens? When the curve balls arrive?"

"Well, statistically speaking, they've got a fifty-fifty chance of success."

"And what if a baby becomes part of the equation? Before they get to know one another properly?"

Troy thought for a moment. "Let's hope the only short-term investment they make is in Zach's fixer-upper. I know he's already put some money into it, but it still needs a lot of work. The electrical needs to be replaced eventually. The guest bath needs new plumbing; the toilet is the original, I think. That will keep them busy."

"Or drive them apart." Amy laughed. *If we're lucky.* "Remember when we painted the nursery together and got into that huge fight? We should have known that day it was the beginning of the end."

Troy laughed. "You hated the color, but we couldn't afford to change it."

"*You* didn't want to spend the money." Amy remembered sobbing as she stared at the green paint on the wall that was the same color as split-pea soup—she was so mad at Troy she'd slammed the nursery door and vowed never to walk into it again. "Maybe that's what we do—we encourage them to DIY the toilet. That will be a good test. They might end up wanting to kill each other and decide they're not ready for marriage."

"That's shitter sabotage!" Troy exclaimed.

"If the toilet fits." Amy smiled.

"I know you don't want to hear this, but this isn't a situation you have any control over. You'll have to wait and see how this plays out, *naturally*."

"But that's such a boring and adultish thing to do." Amy fake-pouted.

"I know. But it's important we let them make their own choices," Troy said.

Amy felt a slight lift in her shoulders—Troy's positivism infecting her. Maybe it *would* be okay? "Fine," she conceded. "But if I have to break some pipes at his house to see what Zach and Olivia look like under pressure, I'm okay with that."

"I'm sure they'll have their fair share of stress without your help," Troy asserted. He said it with such confidence that Amy started to ask a follow-up question, but he cut her off and said he was late for an appointment.

"Bye," Amy said to her empty living room, surrounded by old memories and the shadows of her past.

CHAPTER FIVE

June turned sideways in front of her full-length mirror to inspect how the coral-and-white wide-striped palazzo pants hung on her short frame. She'd paired them with a white tank top and her favorite long chunky necklace, which she'd picked up at the local farmers market last year. She frowned at her reflection. Was the necklace too much? Was she trying too hard? June rubbed the back of her neck, pulled everything off, and threw it all into the giant pile of outfit rejects. She stood in her Spanx and smirked. Maybe she should walk into the brunch in nothing but her shapewear. That would certainly break the ice when she met Zach's parents for the first time tomorrow morning.

June sat on the edge of her bed and wished she could get Zach's mom out of her head. Or the idea of her anyway. Olivia had called June after meeting her. Her daughter had gone on and on *and on* about how Zach's mom *is so amazing. So chic! Her shoes are to die for! You know that actress on* Unreal *with the dark hair and the olive skin? She looks exactly like her! So gorgeous!* June didn't know the actress or the show, but she'd Googled them both after they'd hung up and instantly wished she had time to lose five pounds before meeting this woman.

June hated that she was focused on her own insecurity instead of her daughter's relief that she liked Zach's mom. June knew all too well from her experience with William's mother—who merely tolerated June, if she could call it that—how hard it could be on a marriage when your husband's mom treated you like the third runner-up in some pageant you weren't aware you'd entered.

June decided there was zero chance she could make herself look like a supermodel, so she tried on the last outfit again and hoped it sent the message she was looking for: *I'm an effortlessly fashionable bookseller who didn't change six times before settling on this.* She smoothed her wrinkled pants. Hadn't she read somewhere that ironing was "out"? Or was that something Chloe had clapped back with when June asked why her clothes always looked like she had pulled them from a balled-up pile on her bedroom floor?

She'd learned that term, *clapping back*, from Chloe. June had listened intently as she'd demonstrated how to separate the clapping emojis to drive home a point on Instagram. But June knew she would never *clap back* the way Chloe wanted her to—she didn't have social media. She'd refused to create a personal profile on any of those apps, not even Facebook—the one a friend promised her was safe and fun for people *their age*, saying it was the place to track down lost friends or loves.

June wanted no part of that. The past belonged in the past. It was hard enough to keep old wounds from surfacing. She didn't need to see new pictures of the people who'd hurt her. She had no desire to know how their lives had turned out after they'd betrayed her for each other. She got that some people wanted to voyeur into the lives they'd walked away from, but June would rather stay on the path she chose. The one that moved forward.

Chloe had been mortified when she'd started working at All Booked Up and asked June for the store's Instagram handle and June said it didn't exist. Chloe had scrunched up her face. "You, like, have to have one. I can make it for you in, like, five minutes." June had reluctantly agreed, mostly so they could stop talking about it. Chloe had recently told her the bookstore account @allbookedupbookstore was up to eleven hundred followers. June had no idea if that was a good number, but Chloe seemed satisfied. June understood that many people found out about books through social media and preferred to read them electronically. But June liked to walk into a library or a bookstore (like her own!) and browse. She needed the feel of an actual book in her hand, found comfort in its smell, and enjoyed having the option of—gasp—dog-earing its pages like a monster.

June decided to casually drop *clapping back* in conversation at the brunch. Show Olivia that she *got* her and, for once, feel like she was in on the joke. Her daughters' vernacular often sounded like a foreign language. They'd tease her when she'd ask what certain words meant. Like recently when they'd said the boba at that new place was bussin', and she'd asked for a translation. After their giggles stopped, they said, "That means, good, Mom!"

She'd tell a story about a customer who'd tried to return the obviously used copy of *Daisy Jones and the Six* last week. June imagined herself describing the bent cover with water marks on its pages—clearly enjoyed in a bath or a swimming pool—between bites of the egg white omelet she'd order, though she'd really want the pancakes. *'This is a bookstore, not a library!' I clapped back.* She wondered if Zach's mom would understand— if she spoke her son's mother tongue or would be as clueless as June.

Chloe popped her head into June's doorway. "Is that what you're going to wear to the big brunch?"

"Yes, is it okay?" June asked, suddenly worried she had it all wrong.

Chloe gave her a once-over. "It's bangin'."

"The stripes aren't too much?"

Chloe shook her head. "No. You look great. I promise."

"Are you sure you can't come?" June asked hopefully.

"I have that group marketing project due next week and tomorrow's the only time everyone could meet. I will get fifty points deducted off my score if I bail."

June's phone rang.

Chloe saw William's name on the screen. "Oh, and Mom?"

"Yeah?"

"Olivia wanted me to remind you to please be on time tomorrow. Tell Dad I said hi."

June suppressed an eye roll. "Yes, ma'am," she said. She waved at Chloe and sent William to voice mail. She didn't want to explain to her daughter that she had no intention of answering his call, being too exhausted to have another discussion about the engagement.

For the past week, they'd been stuck in a cul-de-sac, neither one moving off their position. So around and round they'd go.

June was working at being supportive of Olivia's choice with the same intensity and focus she'd once given the Weight Watchers program. (She still knew the points total for every menu item at El Pollo Loco.) Although she agreed with many, if not all, of William's reasons that Olivia and Zach shouldn't get married so quickly, she vowed to stay on her daughter's side.

June wanted to be the nurturing, loving mother she'd longed for when she announced her own engagement. She'd already stumbled when Olivia first told her, but she'd since recovered her footing, telling Olivia she was sorry she'd come on so strong. They'd since moved on to the fun discussions, like what kind of dress Olivia wanted to wear. But still, William made a strong case for why Olivia shouldn't rush things, and it was hard for June to argue. She hoped William was leaving her a message saying he would be at the meet-the-parents brunch wearing his big-boy pants, ready to support his daughter. That he agreed with the point she'd made to him yesterday.

"June. This isn't a time to be soft," he'd said. "We need to tell her we won't pay for the wedding until she finishes law school. If she really loves this Z guy—"

"His full name is Zachary."

"Well, Olivia kept calling him Z when she *finally* spoke to me. What is it with the Z and V? It's so—"

"They're in love," June protested, not daring to let on that she doesn't get the letter thing either.

"You never called me W."

"It doesn't exactly roll off the tongue."

"Anyway, if she really loves *Zachary* as much as she says she does, she should wait. What is the damn rush, anyway? If she does this now, she'll never get her law degree," he barked.

June knew from the time of day that William was driving to the hospital for an overnight shift. She could picture him: his smooth hands gripping the leather steering wheel of his Tesla, his eyes narrowing at the thought of his oldest daughter not becoming the kickass defense attorney she'd imagined being since the age of nine. Or that William had imagined her being. It was hard to remember in whose mind her law aspirations had begun.

June took a deep breath. "She said she'll finish school, and I believe her."

"Of course you do," William laughed. It sounded bitter, making June think of an unripe peach. "You always believe everything the girls tell you."

June ignored the dig. "She's not a child anymore. We can't—"

"If she's not a child, then why are we still supporting her financially? Isn't that the very definition of a dependent? I thought we agreed she was off the dole when she finished undergrad, but somehow *I* got her Amex bill in the mail this week. Do you have any idea how much she racked up in Italy? No, of course you don't. *You* didn't write the check."

June pushed her thumb against her temple, not wanting to point out that Italy had been a graduation present—which hardly fell under the umbrella of support—because that would lead to a fight about it being June's idea to send Olivia to the Amalfi Coast. And that had created this mess. Not to mention June knew Olivia was practically living with Zach at this point. Arguing with William was futile, his mind being as sharp as the surgical instruments used in the operating rooms he frequented. He often acquiesced when he argued with June, but when he chose to dig his heels in on something, she had very little chance of winning.

In all the years she'd known William, she'd never seen him this worked up. About anything. It was like his emotional dam had finally burst—the feelings and reactions she'd begged for during their marriage were now gushing from him and drowning her. Thankfully, he hadn't unleashed any of this on Olivia.

Yet. June knew it was only a matter of time—she had to stop him.

"I'll pay for the wedding, then," June said, and hoped that if he agreed, Olivia would be okay with something small. Maybe a ceremony on the beach a few blocks from June's house? A quaint reception on the patio of the Italian restaurant across from the bookstore? June's business did okay, but there was no way she could afford to pay for the type of dress she and Olivia had discussed, let alone a lavish wedding.

"How will you do that?" he asked, not unkindly.

"I don't know. I'll figure it out. Take out a loan. Sell some stock. Whatever." June picked at her cuticle. "I don't want to push her away." June felt tears coming and squeezed her eyes shut.

William went quiet, and they sat in comfortable silence until he spoke again, his voice softer. "You aren't Olivia. And you definitely aren't your mom."

William's insight unleashed a burst of affection for her ex. They were no longer a couple, hadn't been for over a decade, but they had lived a life together. They'd raised two children. They'd loved them fiercely, each other somewhat less so, which ultimately had led to the unraveling of their marriage. But after all this time, he hadn't forgotten that it was her complicated relationship with her mother that, for better or worse, influenced many of her decisions with Olivia and Chloe.

June sighed. "Fiona said the same thing."

"One of the many reasons I like that woman. She has good sense." She could hear the smile in his voice. William had met Fiona a handful of times over the years. He liked the way she teased him about his resting bitch face and polo shirts that were so starched they could stand on their own.

"Anyway, I know I'm not my mother. But if we—if *I*—try to stop her, I might as well be wearing a strand of pearls and a twinset and grab an ax to properly shatter my daughter's dreams. Eileen is an expert at that," June said.

"Don't be so dramatic—"

June pressed on. "We need to let Olivia make her own choices, even if we don't believe they're the right ones. And we can't use purse strings to control her. Can you please try to get on board with this? Fake it till you make it?" June half laughed but was met with another long silence. She went in harder. "The brunch is tomorrow, and our daughter will be devastated if you don't go. But if you choose to attend with the intention of blowing this thing up, I suggest you stay home."

June heard the click of the hospital parking garage arm lift. And then the squeal of the tires as he pulled into his assigned space. After all these years, she still easily recalled the daily pieces of William's work life.

"Fine. I'll think about it," he said, his voice tight.

* * *

William groaned when he heard June's scratchy voice explaining that she wasn't available right now. He knew she'd sent him to voice mail. The phone had only rung twice. He'd been up half the night thinking about Olivia and this guy named Z who had managed to disrupt her perfectly planned life in mere weeks. *Weeks!* This wasn't his daughter. Chloe, maybe. But not Olivia. Olivia was climbing her ladder. And this guy had knocked her off while they drank cheap Chianti. (At least the Amex bill reflected that she wasn't opposed to the house red.)

He took a few long breaths. He couldn't let himself get worked up again. He had to hold it together.

When Olivia finally got up the nerve to FaceTime him directly and discuss her news, William had white-knuckled the entire conversation, literally gripping the edge of his desk with such a fierceness that his hands had felt numb when they hung up. He'd listened as Olivia rambled about how smart, athletic, and courteous Zach was. But Olivia didn't know what this guy was like when times were tough. She hadn't even had a head cold while she'd known him. What would he be like when she was sick? When *he* was? She had zero information on anything about this man that mattered. All William heard about from Olivia were the hikes at sunset, the ferries to Capri, and limoncello. As he nodded and made supportive noises, he found himself thinking Olivia might as well have met Zach on that ridiculous reality TV show *The Bachelor*. They had about as much chance of surviving a life together as those people.

As a doctor, William believed in statistics. In science. If the possible success of his daughter's marriage to Zach was the hypothesis of a clinical trial, he had no doubt they'd fail to reach statistical significance. He couldn't say this to June. She hated when he brought numbers into emotional situations. Not to mention she was hoping Olivia would have one of those unrealistic happy endings from the novels in the window display of her bookstore. William would love nothing more than for his daughter to have the same, but it wasn't likely to happen with a man she barely knew.

William tucked his navy polo into his khaki pants, tightened his belt. He knew June was right. That he shouldn't go to the brunch tomorrow if he wasn't going to support the marriage. But could he do that without meeting Zach first? In Olivia's defense, she had set up a dinner, but William had needed to cancel last minute due to being called in to the hospital. William now found himself in a position where he had to accept this wedding before he knew how this kid carried himself, before he felt the firmness of his handshake, and most importantly, before seeing the way he treated his daughter.

June was asking William to go against every principle he believed in simply because he loved Olivia. Could he do that?

William wrapped his watch around his wrist. He knew he was the unflinching parent. The stricter of the two. But still, there was nothing he wouldn't do for his girls or June.

Last Memorial Day weekend, he'd somehow juggled his schedule at the hospital to run the bookstore for two days when June, Chloe and the entire staff had caught a nasty virus. She'd called him in tears, a palpable desperation in her voice. She couldn't afford to be closed on a busy holiday weekend. The walk-in sales would carry her through the slower times. Could he please watch the store? She wouldn't ask unless it was her absolute last resort, she pleaded. Olivia would help him.

For those two days, he wasn't William, the astute anesthesiologist known for distributing meds during surgery with steady nerves, but "Bill" (he put it on his name tag as a joke and then found he quite liked this alter ego), the chatty bookseller who funnily enough had not read most of the books in the store. Not typically one for small talk, he had yakked it up with browsing tourists while Olivia ran the register, and after closing he'd drunk beers and chowed on nachos at the dive bar next door. He wouldn't admit this, but a part of him had been sad to pass the keys back to June when she was finally able to get out of bed. He had wondered what it might have been like, in another universe, to live Bill's life.

William was many things. He was sharp like a razor but could also be melted like butter. He was wound tight like a ball of string but understood he was sometimes dangerously close to unraveling. But mostly he was a father, who *of course* wanted his daughter to be happy.

But could he do *this* for Olivia? For June? Was he capable of eating eggs and bacon with this kid without pulling his father aside and asking if he was as unsure about this as William was? What harm could that do? From what June had gathered from Olivia, both of Zach's parents had said they were supportive of the engagement, but William wondered if they, like him, had simply been biting their tongues.

William secured the top button of his shirt and decided he would attend the brunch tomorrow. That he would give his ex-wife and daughter what they needed. But to get through it, he would definitely have to put on his proverbial bookstore badge and channel his inner Bill.

CHAPTER SIX

It made sense that Amy didn't see the display of truffle popcorn. She was editing a TikTok video about a charity event the Rose Parade princesses had attended earlier that day. Her head snapped up at the sound of the first bag falling to the floor, and she watched in horror as the rest followed suit, tumbling into the narrow aisle in Trader Joe's.

"Shit!" she mumbled, accidentally deleting the video draft before shoving her phone into the side pocket of her patent-leather handbag and leaning down to pluck the popcorn off the floor. Two young male employees in Hawaiian shirts materialized in the aisle. *Is it their sole task to guard this display?* They scooped several bags at a time, their pectorals bulging out of their button-downs. The one to her right, with the dark hair and straight teeth, reminded her of Zach. If working with his dad in real estate hadn't been his high school job, Amy could have imagined him at the register, chatting up customers about their day as he scanned the bar codes on coveted pints of boba ice cream and frozen bags of cauliflower gnocchi. He'd love the thrill of ringing the bell whenever it was time to open a new register. Zach excelled at everything he tried. Real estate whiz. King of the Trader Joe's aisle.

Husband?

Amy had thought a lot about what Eternal Optimist Troy had said on the phone the other night—that Zach loved Olivia and there was something to be said for that. She knew Troy was right, but something about Zach getting engaged was forcing Amy to face that he was a grown man. The problem was, she couldn't seem to shake the image of him as a nine-year-old in his Little League uniform, running up to her with red cheeks, excited about the double-double animal-style cheeseburger he was going to get at In & Out—their post-game tradition. They'd had a lot of traditions over the years—none of which had involved anyone else. How would Olivia fit into their monthly pizza nights? Their Thanksgiving weekend Christmas tree trimming? Their annual Harry Potter movie marathon?

What Amy couldn't admit to Troy was what the wedding announcement was really doing to her. It was reminding her that she was losing Zach.

She was too embarrassed to tell Troy about something she'd said to Zach when he was planning his trip to Italy. When he told Amy he was taking a solo vacation to the Amalfi Coast to celebrate closing on a stunning $11 million estate in the coveted area above the Rose Bowl, Amy had suggested he take her along. But instead of agreeing, he'd laughed, thinking she was joking. That had stung. She'd covered her disappointment and chuckled right along with him.

She knew she couldn't have him to herself forever. That he needed to build a family of his own. But knowing something and accepting it were two very different things. She *might* have spent the weekend he left for college intermittently crying and pouring through photo albums and watching his baby videos, but still, she wasn't *that* mom. It wasn't like she'd slept in his bed. She still had a few lines that wouldn't be crossed. But it had always been the two of them, and now, apparently, it would be three. Olivia was sweet, but was she wife material? Amy certainly hadn't been when she was Olivia's age. Was she good enough for Zach? Amy had no idea. And neither did her son. That was the problem.

Amy grabbed a bag of popcorn off the rebuilt display and threw it into her cart to try to save face. She hated truffles, didn't get why those stinky mushrooms had infiltrated every snack product—butter and hot sauce included.

She heard the canoodling before she saw it. As she maneuvered her cart around a woman reading the ingredients on the back of a bag of Gummy Tummies, she was struck by how canoodling had a distinct sound. The murmuring. The quiet smack of the lips. The soft laughter. She shouldn't have been surprised when she turned the corner and found her ex-husband, Troy, cuddling with a woman next to the jars of chili onion crunch and marinated artichokes. But she was anyway. Troy always seemed to pop up when she least expected it. Like at three PM on a Friday in Trader Joe's. And very rarely was he without a woman on his arm.

Amy hadn't seen this blonde before, but all the women her ex-husband dated had a similar Coachella vibe—bedhead hair cascading down their backs and crop tops grazing their belly buttons. Short shorts and long legs. Amy tried to remember when Zach's father had become a cliché—a middle-aged man with money who dated women younger than their son. Amy self-consciously ran a hand through her hair before clearing her throat to alert them that they were blocking her path to the bruschetta mix.

Troy pulled away from the leggy blonde and picked up the red basket off the floor before noticing Amy. Of course Troy had a basket, Amy thought, scanning its contents. Red wine, a bag of baby spinach, a package of mushrooms, a bottle of salad dressing, a box of pasta. Tonight's dinner. Amy pinched her lips together and looked at her overflowing cart—enough food for the next two weeks. It must be nice to have so much free time that you could have a make-out sesh *and* grocery shop for one meal at a time! Troy had called Amy more than once from the golf course before ten AM on a weekday. Amy couldn't remember the last time she'd been anywhere other than her ergonomic office chair at that time of day.

"Hey!" Troy said, finally noticing her.

"Hello, Troy," she said coolly.

"Wow. First, a phone call. Now we're bumping into each other here. How lucky am I this week?" Troy said, widening his hazel eyes, causing the skin around them to splay into evenly spaced wrinkles. Only making him more handsome, *of course*. Unlike Amy's crow's-feet, which she paid someone $300 to erase every three months. Another thing to put in the Troy Irritates the Hell Out of Amy column. "What are *you* doing here?"

"What does it look like I'm doing?" Amy said crisply, and instantly regretted it. It was so like Troy to ask her something like this. Not understanding why *she would want to be* pushing a shopping cart at Trader Joe's when she had an assistant for that.

Troy gave her his *What did I say?* look.

He didn't mean to get under her skin. He never did. But somehow he always ended up there, like a bug bite that Amy would scratch for hours after, a reminder of what he'd done.

After all these years, Troy didn't understand that even though she loved her job, it could be all-consuming, especially this time of year, it was a treat for Amy to roam the aisles uninterrupted (well, usually) and choose her own Manchego cheese. To be that person who had thirty whole minutes to spare to buy groceries for one. Well, technically two, if you counted Zach, who before meeting Olivia was over for dinner so often he might as well have lived there.

Over Troy's shoulder, Amy spotted those almond-butter-filled pretzels Zach liked. She wondered if those dinners would continue, and if they did, would Olivia be joining them? Or would Olivia replace Amy, serving Zach at their place? *Their place.* Forget the wedding. She was still processing that Olivia had already moved into Zach's house.

"I'm used to seeing Alyssa here." Troy looked toward the front of the store, as if Amy's assistant might walk in at any moment. "By the way, last time I bumped into her, I suggested she buy those oven-baked cheese bites. Zach had told me you were sick, and I know you crave the salty stuff when you don't feel good." He winked.

Winked!

A smile tugged at her mouth, but she mashed her lips together so it couldn't escape. It was so hard to stay annoyed with Troy.

"Oh? I'm not sure I remember those," Amy lied. The truth was, she had devoured the melt-in-your-mouth, lick-your-fingers-after-each-one cheese bites in one sitting, but she wasn't about to admit that. She couldn't find it within herself to give him the satisfaction.

"Well, it was good to see you. And thank you for tipping me off that this is the new dating hot spot. Now that I know I can meet a man and stock my freezer at the same time, I'll start coming more often." Amy raised her eyebrows and tilted her head toward Troy's female companion, who was scrolling through her phone.

Troy laughed. "Touché."

Amy wondered if Troy would ever settle down. If he would seek a relationship with someone he might actually marry. Since their divorce a hundred years ago, she'd never seen him seriously date anyone. But then again, neither had she. Tonight, she had a hot date with Hulu.

"I need to get to that shelf." Amy pointed to the Crispy Habanero Peppers behind Troy's ass. She loved and borderline hated the way the chilies made her mouth catch on fire and the lingering tingle they left behind. Not unlike the complicated feelings she had for Troy. She leaned past him to grab *one* jar. She had planned to take two, maybe three, and consume them while watching *90 Day Fiancé*, her lips burning as she stared at the screen of her iPad, fascinated by strangers with multiple-decade age gaps who moved across the world to marry each other. Although right now, that other-side-of-the-globe thing sounded appealing. If she lived in another hemisphere, she wouldn't bump into her ex-husband and his arm piece while trying to buy her stuff-my face-while-in-bed snacks.

The blonde finally looked up from her phone and jammed her finger in the air toward the jar in Amy's hand. "Oh my god, I saw those on Instagram!" she squeaked.

She's alive! Amy thought.

"There's this account I follow. Trader Joe's list." She looked at Troy, as if this would interest him. His blank face showed it clearly didn't. "She has over a million followers," the blonde said in awe, waiting for a reaction. When she didn't receive one from Troy or Amy, she continued. "She was raving about these—she's posted like three times about them." She jutted out her glossy lip. "But I worry they'll be too hot."

"You're too hot," Troy asserted, without a trace of embarrassment. Which was fine, because Amy was embarrassed enough for both of them.

"Thanks, baby." The woman leaned her hip into him. "Let's try them tonight."

"Here. You can have mine." Amy tossed the jar into their basket. The peppers had forever been ruined, along with that Trader Joe's Instagram account, which Amy also religiously followed. She'd met the woman at a publicity event and had giddily taken a picture with her and a bag of pickle potato chips. Not that she'd ever admit to it.

Troy gave Amy a look as if to say, *Be nice.*

"You're so sweet!" The woman beamed. "I'm Sloane," she said, offering Amy a little wave. "How do you guys know each other?"

"We were married and have an adult child together," Amy said, drawing more pleasure than she should from watching the information sink in. That Troy had once been involved with (gasp!) a woman his own age! One with real boobs and two wrinkles between her eyes that used to form the number eleven before she gave in and started getting Botox.

Sloane looked at Troy as if this was news.

Amy swallowed her laugh.

But Troy rolled with it. "Guilty as charged. You've now met my beautiful ex-wife, Amy." He leaned in and pecked Amy's cheek. "How are you? Everything set for tomorrow? What can I do to help?"

Despite his *many* irritating characteristics, Amy liked that Troy maintained a respect for her. She believed this came with the understanding that the Sloanes of the world would continue to come and go, while Amy and Zach would be permanent fixtures in his life.

Sloane seemed slightly put off by Troy's reverence. "What's tomorrow?"

"Our son recently got engaged—"

"To a woman he's known for barely two months," Amy interjected. *Who can't be a day older than you!*

Troy placed a hand over his heart. "He's a romantic. Takes after his dad."

Amy pursed her lips. "I sent you an email. I made a reservation at Nick's for eleven AM," she said as she felt her phone buzz in her purse. "I hope the parents aren't boring people, or it's going to be a long morning."

A flicker of something crossed Troy's face, but his lips moved quickly into a genial smile. "I'm sure they'll feel like old friends in no time."

Amy narrowed her eyes. "Zach told me the dad is a doctor. Even worse, an anesthesiologist. I'm sure he'll be arrogant."

Troy pulled his eyebrows down. "You're tough!"

"Have you met me?" Amy joked. "And I hear the mom sells books? I don't trust people who have time to read." Amy laughed before Troy could scold her again. "I'm kidding." Her wrist buzzed, and she read a message on the screen of her Apple watch. "Anyway—I'm sure it will be interesting."

"That, I agree with one hundred percent." Troy rearranged the metal bar of the basket on his arm. "Well, we'd better get moving. I'm making dinner for Sloane tonight."

Sloane beamed.

She bounced back quickly after finding out her sugar daddy has a family, Amy thought. But she also felt envious of Sloane;

imagine your biggest worry being how you'd recover if you ate a pepper that was too spicy. Amy could barely remember herself at Sloane's age—before she gained a son, arguably the greatest love of her life, but lost someone very important in the process. Amy knew this was normal, that people moved in and out of your life like butterflies on a spring day, but the friendship that was ripped away when she became pregnant with Zach was something that still affected her life. And the choices she made. Like her solo date with her TV tonight. It was easier than getting on some dating app, swiping right, agreeing to meet for drinks, and inevitably becoming so bored that you'd count the minutes until you could feign a headache and go home.

The old Amy had been more pliable, more open to relationships, especially friendships. Like the one she'd had in college. She'd thought it would last her entire lifetime. But the current Amy had convinced herself that investing in other women so deeply held too much risk. The ghost of that dead relationship was a shadow she could not—no, *would* not—shake.

Amy pointed to the peppers in Troy's basket. "Be careful," she said, glancing at Sloane. "I'd hate to see you get burned."

* * *

Later, as Amy loaded her groceries into the trunk of her silver Audi, she thought about the brunch tomorrow. How different it would be from when her parents met Troy's. His mom and dad hadn't come to the wedding at city hall, but when Zach was born, they'd told Troy they'd decided to let go of their anger at him for everything that had happened, "for the sake of our grandchild." Amy had been relieved, wanting them to be a part of Zach's life. But she was so exhausted after giving birth that she only remembered her and Troy's parents exchanging stilted hellos in the hospital room as they took turns holding Zach. Had the four of them gone out into the hall and let their feelings of disappointment pour out? Or had they all made pleasantries over their silent acceptance?

Amy wondered if either of Olivia's parents felt the way she did—that this thing between her son and their daughter was happening at warp speed and someone needed to drain the fuel out of the rocket, stat.

Amy was the most curious about how Olivia's mom felt. Could the two of them bond over this and come up with a plan to stop the wedding? Olivia had told Amy that her mom was incredibly laid-back, so it wasn't looking good that she was going to be in Amy's corner. And Olivia was obviously painting an accurate picture of the woman, because her mother was comfortable letting Amy take the reins on arranging the brunch. Amy wouldn't have been able to give up control if the roles had been reversed. At least, if the wedding did happen in the ridiculously short time frame Zach and Olivia were hoping for—Valentine's Day, in less than six months—Olivia's mom might want to take a lesser role in planning it. Because Amy wanted to be *very* involved. Although she couldn't figure out how in the hell she was going to juggle wedding planning and preparations for the Rose Parade.

According to Zach, Olivia had suggested Valentine's Day because of law school. She said the deeper she got into her classes, which she'd only recently started, the harder it would be to handle them plus a wedding. Zach had no issues with this—"the sooner, the better," he'd said, while Amy bit down on her tongue so hard she was surprised she didn't draw blood. But Amy wondered if Olivia wasn't being more cunning than he realized. If she was hooking him early before the honeymoon period was over. She almost couldn't blame her. Because you didn't let a man like Zach get away.

Amy slid into the driver's seat, pulled out her tablet, and scrolled through her emails. Twenty had arrived in her in-box since she'd checked out at the register. They were almost all about a scandal involving last year's Rose Queen, which had originally been posted by a gossipy Instagram account and then picked up by E! News. She'd been caught shoplifting some clothes from an overpriced boutique on Robertson. It wasn't a huge deal, more of a nuisance than anything. Amy had already issued a statement saying it had all been a misunderstanding and called the store owner to pay the balance of the clothes, with a healthy tip added. Then she'd gotten on the horn with the young woman's mother to get the girl set up with some counseling. That part would be private. But it wasn't the first time the young woman had shoplifted, and she'd had a credit card in her purse both times she did it. Amy had come to care about the Rose Princesses, and she didn't want to see them destroyed by one mistake (or in this case two).

This was what Amy did. Made bad news go away. She was the Rose Parade "fixer." As she shifted into reverse and carefully backed out of the crowded parking lot, Amy evaluated whether Zach's sudden engagement would need fixing.

CHAPTER SEVEN

"A little to the left," Troy called out as Zack drove the stake into the grass with a rubber mallet. "And maybe we should also put one more open-house sign on Alder lane? So they know to take the right at the light?" He glanced back at the open trunk. "I have another one."

Zach straightened up and checked his phone.

Troy could see Olivia's name on the screen.

Zach typed something and smiled. Troy wondered what they texted about constantly. All morning, Zach and Olivia had gone back and forth while he and Zach had driven around to put up signs. It was as if they couldn't stand to be out of touch, needing to feel a connection through words. It made Troy smile to see his son so happy. He remembered the feeling of being so in love that it felt like you were the only two people in the world. "I should go in a minute. I'm meeting Olivia at the house so we can drive together."

Troy checked his watch. The brunch was in an hour. His heartbeat quickened. He could tell how nervous Zach was—he'd barely said two words to Troy this morning. Troy was nervous too. He hadn't been able to eat any of the dinner he'd made for Sloane, and he'd barely slept all night. His inability to eat or sleep went so much deeper than his only son getting married. But he had no one to whom he could confess the real root of his worry.

"I'll drop you off and take care of the last sign myself," Troy said, and watched as relief flooded his son's face.

"That would be great."

"I appreciate that you helped me at all. This is a big day for you."

"No problem." Zach looked at his phone. "Olivia is blowing me up. I guess she's worried—she can't get a hold of her mom . . . and she's confused about why I have to help with this open house this morning *of all mornings*. Not that she doesn't understand this is my job. It's a lot—the parents meeting each other—"

"Everything's going to be fine," Troy interrupted, although he wasn't so sure that was true. He wondered why Olivia couldn't reach her mom. Zach had told him how close they were—that they talked on the phone at least once a day. Was she having second thoughts? Did she have a bad feeling about the brunch?

Troy sure did.

"I'm sure everyone's a little on edge, including Olivia. She will get used to you working weekends and sometimes on days when other important things are happening," he said instead.

Olivia would come to understand that Saturday and Sunday afternoons were prime time for open houses. For people to peruse the inventory in their neighborhoods. After all these years of selling real estate, Troy still enjoyed them. Most agents of his caliber passed them to junior agents to pick up new clients, but Troy could often be found arranging chocolate chip cookies on a platter in a newly remodeled kitchen. Real estate had saved him years ago, when he suddenly became a breadwinner to a wife and child. Back then, closing a deal meant he and Amy could pay their rent, buy diapers, and gas up the used BMW Troy had purchased to drive clients around. One they couldn't afford. But he knew no one was going to buy a million-dollar house from a guy behind the wheel of the clunker he'd driven before that.

Now he was arguably one of the most successful agents in Pasadena (at least that's what all his power broker awards said), and Troy still felt that old hunger when the right offer came in. It made him happy to watch Zach stoke the same fire.

*　*　*

"How are *you* feeling about everything?" Troy dodged the traffic to backtrack to where Zach's Land Rover was parked. They pulled onto Marengo Avenue, and he saw his son's shoulders tense as he checked his phone again. He remembered meeting Amy's parents for the first time—asking Amy's dad for her hand in marriage *after* he'd gotten her pregnant and put a ring on her finger. Not his finest moment.

Troy wondered what kind of man Olivia's father was. If he would slap Zach on the back and welcome him to the family. Or if he would be more reserved until Zach proved himself. Troy had loved Olivia from the moment he'd met her last week. She made Zach's face light up. He could see in his son's eyes how much he loved her. Troy knew that look.

Zach shrugged. "Yes and no. Olivia's mom is great. When I met her, we talked about books for hours. She's so easy."

Troy smiled. "So she'll be there, then. She's probably busy getting ready."

"But her dad canceled on us when we were supposed to have dinner. Olivia said it was work, but I wondered . . ."

"He's a doctor, right?"

Zach nodded.

"I'm sure that's all it was. You're used to real estate, which is flexible. Medicine, I'm sure, is not."

Zach didn't appear to hear him. "She says her dad is protective, but also a man of few words, I guess. He hasn't said much to her about how he feels about her getting married. I was nervous that I hadn't done the whole ask-her-dad-first thing, because I know from you how important that was with Grandpa, but she isn't worried about it. It's more of an old-fashioned thing anyway."

Troy pressed his lips together to keep from giving a lecture about the importance of tradition.

"But it's not like I was going to FaceTime the guy out of the blue from Italy and ask to marry his daughter. That wouldn't have gone well. In person is always better, I think," Zach said, more to himself than to Troy. Troy was sure Zach had spent a lot of time talking himself into that. His son went silent.

"You fell in love—you followed your heart. You love his daughter. He loves his daughter. You have common ground there."

"I hope you're right," Zach said. "What was Grandpa like when you met him?"

Troy thought of how sweaty his hand had been when he clasped Amy's dad's. How fast his heart was beating. How he'd nearly shit his pants he was so nervous. "He was also protective, but it went well," Troy lied. The truth was, he'd gone through the most intense grilling of his life. He had no good answer for why he hadn't asked Amy's dad for his permission before he'd asked Amy. It had all happened so quickly that it hadn't crossed Troy's mind to seek out Amy's dad's approval first. He'd been more focused on doing the right thing—making them a family. "I'm sure her mom and dad will both love you. What's not to love? Great job, nice guy." Troy pointed a thumb at himself. "Good genes."

Zach laughed.

Troy collected his thoughts. "You're going to be a great husband. Father. Much better than I ever was." Troy knew he was fishing. He felt Zach's eyes on him. It had taken Troy longer than it should have to figure out how to be a good dad. He'd let Amy take the brunt of parenting responsibilities for too long. It was something he still thought about between sleep and waking. At the time, Troy had told himself he was building a better life for the three of them, but in the process his wife had lost faith in him, and his son had seen him more as a babysitter than a dad. It wasn't until the divorce that Troy had been forced to make time for his son (Tuesdays, Thursdays, and every other weekend were not enough) and quickly realized he had been wrong—that making money to build a better life only meant something if you could share it with the people you cared about.

He'd taken on a buyer's agent to help him on his nights and weekends with Zach and never once regretted sharing the commission. His obsession with success began to ease, as did his parameters for what defined it. Not that Troy didn't love money. He certainly did. But he loved his son much more.

Now Zach was getting married and was likely going to become a father himself one day. Troy thought about the brunch this morning and worried that once everyone was in the same room, all the hard work he'd put in with his son would unravel. That because of Troy's curiosity, his unresolved feelings, his angst, whatever you wanted to call it, he might have jeopardized the most important relationship in his life—the one with Zach.

Troy frowned and kept his gaze on the road ahead. If Zach met his eyes, he would see that he was hiding something. Not that Troy would be able to keep his secret much longer. His son was going to find out the truth in—he checked his watch—under an hour. And when he did, would Zach believe that Troy hadn't meant to tip the domino that was about to knock everything down?

"You turned out to be a pretty good dad," Zach offered generously. "I owe you one. If you hadn't insisted I go to Positano . . . I mean, it wasn't on my radar, if you can believe that—"

"You don't owe me a thing," Troy interrupted. Maybe being the reason his son had met the love of his life would outweigh his lie by omission. He conjured his best real estate agent grin. "I am pretty awesome, aren't I?"

"Well, I wouldn't go that far." Zach flashed a wry smile, then went quiet. "You know, I haven't told Olivia that you're the reason I went there. That we wouldn't have met if you hadn't told me . . ." His voice drifted off.

Troy had figured as much. If Zach had told Olivia, that would mean they had started to put the pieces of the puzzle together. "Why not?"

Zach rubbed his freshly shaved chin. "I guess I didn't want to seem like a stalker? She already thought I was creeping on her when I came up to her with my camera. And now she's sure that us meeting each other was fate. The thing is, I agree. You did play a part, but I know I'm meant to be with Olivia. If I tell her the full story now, she'll wonder why I kept it from her in the first place. And what we have really does feel magical—I don't want to ruin that for her."

Troy held his tongue to keep from pointing out that the magic would disappear anyway. They were in the real world now. Based on Olivia's comment about Zach working today, he was sure his son also hadn't told her the full story of what his work life was like. That real estate was far from a nine-to-five job. Olivia had no idea what happened when a deal went south, how Zach still crumbled under pressure—something that could only be rectified through experience. Olivia and Zach didn't know much about each other, but Troy, even after everything he'd been through in his own relationships, was choosing to believe that they would persevere, regardless of what they learned at brunch today. For that reason, he encouraged his son. "That magic you're feeling? Hold on to it. For as long as you can."

"Did you ever have it? With Mom?"

Troy hadn't thought about the beginning of his marriage to Amy in a long time. But when she'd called him the other night and shown him those pictures from their wedding day, it was as if he were right back there in his cheap suit, the gold band around his ring finger feeling like it was cutting off his circulation. But there had been magical moments along the way. Like when they'd heard Zach's heartbeat the first time. Or when they discovered his gender and Troy cried in the ultrasound room as he squeezed Amy's hand. In those early months after Zach was born, Troy and Amy would fall asleep on the old chenille couch that Troy had bargained down to twenty-one dollars at a yard sale, Zach swaddled on top of Troy's chest. But the only real magic in their marriage had been sparked by their son. "Sure, Bud. We had magic. But we did a shitty job of holding on to it. Obviously."

"Obviously," Zach echoed as he checked his phone again. "Olivia is ready to head to the restaurant."

"I'll make sure you're there for her in time." He sped through a yellow light, refusing to let his son down ever again.

CHAPTER EIGHT

Olivia squeezed Zach's hand under the table. Her heart felt like it was going to spring out of her chest and land next to the salt and pepper shakers. Where the hell was her mom? She was nine minutes late. Olivia glanced at her phone—no response to her last text. She'd sent four at this point. She wanted to ask her dad to check on her, but Zach's mom was in the middle of telling a story about the Rose Parade—which Olivia sensed was going to be a constant theme—and Olivia didn't want to interrupt. She also didn't want to draw attention to her mom's tardiness.

Olivia tapped her fingers on the table. Her mom was late more often than she wasn't. Sometimes she opened her bookstore after the time listed on the front door. Not that there was ever a line of people around the block waiting to buy Reese Witherspoon's latest book club pick, but still. Olivia had always found that semi-unprofessional. "I own the store," her mom would snap defensively if Olivia brought it up. Like when she almost missed Olivia walking across the stage to get her diploma at her college graduation. *Our last name is Abbott, Mom!*

Knowing punctuality was not her mom's strong suit, she had begged her to be on time for this brunch. She'd had Chloe remind her. Her mom had promised her that she would—she'd picked out her outfit yesterday! So where was she? Olivia wanted her mom and dad to make a good impression on Zach's parents. But no, her mom couldn't be bothered.

Olivia squeezed Zach's hand harder. He squeezed it back and gave her a look that said, *She'll be here. Don't worry.* But he didn't know her mom—not like she did, anyway. He didn't have a clue that her mom might be twenty or thirty minutes late without a good excuse.

Olivia took a sip of her water, wishing it were wine. She glanced at her dad. He sat straight in his chair, looking as stiff as his hair, which was slicked back like a helmet. But at least he was there—and had been cordial when Zach pulled him aside and apologized profusely for not asking for Olivia's hand properly. She'd hugged him afterward and whispered, "Thank you, Daddy," and he'd given her a conspiratorial wink, which she took to mean he was trying his best to be a good sport.

Now William was engaging with Zach's dad, and it seemed to be going well. She overheard bits and pieces about the Dodgers in between more of Amy's anecdotes about the sustainable rose floats.

"Can I talk to you for a sec?" she said to Zach.

He nodded and smiled. Olivia soaked him in. She loved the crisp white shirt he had tucked into his slim-cut pale-blue pants that hit below his ankle. His socks with bacon and eggs peering out in the space between his pant leg and the top of his shoe. "Nice socks," she grinned, and grabbed his hand. She'd already bought him two pairs for Christmas that she was so excited about she'd probably cave and give them to him sooner.

She'd had them custom made. One was covered in a pattern of pictures of Olivia grinning as she was about to put a giant slice of pizza in her mouth. And the other had multiple photos of Bart, the cat from Positano.

"Any word from her?" Zach asked, when they were away from the table.

"No." Olivia sighed. "But you think she's coming, right?"

"Of course she is. She told you she was, didn't she?"

Olivia nodded. "But what if—"

"She didn't change her mind. She isn't having second thoughts. She supports you—us. She's just late," Zach said confidently.

Olivia's eyes brimmed with tears. She sucked in a deep breath to keep them from spilling over.

"I love you so much."

"I love you too, V." He kissed her softly. "Want me to call her? See what her ETA is?"

Olivia shook her head, pushing down her mounting frustration. "No, we should get back to the table, to the people who arrived on time."

* * *

June gripped the steering wheel hard. She watched through her side mirror as the police officer approached. He was a tall, broad man, with a bushy mustache and a steely stare. She doubted she'd get out of this one without a ticket. She had been going over ninety up the 110 freeway because she was late. And now she was going to be even later. She thought of Olivia, how pissed off she must be—again. First the questions; now this. She knew they'd inevitably argue about her inability to be on time—"for anything." She'd mention those *two times* June had opened the store late. June needed to send Olivia a quick text so her daughter knew she was alive, but she didn't want the officer to see her pick up her phone. She whispered, "Hey, Siri," to see if she could shoot off a voice text, but the robot assistant ignored her. She sighed, grabbed her identification, and rolled down the window.

"Do you realize you were nearly topping a hundred miles per hour?" the officer asked, his face blank.

"I do." The story poured out of her. Her daughter. Positano. Engaged after weeks. Brunch to meet the other parents. It turned out Officer Mustache had a daughter about Olivia's age. He cringed at all the right parts of the story.

"License, registration, and insurance?" he asked, after she was done rambling.

June's shoulders slumped. She'd thought she had him.

He walked back to his police cruiser.

June slyly swiped her phone, and it lit up with notifications. There were several texts from Olivia, all asking where she was. They started out fine—her daughter asking for her ETA, then checking in a second and third time to see if she was close. But in the last text, she'd written, *Where are you.* The period at the end of her question meant only one thing: she was pissed. June had once asked her girls why their texts were often one long run-on sentence. "Periods are bad, Mom," they'd explained. "We only use them when we're mad." June started to reply to Olivia, but the officer was already returning.

"It's your lucky day—or maybe it's not, considering the brunch." He chuckled. "I've decided to let you off with a warning, but"—he raised his heavy eyebrows—"you have to assure me that you'll drive the speed limit the rest of the way. And for what it's worth, I hope those two kids come to their senses. I'm twice divorced."

"I'm twice engaged, once divorced." June laughed.

The officer's eyes glinted with amusement. "Good luck to you."

June did the math in her head. She was about ten minutes away from the restaurant. She would be almost half an hour late.

She started up the freeway again, the officer following behind to help her merge into oncoming traffic. He guided her to the slow lane, where June knew she must stay. She blew out a long, noisy breath. Make that thirty-five minutes late.

June yelled at Siri to dial Olivia, praying she wasn't too mad. Maybe her daughter was halfway through a mimosa by now. Maybe calling the guy who'd pulled her over Officer Bushy Stache when she recounted the story would help.

*　*　*

"How can she still not be here?" Olivia hissed into Zach's ear.

He rubbed her leg in response. "It's okay. Now she can make a grand entrance!" he joked.

Olivia didn't laugh.

Olivia's phone buzzed. It was her mom. *Finally.*

"Is that her?" Amy asked, and Olivia nodded. They had been discussing June's absence for the last couple of minutes, as it could no longer be ignored. Nine minutes had led to fifteen, which had led to Amy politely asking Olivia and William if she was coming at all. They'd both assured Amy and Troy, though he didn't seem concerned, that June was probably running a little behind. That she'd be there. That the 5 and 110 freeways were both backed up, according to William, who'd checked Waze before he'd left. He had come all the way from San Diego and been on time. Something everyone was thinking but no one was saying. Olivia had texted Chloe in a panic, but Chloe said she warned their mom not to be late. "I was a real hard ass about it before I left for my class," she'd insisted.

"William, you came from San Diego?" Amy cringed. "I had no idea you lived all the way down there." She looked at Olivia. "But I knew your mom was in Long Beach. I didn't think about it—I've been so busy with work. I'm sorry. I should have found a place more in the middle."

It wouldn't have mattered if we'd met in my mom's living room; she'd still have been late, Olivia wanted to say. Instead, she said, "No, you're fine. I know you guys love this restaurant. And we're excited to try it, right, Dad?"

William nodded obediently, though they'd never discussed it.

"I hope everything is okay," Amy added as Olivia excused herself to take the call.

The server arrived for the third time, having been waved off the prior two. Everyone had agreed it was okay to order drinks while they waited.

"Get me a bloody?" Olivia asked Zach over her shoulder. She'd planned on a white wine spritzer. But this situation called for vodka. *Make it a double,* she wanted to add.

* * *

Amy watched Olivia walk outside and heard her say, "Mom?" Her tone was sharp.

Amy wondered how a mother could be late to her daughter's engagement brunch. Late to meet her daughter's future in-laws? She couldn't remember being late to anything. Fifteen minutes early was on time in Amy's book. She was trying not to judge Olivia's mom but hoped, for Olivia's sake, that her mom had a good reason.

"I'm going to use the restroom," Zach said.

Amy looked at Troy, but he didn't notice; his face was buried in the menu. He'd barely said two words, which was so unlike him. Usually she couldn't get her ex-husband to shut up. But right now she was grateful for his silence.

William was checking something on his phone. This was Amy's opportunity to see where Olivia's dad stood on the *Our kids are getting married after knowing each other for two months* issue. She glanced over her shoulder. Olivia was still outside, and by the way she was pacing and waving her free hand in the air, it didn't appear the conversation was going well.

The server set a glass of red wine in front of Amy, and she took a hefty drink.

"So, William, how did you react to the engagement news?"

William sipped his club soda and lime. He'd mentioned he would be on call at the hospital later that evening, but he was literally buttoned up—his shirt choking his neck, the top button begging to be undone—and Amy pegged him as a teetotaler. Not that there was anything wrong with that. William was quiet for a moment, then raised his eyebrow slightly and did something with his eyes. It looked like he rolled them, but Amy couldn't be sure.

"I think it's great!" Troy bellowed. "Young love."

Amy cursed under her breath.

William's mouth closed.

As did Amy's window of opportunity.

Olivia and Zach arrived back at the table at the same time, and Olivia smiled sadly at Zach. He gave her such a loving look that Amy's heart melted a little. She instantly felt bad for the conversation she'd tried to initiate.

"I think we should order. My mom's still at least twenty minutes out," Olivia said, grabbing her bloody mary and taking a drink before sitting down.

"Is she okay?" Amy asked.

"She's fine." Olivia paused, as if trying to decide how much she wanted to tell everyone. "She got pulled over."

As Olivia told the story, Amy felt for her. The poor girl. She seemed so embarrassed. When she'd said her mom was laid-back, Amy had had no idea it bled into other areas, like timeliness.

Olivia got to the part about Officer Bushy Stache, and Amy swallowed a laugh. Olivia clearly didn't think it was funny, but Amy saw the humor. She imagined the stache as a handlebar. And her mom had gotten out of the ticket! Maybe Amy could overlook the lateness issue and come to like this woman. She sounded as if she could be funny and savvy. Qualities Amy adored. Maybe Olivia's mom could become a friend. Someone Amy could drink a glass of wine with. That would be nice. Amy would give her a fake earlier time to arrive whenever they met. That should solve the problem.

*　*　*

June did everything in her power not to press the gas pedal to the floor. She felt the officer watching her, though he'd exited the freeway already. Finally, she reached the end of the 110, and Waze told her she was only four minutes away.

At the stoplight, she checked herself in the rearview mirror. She was flushed. She took a drink from her water bottle and breathed deeply. Hopefully everyone would be eating and drinking by the time she walked in. She'd made Olivia promise to have everyone order. June wasn't hungry anyway, after the stress of being pulled over. She wondered how William was doing—if it was obvious he was hesitant about the wedding. She prayed he hadn't let on. That he was doing his William thing, listening and observing before passing judgment.

June parked and walked toward the restaurant. Through the window, she spotted William sitting next to Olivia and Zach. They were eating, and Zach appeared to be telling a story. Olivia looked at him and laughed at something he'd said. William's face was typical, unreadable as he speared a sausage. June could see the back of Zach's parents' heads. Her heartbeat began to quicken. She straightened her spine and pulled open the front door.

Olivia spotted June. She smiled, but June could still see the irritation in her daughter's eyes. She smiled back. Zach stood and waved. June approached the table. Zach's parents turned to greet her.

June stopped.

If a record screech sound effect had been available, this was where it would play.

She could feel the color drain from her face. Her mouth dried up. She couldn't move. Her mind twisted and turned, trying to figure out how they'd all ended up here. What shit the universe was trying to pull.

"Mom?" Olivia asked, her eyebrows knit together. June could see the thought bubble appear above her daughter's head. First, her mom was late. Now she was acting like a crazy person.

June couldn't respond. If she had been able to find the words, she still would have been physically incapable of speaking. It would have been like trying to talk under water.

Amy's jaw dropped, and she shot a look of confusion at Troy.

Troy. June's Troy. The love of her life. Until.

Oh my god, June thought, putting the puzzle pieces together. She looked from Zach to Troy, now recognizing the strong jawbone they shared. The hazel eyes that changed color depending on the light. For some reason, she immediately recalled gifting Troy a sage Ralph Lauren turtleneck for his twenty-second birthday, a major splurge, so she could see his eyes turn from ginger to bronze.

And Amy. Her former best friend who somehow hadn't aged. She still had the same symmetrical upturned nose and wide-set velvet-brown eyes. If she had wrinkles, June couldn't spot them.

Zach also wore his genetics well. Her daughter's fiancé seemed to be the perfect blend of the people she had spent the better part of her life trying to forget.

After all, he was the child Troy and Amy had together. After they ruined her life.

"June, it's good to see you," Troy said easily, and started to approach. June stepped backward. Troy froze.

Good to see me? So casual. So impersonal. Like acquaintances who'd bumped into each other at a farmers market, not fully stopping to talk as they headed toward the organic vegetables. June felt as if she were rising out of her body, watching.

"You guys know each other?" Olivia asked, her voice an octave higher than normal. Her eyes darted to the cast of characters in this bizarre freak show. She looked at her mom, then Amy, then Troy. Finally landing on Zach.

But Zach's face was covered in as much confusion as Olivia's. "What is happening?" Zach asked, turning toward Troy.

June thought she saw them exchange a strange look.

The server arrived with a pitcher of water. "Does anyone need anything?"

William finally spoke. "An explanation would be nice."

June felt as if what was left of the air in the room had been sucked out. She heard forks and knives clanking against dishes. Laughter rang out from a group at a neighboring table. A server passed by with a tray of mimosas as she called out, "On your left." June moved out of her way. She looked at William.

She'd never told him the full story. He only knew part of it—the excerpt she could tell him without crumbling, the feelings still having been so raw when she met him and then buried deeply after they decided to marry. She could barely look at Olivia. Her daughter wasn't privy to any of it. Olivia had no clue about the life June could have lived if it hadn't been snatched by Troy and Amy.

A life that would have meant Olivia didn't exist. June's heart seized at that thought. Her eyes made their way back to Troy, who was tugging at the collar of his shirt as if trying to get more air. June drew the courage to look at Amy again. She swallowed hard—a wound breaking open inside of her when their eyes met.

June wondered who would explain how the three of them were linked. She sucked in a sharp breath. It wouldn't be her. It shouldn't be her. She couldn't be the one to tell it—because once the story was out there, everything would change. It could shatter her daughter's life. Zach's. How would they be able to get married once they knew?

CHAPTER NINE

Amy was the first to speak. Her heart was beating so fast that her chest felt hot. She inhaled deeply through her nose and caught the eye of a woman with a sleek ponytail gawking at them from the next table. "This probably isn't the best place to get into everything." She glanced at William. "To explain how we all know each other."

As Amy spoke, she tried hard to push away the memory of the plush pink rug against her cheek as she curled into a ball after throwing up. Two decades later, she could still picture Troy's sheet-white face after she opened the bathroom door and behind him, on the table, the answering machine. Its red blinking light announcing a message she knew was from June, Amy's best friend and *Troy's fiancée.*

Amy had hurled again as she absorbed the fact that she had slept with Troy the night before. It had been an accident. Well. Sort of. She had gotten so drunk on Long Island iced teas that she didn't remember much—not even his penis. Thankfully, she hadn't been able to describe one distinguishing feature.

If Troy's penis had been arrested and Amy was tasked with identifying it in a police lineup, she would have failed miserably. His dick would have gone free—on to a life of committing more penis crimes. But not remembering it didn't mean she hadn't touched it. That it hadn't been inside her.

Or that she hadn't ruined the most significant friendship of her life. She'd deeply regretted the act the minute she opened her eyes, but the damage had been done. She knew immediately that she would tell June the truth and there would be no wiping the slate clean. Or blaming the fact that Troy had been so distraught after being rejected by June's mother, Eileen, when he tried to convince her to accept his engagement to June that drinking nine Long Island iced teas between the two of them (Amy found the crumbled receipt in her purse later) seemed right. There was no rationalizing that one friend drunkenly consoling another had slipped quickly into something else— that Amy had meant to pull back from the comforting hug she'd given Troy that had led to him brushing her neck with his hand and pulling her face to his. In the moment, it felt unstoppable. Like it was happening only because Troy was hurting. But playing it back the next morning, as her head pounded with every breath she took, Amy had seen it for what it really was: two incredibly weak people who had horribly betrayed a wonderful person.

Amy wiped away the memory and found her voice again. "Why don't we head somewhere we can all talk—maybe my house? I live close by." She looked at June, wanting to give her the chance to speak next—to say something, anything.

Amy held June's gaze and hoped her eyes conveyed the plea for forgiveness she was seeking. In her former best friend's eyes she saw decades of stories, joys and sorrows that Amy had missed. June was stone-faced—her silent rejection of Amy's invitation evident.

Olivia gripped Zach's arm, as if she needed him to keep her upright. Their faces were flooded with confusion as their parents' pasts came to life before them. Troy looked as if he'd seen a ghost—and maybe he had. Maybe they all had. And William's stare was fixed on June, his shock making it clear he'd never heard of Amy or Troy or any of this.

Amy tried again, her voice shaky. "I'm so sorry about everything that happened, June. I've thought about you for so many years. I can't believe you're here—"

* * *

Amy's apology sliced through June. Her chest stung in response. "Please stop!" June cut her off, and Amy flinched.

June's cheeks felt like they had caught fire. Her heart was slamming inside her chest like a bird trying to break free of its cage. "I don't want to hear it. And there's no way I'm going to your house. I don't want to know where you live. I don't want to know anything about you." She pointed at Troy. "Or you." Her lip started to quiver, and she forced it to stop. She would not cry. "I have nothing to say to either of you!" June caught the attention of a baby in a nearby high chair, his eyes wide with fascination as he watched her while mashing some unidentifiable food into his tray. June must have looked and sounded like a wild animal to him—her cheeks flaming red, her nostrils flaring, her voice sharp.

June felt like she was in a bad dream. That any minute she'd wake up soaked from sweat but relieved it hadn't been real. She'd had nightmares about Amy and Troy over the years, triggered by news that there was a reunion at their college or that a mutual friend had gotten engaged. She couldn't believe they were standing three feet from her now. She had walked into the brunch ready to make apologies for being tardy. Then she'd planned to charm the people who would soon become part of her family. But now she was staring at a man who would have become her own family had they gotten married. And a woman she had *already* considered family. She'd been the sister June never had, the one with whom she'd made a pact that no matter what happened in their lives, no matter where they were in the world, they'd spend their fiftieth birthdays together. June practically choked on the irony—those birthdays would happen next year.

Reunited, and it felt so *not* good.

June finally allowed herself to look at William. She could see in his face how lost he was. She knew he was wondering who in the hell these people were. He would soon put the pieces together and figure out that Troy and Amy were the reason June had never been able to give William her full heart. Part of why their marriage had ended.

Sure, they'd had other issues—one being that William's job always came first. June often snapped that if he was going to have two wives, why couldn't the other one be *human* and hot so they could at least have a threesome? And William was a man of very few words, especially when they argued. If avoiding conflict was an Olympic sport, he'd have grabbed the gold.

Once, toward the end of their ten-year marriage, when June had pushed him to the edge, he'd accused her of never being *in love* with him. June had denied it—of course she'd fallen in love with him, and still was! He'd swept her off her feet. But later, when she lay alone in their bed, William downstairs on the couch, she'd stared at the rotating blades of her ceiling fan and wondered if he was right. And she'd allowed herself to do something that was strictly off-limits: think of Troy and Amy. Losing them had taken a giant piece out of her.

The pain of that loss had sat dormant in the dark corner of her heart until today.

Everyone's eyes were fixed on June—Olivia and Zach wanting an answer. Amy wanting an answer. William wanting an answer. And Troy wanting what? She didn't know. She saw flashes of the cake tasting for her wedding to Troy in 1996. Amy had shown up at the bakery late, on the morning after she'd slept with Troy. June had been worried—she had spilled her guts about a fight she'd had with Troy into Amy's answering machine and was surprised when she hadn't heard back. She'd watched the latest episode of *ER*, glancing at the cordless phone in her lap every few minutes, willing it to ring. It wasn't like Amy not to call her back. When Amy finally showed up at the bake shop, June teased her that she hoped she hadn't called back because she'd hooked up with a hot guy.

Amy turned pale, and June's stomach twisted like the glazed donuts behind the bakery counter as she listened to Amy explain. Amy's confession spilled out so quickly that it took June a few seconds to register what she'd said. And once she did, she took the beautiful piece of red velvet she'd been looking forward to eating and shoved it into Amy's upturned nose, the red spongy cake crumbling down her cheeks, the white frosting obliterating her eyes. Then she stormed out. Her purse caught on the door as she tried to escape. She had to stop, untwist it, and power forward again. But she'd never looked back.

Now she felt the same pressure in her chest that she had that day. Like she needed air urgently, but her windpipe was blocked. She turned and strode out of the restaurant, her legs stretching to keep up with the pace her mind had set. She held her purse close so it didn't catch on the door this time. And again, she didn't look back. But she heard the voices.

Olivia's as she chased after her mom.

William's as he chased after Olivia.

June rushed to her car, her arms pumping like a power walker trying for a personal record. She could hear her family approaching, but she kept moving forward as best she could in the impractical four-inch heels she had chosen in a desperate effort to impress the mother of her daughter's fiancé, who'd turned out to be Amy! June still couldn't believe Olivia had been talking about *Amy* when she'd bragged about how gorgeous her future mother-in-law was, the amazing clothes she wore. She didn't want, or know how, to explain her connection to Amy and Troy to Olivia or William.

Maybe she could get into her vehicle and race off—well, drive at the top of the speed limit, because if she didn't, Officer Bushy Stache probably had radar and would track her down and give her a ticket. She reached her Subaru Outback, panting. She was out of shape—another cruel reminder of the decades that had passed. In college, she'd played tennis (for fun!) and taken step aerobics classes while wearing G-string leotards (nonironically!). It was time to get a Peloton. After seeing Amy's lithe body and toned arms, June was suddenly willing to pay its hefty price tag. Amy probably had that Mirror thing too.

June leaned against her car and watched Olivia and William approach with matching expressions—furrowed brows, cocked heads, wide eyes.

She caught her breath and gave them the CliffsNotes version of her past with Zach's parents. Girl met boy in college. Boy asked girl to marry him. Boy slept with girl's best friend.

Girl's best friend got pregnant and married boy. Girl never spoke to either of them again. She knew this explanation was no better than a Band-Aid placed over a gaping wound that required stitches, but right now it was all she could muster.

* * *

Inside the restaurant, Zach grabbed the edge of the table, and water lopped over the edge of his glass. His parents had just explained why June was so upset. "How could you guys have done that to your best friend?" He pointed to Troy. "To your fiancée?" Zach shook his head. "Now it makes sense why you got divorced. This dirty little secret must have made staying married impossible."

Zach felt sick as he said the words. As he realized *he* had been the result of the dirty little secret. That his birth had ruined several relationships. "You love to tell the story about meeting while drinking Long Island iced teas. Is that all bullshit?"

Zach rubbed his temple and looked out the window past his mom and dad. Olivia and her father were talking to June. He wondered what Olivia was saying. How she was feeling. All Zach knew was that he was angry. "I should have known. People don't drink those!"

"The Long Island iced tea part is true," Amy offered weakly. "It's what led to the other part of the story." She stared down at the white tablecloth.

Zach noticed some of her red wine had spilled on it, and for no logical reason, that made him angrier. "You mean the getting-pregnant-with-me part of the story?" he snapped.

His mom jerked back, clearly shocked by his aggressive tone. He didn't speak to her that way. He didn't speak to either of them that way.

Troy leaned across the table and touched Zach's shoulder. Zach shrugged it off.

Zach saw a shadow of sadness quickly pass across his dad's face, and that was hard to see. He didn't want to hurt his parents, but he was hurt. He felt stupid. He cringed as he recalled telling Olivia the Long Island iced tea anecdote. How they'd Googled the ingredients after and laughed at how gross the drink sounded.

Troy and Amy hadn't worked out as a couple, but he'd always loved his parents' story—they told it with humor and heart. He'd believed they were two people who'd met in a bar, drunk too much, and ended up with hangovers *and a baby*. He'd always believed they had the best intentions to make it work when they got pregnant, simply because they were two good people trying to do the right thing. But had it been guilt that motivated them instead? Guilt over what they'd done to June?

"*Technically*, we did meet and drink Long Island iced teas, but it wasn't *how* we met. We already knew each other," Troy said.

"Your dad called me because he and June were having some problems. Neither of us were looking to betray June. It just happened."

Zach gave his mom a hard look. She seemed like she was in a daze. His normally impervious mother's eyes were watery. She was actually showing emotion! He hated seeing her so upset, and hated knowing he was partially to blame, but at the same time, hadn't she caused all this? "Why couldn't you tell me the truth?"

"Not exactly bedtime story material," Troy quipped.

Zach shook his head. "So this is a joke to you?"

"Not at all." Troy twisted the napkin in his lap.

Amy jumped in. "We knew immediately that we did something terrible. We regretted it right away. We hated that we hurt June. We still do." She shared a look with Troy. "But it's complicated. Our betrayal gave us you. And we never wanted you to feel like you were a mistake. So that's why we left that part out. Never thinking it would come back to haunt us."

Zach looked at his dad. Troy had deliberately conducted a séance. He'd brought the ghosts back. But why? Why would his dad tell him about an "old friend's" daughter being in Positano but not say who that old friend was? That the old friend was his ex-fiancée whom he'd cheated on? He had to find out what the hell his dad had been thinking when he knew how these people fit together—into a terrible mind-numbing five-thousand-piece puzzle that *no one should ever finish!*

But at the same time, Zach couldn't imagine his life had he not gone to Positano. He couldn't imagine not knowing Olivia. Not being her husband one day. Because of another mistake Troy had made, Zach was now engaged. He could almost understand how his parents felt about the misstep they'd made that had created him. Troy had been wrong to send Zach to meet Olivia, but Zach was happy he did.

Zach clenched his jaw. What version of the story was Olivia hearing from June? What if his parents were lying to him and there was a worse version that his fiancée was now hearing?

Zach was struck by a scary thought. What if Olivia held his parents' betrayal against him? How could she not feel protective of her mom? And wouldn't that make her mad at *his* mom and dad? And him by association?

He closed his eyes. He hadn't known Olivia long, but he *knew* her. She wouldn't let this change things. She couldn't.

Amy took a drink of her wine. "Let me ask you this: would you have wanted the truth? To hear that we did a terrible thing to some woman you'd never met?"

But I've met her now, Zach thought, and shot another look at his dad. His dad broke eye contact and started fidgeting with his watch.

"I don't know," Zach said. He could see his mom's point. How would it have helped him to know his parents were cheaters? But now he'd met June. Who had once been engaged to *his* dad and was going to be his mom. Zach wanted to puke. Was he somehow related to Olivia? It felt like it in a weird way.

* * *

Troy had practically murdered his napkin and wound his watch so tight it was probably broken. His son's face was etched with worry. It wasn't lost on Troy that Zach was not much older than he had been when June called off the wedding. Troy could still remember how he'd felt when June told him it was over—it was as if his heart stopped beating, the muscles in his rib cage stopped working, the air in his lungs stayed trapped. He'd doubled over in response.

"I can't do this anymore," June said, rubbing her eyes, which were nearly swollen shut. He knew she'd been crying, but she never shed a tear in front of him.

Troy reached for her, but she repelled him. He flinched from her disgust. But he didn't blame her. He felt the same way about himself.

"Please, June, I'll do anything." He'd pressed the words out one by one, the air still caught in his diaphragm.

"Then undo it. Make it so it never happened. Turn back time." June's words were sharp, each one cutting through his heart. It was the one thing he couldn't do. She slid the engagement ring from her finger.

He flashed to the proposal. To her happy tears. To the smiles. The laughter. The race home to get to the phone so they could spread the news.

June had insisted they call Amy first.

* * *

Troy met Amy's gaze now—he knew her so well that he could read the look in her eyes perfectly. It said, *We'll never be able to make him understand, because he wasn't there.* He and Amy always said they'd felt like two survivors of a catastrophe. Damaged, lost, guilty, and alone.

Troy thought back to the morning after he'd slept with Amy. Amy's arm was draped over his chest, the way June's might have been. Their clothes were strewn across the floor as if they hadn't been able to get to the bed fast enough. Before Troy met Amy at the bar, he'd driven up to Santa Barbara and tried to convince June's mom, Eileen, that he could be a good husband to June, a good son-in-law to her. June had been moving forward with wedding planning, claiming that Eileen was never going to give her approval and probably wouldn't attend the ceremony. But Troy knew June was trying to be tough. He decided the best gift he could give June would be getting her mom to see their side.

But Eileen had rejected him. She'd made him feel so unworthy of June that Troy had countered with the most unworthy act anyone could think of: sleeping with your fiancée's best friend. He had fulfilled Eileen's prophecy. Not consciously. He hadn't gone to that bar to meet Amy with a plan to have sex with her.

But he had.

How could he explain this to Zach?

"I begged June to forgive me," Troy said to Zach. He flicked his eyes to Amy. "To forgive us. But she wouldn't. She gave me the ring back, and that was the last time she spoke to me. I called so many times that her answering machine was full. I went to her place. I tried to make things right, but she wanted to move on."

"I tried too—so many times . . ." Amy said, then turned her face quickly away to the parking lot, where June was still standing.

Troy followed Amy's gaze to June. She was running a hand through her blonde hair, and god, she looked beautiful. She hadn't changed a bit. He couldn't believe she was there, only a hundred feet away. He felt like two people: a man thrilled to be reconnected with his lost love, and a father scared to lose his son.

"I still think about her often," Troy said, shocking himself. He hadn't meant to admit that.

Zach's eyes sank, and he sighed.

He knew what his son was thinking. That Troy's selfishness was responsible for all of this. Zach looked worn down, and that made Troy feel worse.

Amy turned around. "You think about her?" She cocked her head. "Often?"

Troy nodded, not daring to say how often. Nearly every day for as long as he could remember. He'd searched for June for years, and finally, he'd found her daughter. "Don't you?"

Troy and Amy never spoke about June. The last time he could recall discussing her was a year after they'd had Zach. Amy had gone to see June. When Amy came back to their apartment, she shook her head and cried into Troy's shoulder.

June had refused to give her a second chance. Amy had removed Zach from his car seat, brought him to her chest, and kissed her son's forehead. "Promise me we'll never talk about June again." Troy had agreed and put his arms around Amy and Zach, wiping away his tears before Amy could see them.

"I try not to. I avoid all the things that remind me of our friendship. The movie *Beaches*—"

"You guys rented that so many times I thought Blockbuster might give it to you," Troy said.

Amy smiled a little. "And Macy's. June loved it there. Every time she had extra money, that's where we went shopping—to buy another choker. I can't step foot in one. Or eat red velvet cake. Can't touch the stuff."

"That's why you freaked out when Dad got you those red velvet cupcakes for your birthday a few years ago," Zach said. "It makes so much more sense now."

Troy remembered that night. He and Amy had been divorced for a long time, but he still brought her something sweet every year. He'd surprised her with the cupcakes, and she'd started ranting about him not remembering why she couldn't stomach them. She'd tossed the box in the garbage and stormed off.

Amy nodded. "I know it was dramatic. But I had buried it the best I could, deep in here." She touched her chest. "I guess I got triggered."

"By cake," Zach said.

"By cake," Amy repeated.

"You guys could have benefited from some serious therapy."

"I'm sure you're right. But I thought it would be easier to pretend it never happened."

Troy understood. He'd tried to forget, so many times, but then something would spark the memory of June. She could be in a song by the Gin Blossoms or that annoying one by Meatloaf about doing anything for love. She could pop into his mind when he went into a bookstore and remembered her love of reading. Once, he'd thought of her when he saw a woman clutching her pearls in a movie. It seemed like *anything* could set off a memory.

At first, he wrote June letters he couldn't send because he had no idea where she lived. Then, when the internet became a thing, he wrote her emails that would sit in his drafts folder because he didn't have an email address. And later, he did Google searches and then social media searches but would come up empty every time. He'd looked for June off and on for over a decade. After he and Amy divorced, he'd allowed himself to fully wonder, *What if?* He'd always thought he and Amy were meant to be because they had Zach. But what if he had also been meant to marry June—only later?

Troy had hoped that one day he'd find her and maybe they could reconnect—as crazy as that sounded. But no matter what Troy tried, he couldn't find June. The woman had zero digital footprint. Not even a LinkedIn.

Then about six months ago, he'd run into a friend from college at a real estate convention. Troy had casually asked about June and found out that she was divorced and had two daughters named Olivia and Chloe. And that her last name was now Abbott. He'd immediately Googled June with her new last name, but the first two pages were all references to a June Abbott who had become the first female CEO of a seedbox company. So he'd given up. He did find Olivia, though, gasping when he saw the uncanny resemblance to June at that same age. Olivia was on Facebook and Instagram and her profiles were public. Troy checked constantly to see if she posted anything about June. But she never did, only posting about going out with friends. When he saw the post from Olivia about her trip to Positano, he decided that was the sign he needed. His son and June's daughter were in Amalfi Coast at the same time. It had to mean something.

When Zach called Troy the next day from Italy, Troy found himself blurting out that an old friend's daughter was also there and sending a stolen Facebook screenshot of Olivia posing on the dock near Spiaggia Grande beach. Troy wasn't sure if it was Olivia's enigmatic smile or Zach's desire to explore Positano, but Zach agreed to go without asking any follow-up questions.

And now they were engaged.

"Do you guys regret getting married?" Zach asked now, the question surprising Troy. "Regret having me?"

"No!" Amy and Troy said in unison, and Troy's heart crumpled. Troy wished he could clear the air right now. He'd tell Amy the truth about how they'd all ended up at this brunch. He'd run outside and tell June he'd never stopped thinking about her. Maybe he'd never stopped loving her? Zach would see how much love he had for June, and it would all make sense. But he knew he couldn't do that—that it would make everything worse. And this wasn't about him. It was about Zach and Olivia.

"We could never regret having you. Ever," Amy said firmly, her eyes blazing with tears. She put her hand over Zach's. "You have to believe me."

Zach looked up at her. "I do. This is all so weird."

"We got married because we thought there was enough love there," Troy said. "We were young and confused. But neither of us regrets trying to be a family. Not for one second." Troy touched his son's shoulder again. This time Zach didn't flinch.

Troy couldn't say the rest. There was no way he could make his twenty-six-year-old son, who wasn't much older than Troy had been when he'd gotten Amy pregnant, understand that he could be happy he'd married Amy and fathered Zach but also regretful that he'd lost June in the process. That the juxtaposed feelings were not mutually exclusive.

*   *   *

Amy felt like she'd been whipped around by one of those terrible carnival rides that Zach had begged her to go on with him when he was a kid. What was the one that made her brain feel like it was bouncing around inside her skull? The Tilt-A-Whirl! She was trying hard to process the information that had been dumped on her in the last thirty minutes. Zach was somehow engaged to June's daughter. And he was questioning everything. Their integrity. Their choices. If they wanted him. That one wrecked Amy to hear.

And Troy still thought about June? That was news. They had agreed not to speak of her, but she couldn't control whether he *thought* of her. Had Troy been thinking about her while he was with Amy? Was that why they had never been able to connect emotionally? Why their marriage had failed?

It made sense why the thought of June had stayed with Troy, but after all these years, it still stung to hear. Maybe because Amy had always known she was Troy's second choice. And only because she'd been pregnant. Amy had tried to convince herself their marriage was meant to be despite that. After she'd had Zach, it had taken her months to get a handle on mother mode. She'd finally gotten Zach to sleep through the night, with very little help from Troy—*he was the one who had to get up in the morning*—and then Amy had moved into wife mode.

She'd bought magazines with cutout recipes. On the rare nights they didn't heat up a frozen dinner, she used them to cook a few basic meals. She felt chronically exhausted, but she nodded in all the right places when Troy would tell her about his latest listing that had an S&M room or lament about an escrow gone sideways. She stayed home with Zach the first year and waited for Troy to gather traction as a broker before going back to college to finish her degree.

As a new agent, Troy worked most nights and weekends showing houses, and when he was home, he used all the energy he had left to play with Zach, which Amy happily let him do, as she did nothing but spend time with her son. When she and Troy fell into bed each night, they didn't reach for each other. Amy felt like they were in a perpetual state of survival, simply trying not to drown in the life they were far too young to be living.

She glanced at Troy now as he ordered a whiskey, neat, and wondered if June was why he hadn't seriously dated anyone since their divorce. Amy understood that when your heart was irreparably broken like both of theirs had been, there would be aftershocks. Amy had never stopped feeling those releases of stress that came after. She knew that losing June had become entrenched in her chemical makeup, imprinted in her DNA. That it affected her friendships—or rather, her lack thereof. The hole in her heart that used to be filled by June remained deliberately empty. She didn't feel worthy of asking for someone's trust after what she'd done to June. And she refused to give away the last pieces of her heart that she had left.

She had a few girlfriends that she'd met through work; they feasted on Mastro's butter cake during occasional happy hours. They sent each other screenshots and texted ridiculous posts from their neighbors on Nextdoor. But she kept them outside an invisible emotional barrier. And she'd thought that was enough. Until today. Seeing her old friend again had shined a spotlight on the truth: none of those women were June.

* * *

In the parking lot, Olivia's face was blotchy from crying. William was raking his hands through his hair.

"I can't believe you never said anything," William said quietly. "When you talked about your ex-fiancé, I had no idea it ended like this." He waved his hand toward the restaurant.

"I know. I'm sorry. I didn't want to discuss it—I wanted to move on," June said.

"I hate to break the news, but it doesn't seem like you have," William said gently.

"I honestly thought I had." June opened the door to her Subaru and sat sideways in the front seat. Her feet were killing her. She looked at Olivia. "How are you doing?"

"I don't know." Olivia was feeling every emotion under the sun. She was upset for her mom, but she was also scared for herself, that this could mean she'd lose Zach. Was she going to have to take sides? Would she lose the love of her life? She looked across the parking lot. Was she supposed to leave with Zach or go home with her mom? She felt stuck to the concrete, unsure of which way to move. Another tear escaped the corner of her eye. "I wanted this morning to be perfect."

"Oh, honey," June said. "I'm so sorry. I wanted it to be perfect too. I feel like I ruined everything for you."

"You didn't," Olivia said, but she was conflicted. Who *had* ruined it? Was it Amy and Troy, who had been selfish assholes all those years ago? Or her mom, who had clearly never moved on from the pain their actions had caused and melted down inside the restaurant like butter in the microwave?

Olivia noticed her mom was chewing her lower lip hard. Her decision was made. She motioned for her mom to get out of the driver's seat. "Let's go. I'll drive you home," she said.

Relief washed over her mom's face. She clearly wanted Olivia to leave with her. Choose her.

Olivia hugged her dad good-bye. She grabbed her phone and shot off a text to Zach.

*Sorry my mom needs me I'm going to drive her home
I love you*

Olivia hit send and then immediately added another.

Also your dad had sex with my mom wtaf

She added a barf emoji for good measure. And she never sent emojis! That was her mom's department.

His response came through quickly.

*I totally understand we'll get through this I love you
so much*

A second later, another text came in.

*I think we may have to get our memories wiped so we
never think of them having sex*

Olivia stifled a laugh as she started her mom's car, relieved that he understood why she had to leave with her mom. Later, she and Zach could sort through the wreckage of their parents' past.

CHAPTER TEN

"We were like sisters," June confessed to Olivia. They were sitting on June's front porch with Meowsers snuggled up between them. A bottle of wine on the table.

Olivia didn't know what to say. Where to start. Her mind was still spinning. Her mom and her future mother-in-law had been best friends? Her mom had been engaged to Zach's father? Amy had gotten pregnant when she'd slept with Troy behind June's back?

"Have you ever seen the movie *Beaches*?" June asked.

Olivia shook her head. "Never heard of it."

June smiled fondly. "Amy and I watched it so many times I had almost every line memorized. Bette Midler was amazing in it."

Olivia did a quick Google search for the movie on her phone.

"It's about two best friends who are like sisters," June said.

"It says here that one of them dies at the end!" Olivia balked.

"It's about so much more than that—their journey, their bond. It's really good. I swear!"

Olivia nodded but was pretty sure she'd never watch it. It sounded so depressing. She still wasn't over the ending of *All the Bright Places*.

A woman walking two overweight corgis passed by on the sidewalk in front of them. "We used to debate about which one of us was Cecilia and which was Hillary."

"Which one were you?"

"I wanted to be Cecilia, the outgoing one. But I was Hillary. The quiet one."

Olivia skimmed the movie description. "The one who dies?" For some reason, the thought of her mother's movie alter ego's on-screen death made her stomach curl.

"Yes. But it's uplifting. I promise."

"Let's watch it together right now. Do you think it's on Netflix?" Olivia said, pulling up the app on her phone.

June shook her head slowly. "I can't. But you and Chloe should later."

"Why not?"

"I think it would be too hard," her mom said, her eyes darkening with pain. "It would bring up too much emotion." June grabbed a blanket from the basket beside them and draped it over their legs.

"But it sounds like there was a lot of good between you guys—you know, before everything. Wouldn't the movie remind you of that?" Olivia asked hopefully.

"I think that's the problem. It was all so good, until it wasn't. Until it couldn't be anymore." June closed her eyes for a moment. "I've been thinking a lot about my engagement to Troy—for obvious reasons . . ." A distant look crossed her face.

"Your grandmother did not want me to marry him," she said slowly.

"Really?"

"She was not a fan. Never gave him a chance."

"That must have been so difficult." Olivia tried to imagine what it would feel like if her mom didn't like Zach. Rejected the idea of him. It was hard enough that June thought they were getting married too fast. And now Amy and Troy were back in her mom's life, which complicated things more. But if June didn't think Zach was worth marrying, that would devastate her.

"There were so many things. She didn't like him. She thought we were too young. That we weren't ready. That I wouldn't finish college."

"Is that why you asked me if I was still going to law school?"

June winced. "Probably. I'm sorry for that and all of my other overboard questions. I became my mother when I was talking to you! I would like to plead temporary insanity."

"I'll allow it." Olivia laughed.

"But what your grandmother never realized, and that I can only see now as a mother, is you're never ready for the big things, like getting married or having children."

"So you don't think I'm ready," Olivia said quietly, her voice small.

June waved her hand. "This isn't about you, Olivia. Marriage is a huge leap—whether you're twenty-four or forty-eight. And only you get to decide when to jump. I realize that now. But your grandmother—she was much more stubborn."

June sighed. "I had to move forward without her. I'd started telling people Troy and I were getting married. But honestly, I still hoped she'd come around." She took a drink of her wine. "But instead, every time I talked to her, she interrogated me about Troy. Reminded me how much she did not approve of him. Imagine how that would feel."

Olivia thought back to that first conversation with her mom about Zach. How it had shaken her. "It would hurt. I would probably stop talking to him about you."

"And I wouldn't blame you," June said. "It's hard when someone you care about so much isn't on your side about something so important. You want to be in love and you want everyone to accept that love. To trust you know what you're doing. And my mom refused."

"I'm sorry. That sucks."

June smiled, clearly amused by Olivia's word choice. "It really did. But Amy helped me through it. I felt broken. Amy showed up at my apartment and said she had a surprise. She took me to Goodwill to try on ugly wedding gowns." June looked up, as if she were watching the scene play out again. "One of the dresses was so fluffy I could barely fit through the dressing room door." She gave a throaty little laugh. "We drank cheap champagne from Big Gulp cups. We *thought* we were hiding the liquor, but we were so obnoxious as we danced around in our ridiculous taffeta monstrosities that we got kicked out for being drunk and disorderly."

"Really? You?" Olivia tried to picture it, but she couldn't.

"Yes, me," June insisted.

"It sounds like Amy brought out a different side of you."

"She did. Don't ask me how she thought of the idea to take me there, but she turned a terrible day into a good one. And I barely thought about my mom for hours," June said. "Which is saying a lot. Before I met Amy, I'd never had a best friend. I'd never connected with someone in a real way, you know?"

"And now you have Fiona," Olivia said, her eyes soft.

"And thank god for her!" June raised her glass to Olivia's, and they toasted. "I had friends growing up. Girls I hung out with in high school. But none of them were my people. Maybe it was because of my complicated relationship with my mom, but I never felt like I could let my guard down. Fear of being judged, I guess. When I met Amy in college, it was different. *She* was different. I knew right away she was going to be my person." June smiled faintly. "You know how Chloe is yours?"

Olivia nodded. She knew how lucky she was that her person was her sister. That she'd never had to look further than the bedroom next door for advice or support. That their shared history gave them shorthand, a secret language of sorts. It was sounding to Olivia that although her mother and Amy hadn't known each other their whole lives, they'd had a similar bond.

"We met in poli sci, I think it was, and after, she said she was getting a Coke and invited me to come. I was thrilled. It was my first week of school, and she was the first person, besides my roommate, to speak to me." June's eyes lit up. "We were walking across campus, drinking our sodas, and she burped so loudly that every student around us stopped and stared. And you know what Amy did?"

Olivia shook her head, struggling to picture Amy—who Olivia was pretty sure didn't own a pair of jeans or ever leave the house without makeup—belching in public.

"She bowed and kept walking!"

Olivia chuckled. "This is a lot to handle. You. Amy. I can't imagine any of this. Did you run?"

"I wanted to, but I didn't. But I did turn as red as those." June pointed to a rosebush. "All I knew was that I wanted to be friends with her. Be close to her. She wasn't afraid of what other people thought. And I was. I was so busy worrying if people liked me that I never let them get to know the *real* me. Amy made me feel like I could be myself—whoever that person might be." She exhaled softly, as if telling the story was releasing something inside her.

Olivia envisioned her mother as a young woman on a quest to find her friendship soul mate. Feeling lost on a huge college campus and in search of an anchor, then finding Amy, like a beacon of light on a dark night. How good that must have felt. Olivia thought of Chloe while her mom spoke—her sister was like that for her too. An anchor.

She couldn't imagine betraying Chloe the way Amy had her mom.

She couldn't imagine a life without her sister in it.

Her mom picked up her story. "And we clicked, despite being very different."

Olivia tried to imagine Amy and her mom ever clicking. "You still seem very different. Like, if I tried, I don't think I could find two women who seem more opposite."

"That doesn't surprise me. I'm still a lot like I was back then. And I'm sure she must be too. She was an extrovert. I was more of an introvert. Amy was always fifteen minutes early—at least—and I was usually late, which annoyed the hell out of her—"

"Sounds familiar," Olivia interjected playfully.

A frown darkened her mom's face. "I'm so sorry about that. I meant to be on time. I had preplanned my outfit, but when I put it on, the striped pants looked stupid and I changed too many times, and then I looked at my watch and I was already late, and then I got into the car and I didn't have enough gas, and—"

Olivia stopped her. "Mom, we've been over this. It's okay. You don't need to keep apologizing. And anyway, you being tardy to the party is *so not* the main attraction anymore. It was pretty much buried by the whole *You and my future father-in-law used to be engaged* thing."

June half smiled at that. "Yeah."

"So why do you think you guys became so close?"

"Like you said, we're opposite. And opposites attract. We complemented each other. She helped me get out of my comfort zone, pushing me to be social. To go to parties, like this one on a booze cruise. I did not want to go, but she talked me into it, as she always could, and it ended up being one of the most fun nights I had in college. Except for the glitter part." June's eyes glinted at the memory.

"Glitter part? Sounds scandalous!"

A smile touched her mom's mouth. "Hardly. But let's just say that night is why I never allowed you girls to have glitter."

"That really blew when we were in the making-slime era of our lives." Olivia tilted an eyebrow.

"You know what's crazy?" June leaned forward.

Olivia shook her head. Hadn't she already heard the spoiler alert?

"I could never decide what hurt more—losing Amy or Troy," June said softly.

Olivia absorbed this. What that must have been like for her mom—losing the two people she loved most in the world at the same time. Olivia wondered if June had considered forgiving either of them, or both. "What was it like to see Troy at the brunch?"

June took a deep breath. "I almost threw up. It felt like a bad reveal on that show you and your sister like—"

"*Love Island*?" Olivia interjected.

"Yes! That one!" June went quiet. "I think," she said, a few seconds later, "that I probably felt every single human emotion at once."

Olivia put her hand over her mom's. "I'm sorry that all happened to you."

"Thank you for saying that, but the universe has a way of taking care of all of us," June said, scratching Meowsers's head when he leaned into her. "Sometimes the path we're on isn't the one we're meant to be walking."

Olivia hoped this didn't apply to her and Zach.

June met Olivia's eyes and saw the questions swirling in them. "But I don't mean you and Zach!" She smiled. "In my case, I mean that I found your dad, and then we had you and your sister. And that wouldn't have happened otherwise." A tear slid down June's cheek. "So don't be sorry for me for one second."

Her mom's words had a hopeful ring, but they still made Olivia infinitely sad.

* * *

Later, after her mother had gone to bed, Olivia played back the entire story to Chloe at Shannon's Bayshore, a dive bar down the street.

"Do you think she regrets not ending up with . . . what's Zach's dad's name again?" Chloe asked.

"Troy."

"Do you think she regrets breaking up with Troy? Look how close we were to not being born!"

"So it's all about *you* now?" Olivia laughed.

"Of course! I happen to be happy I was born." Chloe giggled.

Olivia watched a group of girls enter the bar, one of them wearing a happy-birthday crown. She smiled at her as she considered Chloe's question. Olivia thought of her mom's past more like a sunken ship discovered at the bottom of the sea. Each item recovered from its depths had memories attached—some positive, some painful. "It's not about regret, Chlo. Mom told me she'd learned lessons from what happened. Like the path you think you should be on often isn't the right one—"

Chloe made a face. "Doesn't she kind of have to say that?"

Olivia laughed. "Maybe, but it was also sincere."

"Okay, enough about Mom. I'm sorry for what's happened to her, but how are *you* doing?" Chloe asked. "You must be freaking out—like how could this happen?"

"I know, I kind of am. All this universe talk from Mom has me thinking. Like why would it bring Zach and me together? What's the point if all it has created is pain?" Olivia swallowed and wiped at her eyes, the tears on a mission to find their escape.

Chloe played with the label on her beer bottle. "There is a point. There must be. Because you're happy. I've never seen you so happy. Not right now, because you're about to cry, but you know what I mean." Chloe smiled.

She looked blurry through Olivia's watery eyes.

"All this other bullshit of people sleeping with other people's people is temporary. They'll get over it. And don't forget about love. It's created love *for you*. That's not nothing."

Olivia pictured Zach proposing to her, his eyes wet as he held out the ring to her. Was Chloe right? Olivia's heart had opened, and it had caused her mom's to break all over again?

Olivia wondered again what Zach was thinking. What emotions he was feeling. They'd texted and FaceTimed earlier, but they were still stunned, emotionally exhausted, and confused by it all. Though Olivia knew it was futile, she'd been hoping that after Zach talked to his mom and dad, he would have more insight to share. That when they compared notes, this insane story would all make sense. But he didn't.

How could she look at Amy and Troy the same way again? They were supposed to be her in-laws. If she married Zach, did that mean she would be saying what they'd done to her mom was okay? She thought about Chloe's words. Was her and Zach's love enough to make this make sense?

"Maybe you're right, but I don't know what to feel. I've never seen Mom like this—not even after the divorce." Olivia remembered hearing June crying in the shower, sobbing in her bedroom when she thought her daughters were sleeping, her red and puffy eyes betraying her the next day. "This is a different kind of sad—hard to explain. It's like she's in mourning. She's not crying, but she's . . ." Olivia searched for the word. "Broken."

Chloe frowned. "Ugh. Poor Mom."

"I'm glad you weren't at the brunch—I'm not sure I'll ever forget the look on her face when she saw Amy. It was like she'd seen a ghost." Olivia pictured it again. "Although I guess she had."

"Maybe this isn't a bad thing," Chloe offered.

"Mom confronting her ghosts?"

"Sort of. Maybe by marrying Zach, you're meant to bring Mom and Amy and Troy back together? Maybe it was meant to come full circle. This way, they can all get over what happened."

Olivia considered that. "Now *you* sound like Mom."

Chloe smiled. "Well, maybe there is something to this whole *universe made me do it* thing?"

"Or do we only say things like that because it makes us feel better about our choices?" Olivia exhaled, and it felt like her chest was expanding for the first time in hours. "Right now, I feel gross. Like this is all my fault. Not the universe's. Mine."

"No way. I will not let you take the blame for this. You and Zach are not the problem here. Speaking of, get up early and go home to him."

"I wouldn't want her to wake up without me here. Don't you have class in the morning?"

"It's a virtual class tomorrow. Go see Zach—you guys need to figure this out."

"I don't have a car here. Can I borrow yours?"

"Of course." Chloe's features softened. "And Olivia? If Mom wants you to be happy, which of course she does, she will figure out things with Amy. You and Zach should tell them to get their shit together. They don't need to be best friends again. They only need to figure out how to be in the same room without someone running out of it."

Olivia remembered her mom dramatically speed-walking out of the restaurant. "Easier said than done."

CHAPTER ELEVEN

When Zach got home from brunch, he was supposed to work on marketing ads for upcoming listings, but instead he edited his photographs from Italy in his darkroom until two AM. He had taken so many photos during the trip, each capturing yet another Olivia. There was one of her leaning back in the sand; the wind had blown her hair across her face so only her smile was visible. He had another of her sitting on the deck of the boat after he proposed, lost in thought as she stared at her ring. And another of her sleeping, the book she was reading open on her chest.

He finally fell into a fitful sleep, but woke two hours later from a nightmare about Olivia falling overboard from their boat in Positano and him being unable to pull her to safety.

Finally, at nine AM, Olivia arrived.

He ran outside and opened the car door before she'd turned off the engine. She stepped out and wordlessly melted into his arms. They stood like that for a long time, her face pressed into his chest, his chin in her hair, not moving when the loud engines of the waste management trucks roared as they emptied the cans on the street.

"It's so good to see you," Zach finally said, kissing her.

"I hated sleeping without you," she said.

"Me too. I finally ended up on the couch." He pushed the nightmare he'd had from his mind. "It felt weird without you in my bed."

"I was in my childhood twin, the scratchy yellow quilt still as uncomfortable as ever. I stared at a poster of Shawn Mendes for half the night."

"He's kind of hot. Should I be worried?"

Olivia smiled sadly.

"How are you? You okay?" He studied her, looking for signs that she was the same fiancée he'd taken to brunch. They'd texted last night that getting married was what they both still wanted. But Zach was still worried that Olivia would change her mind. That she wouldn't want the drama that came with bringing their two families together.

They walked inside and sank into Zach's couch. Zach put his arm over her shoulder, and she leaned into the crook of his arm.

"So Chloe thinks we should tell our moms to put their differences aside."

"What do you think?" Zach asked.

"I agree. It's a lot to ask—and I get that this is all fresh. The Band-Aid was ripped off. My mom is really hurt, but I think she'll do it for me." Olivia paused. "And for you too. For both of us."

She went on to tell him about her talk with Chloe and the good points she had made.

"Do you think your mom will do it?" Olivia asked.

Zach rubbed his chin as he contemplated what the conversation with his mom might sound like. Would she? She was more upset than he'd ever seen her. He'd never told his mother that she *had* to do anything, so suggesting she *get over herself* might not work out well for him. She liked to be in charge—still giving him advice, even when it was unwanted. It had already begun with the wedding planning. Recently, when he was discussing that he and his groomsmen were talking about wearing tuxedos with cummerbunds and bow ties, she'd stopped him midsentence. "Zachary, you must reconsider. Cummerbunds are dated. And a tux feels so formal. I see you in a suit."

He'd nodded noncommittally, not wanting to confess that Olivia had suggested the idea. If he couldn't open his mouth to tell his mom that, how was he going to convince her to make peace with June? In other parts of his life, Zach had no problem asserting himself—with clients, with friends, with Olivia. But his parents? Not so much.

He could imagine the lecture he would get from Logan if he didn't do this. He was already getting so much shit about being told how to dress on his wedding day by his mommy.

Zach turned toward Olivia and agreed to talk to his mom. Saying that of course she'd want what was best for them both. As Olivia visibly relaxed at the thought, a sense of dread rolled through the pit of his stomach. Could he go through with it?

*　*　*

Zach sat in his mom's kitchen, waiting for her to hang up with her assistant. He was shocked she was home on a Monday morning. She'd called in sick. He strained to think of a time she'd missed a full day of work. She'd once gone into the office only hours after getting food poisoning from a shady sushi place, telling Zach she would power through—her penance for trusting a restaurant with only three and a half stars on Yelp.

Zach took a closer look at his mom. She had puffy eyes. Had she been crying? He'd seen more emotion from her in the past twenty-four hours than he could remember ever seeing before. And she was wearing sweatpants! And not the good kind, the Rocky Balboa kind. He squinted—were those his?

"Are those mine?" he asked, when she hung up.

Amy tugged at the waistband. "I had to roll them a couple of times." She dipped her chin. "Okay, full disclosure. Sometimes I wear some of the stuff you left here back in the day. When I want to feel better. It's hard to explain."

Zach took a drink of his coffee as he processed this version of his mom. She was clearly having a moment. "Really? I had no idea."

"Obviously, you had no idea about a lot of things. I'm so sorry." Amy looked down.

"Stop apologizing. You didn't do anything . . . *to me.*" He said softly. After giving it a lot of thought, he'd agreed that his parents hadn't owed him the story of how he was conceived. His mom was right—how would that information have helped him?

His mom's eyes watered. "You must think I'm a horrible person."

"You are the farthest thing from that. You are the best mom I could have ever asked for. You've sacrificed so much for me. You might be a little creepy—the whole wearing-your-grown-son's-clothes thing is a little odd . . ." He glanced at his sweatpants and laughed. "But you are amazing. Don't let this situation make you doubt who you are."

Amy smiled sadly. "You're sweet—but this is more complicated than that."

"June will come around."

"She hates me."

"No, she doesn't."

"You don't know that."

Zach did know some things. Olivia had shared with him some of what June had told her about Amy. It sounded like she had a lot of good memories. But that wasn't for him to tell. "From what Olivia has said about her mom, she has a good heart. I think she will forgive you."

"She didn't before. Why would she now?"

"Because it's been over twenty-six years." Zach's shoulders tightened. "And because her daughter wants to marry me. Maybe she'll let it go because she wants Olivia and me to be happy."

"Is that what I'm supposed to do?"

Zach frowned. "What's the alternative?"

His mom's face hardened. "She wasn't the only one who got hurt. She practically slammed the door in my face when I went to see her after I had you—to beg for her forgiveness. And then yesterday when I apologized, she shut me down. She stormed out. She didn't want to talk—"

Zach swallowed hard and tried to contain his frustration. He felt bad his mom was hurting, that June was hurting, but like he'd said, it had happened over a quarter of a century ago. Wasn't it time to let it go? "She was probably in shock when you said it at the brunch. And it was in front of everyone. You two should talk privately. Try to resolve this."

"I don't know." Amy sat on a barstool and put her palm against her forehead. "I'm not sure I can do it." Her lip quivered. "I can't figure out *how* this happened. How your fiancée turns out to be June's daughter. You meet her in a tiny town in Southern Italy. What are the odds—like one in a billion?"

Dad did this. The answer was at the base of his throat, but he couldn't tell his mom. She would probably put on his high school football uniform, pads included.

Zach hadn't asked his dad why. The answer seemed obvious: he'd wanted a connection to June. And Zach didn't want to deal with what that could mean. Was his dad still in love with her? Was it possible for this situation to get more complicated? Zach didn't want to find out, so he'd kept his mouth shut.

Amy looked up at Zach, her face ashen. "I'm happy for you and Olivia. I am. But I don't think I can call up June and put it all behind me"—she snapped her fingers—"like that." A tear spilled out of the corner of her eye.

Zach watched it slide down her cheek. He started to explain that it wasn't going to be an overnight fix. That it would take time. But couldn't they at least agree to try?

"There has to be another way. It's all happening so fast. Maybe if there was more time before . . ." She didn't finish her thought.

Zach's heart burned. Was she saying they should postpone the wedding? He stared at the dark circles under his mom's eyes, the mottled spots on her face. Maybe he should tell her he and Olivia would wait a couple more months to get married until the dust settled.

But would it ever settle? Would he risk losing Olivia if he suggested they delay the wedding? Would Olivia think he was choosing his mom over Olivia? He'd been there, done that, with other women in his life. He couldn't do it to Olivia.

He remembered his proposal. How Olivia's face had been like a kaleidoscope of emotions—confusion when she saw him on bended knee, then understanding, then love. So much love.

Then she'd demanded he ask. And he'd realized he was so excited he hadn't said the actual words. *Will you marry me.*

He felt a surge of strength. He turned back to his mom. "Then do it for me. And Olivia. Do it for us. And our future."

Amy was silent. Zach waited, his heart beating fast. He'd never demanded his mom do anything for him. Although he was considering demanding she take off his old sweatpants.

Finally, Amy nodded. "Okay."

Zach wrapped his arms around his mom.

"You know I'd do anything for you," she whispered into her son's chest.

"I know," Zach asserted, and hoped asking this of his mom was the right decision. That she and June would be able to put this behind them.

He pushed away the real doubt that lingered: even if they forgave each other, how would they ever forget?

* * *

Later that night, Zach pulled his car into the driveway and sat behind the steering wheel for a few minutes. He could see the light on and knew he'd find Olivia at the dining room table with her law books splayed out in front of her. He'd called Logan after he talked to his mom and gotten the pep talk he needed. To tell V why he hadn't shared the engagement news with his mom before introducing them. He already had one secret he could never tell her, so he needed to share this.

"Hey," he said, kissing Olivia on the top of her head.

"Hey," she said. She was typing notes, but she looked up briefly to smile at him.

He could tell she was busy. This was his out, his excuse to convince himself another time would be better. But he heard

Logan's voice: "If you pussy out on this I will kick your ass." So he sat down across from her and asked if she had a few minutes.

"Wow," she said, when he finished.

"Sorry, I know that was more than a few minutes. Are you going to leave me now? You know, momma's boys are not sexy."

"Oh, you're still very sexy." Olivia put her hand on his upper thigh. "But you know what's not?"

Zach pressed his lips into a line. *Here it comes*, he thought. *The part where she tells me she can't handle it. She doesn't want to compete.* "No?"

Olivia stared at him for a moment. He held his breath.

"The whole she-was-wearing-your-sweatpants thing. That's a serious red flag!" Olivia said, her face neutral. But she quickly broke out into a grin. "But I can work with this."

"You can?"

"Of course. It's not like my family is perfect. Believe me. And the fact that you told me all of this and were vulnerable— that's the sexiest part of this whole thing."

His entire body smiled in relief. "I'm sorry I didn't tell her about you before you met her. It had nothing to do with you."

"I know," she said softly. "It goes way deeper than me! I mean, Harry Potter movie marathons, anyone?" She laughed, then stopped. "But it's also very sweet, Z. You two are tight, like my mom and I are. Hey! That's something they have in common! We found something!"

They laughed.

"Thank you," he said, already knowing what Logan was going to say. *I told you so, dumbass.*

"You're welcome. Now I have to get back to studying. If I fail this test, I will come for you."

CHAPTER TWELVE

As June slid the cardboard sleeve up and down her coffee cup, she thought of the expression *All is fair in love and war* and wondered who came up with it. Someone who'd screwed her best friend's fiancé, June figured.

Someone like Amy.

I know I slept with Troy, but all is fair in love and war!

I know you were supposed to get married to Troy, but all is fair in love and war!

I know I shattered your dreams, but all is fair in love and war!

June scoffed as her eyes darted to the door, and she wondered how early Amy would be. Five minutes? Ten? Fifteen? June had arrived a solid thirty minutes ahead of their scheduled meeting time to make sure *she* was there first. It had required an embarrassing amount of preparation last night, which included, but was not limited to, washing and blow-drying her hair, selecting her outfit, and setting three alarms—two on her phone and one on Alexa. But the hardest had been refraining from drinking a third glass of wine after dinner. (She may have cheated a little by giving herself a giant pour on glass number two.)

June wasn't going to risk a repeat of the brunch. Her lateness had made her the butt of the universe's cruel joke. *I'm going to reunite you with your ex–best friend and ex-fiancé, and you're going to walk into the situation like you're in some movie starring Tori Spelling on the Hallmark Channel.*

Maybe it was time to get a watch. A real one. Did people wear those anymore? Or were they wrapping their wrists with tiny computers that buzzed each time a message arrived? June had a friend whose watch signaled her when it was time to sit, to stand, to breathe. June did not want to be ordered around by a timepiece.

That, she reasoned, was why so many people didn't read actual books anymore. Their wrists were constantly buzzing. What hardcover could compete?

When Amy had texted June, suggesting a meeting—clearly she'd been given the same impassioned speech by Zach that June had received from Olivia—June had demanded (well, strongly suggested was probably more accurate) that Amy come to Long Beach, *her* turf. June sipped her Chardonnay as she watched the bubbles on her phone appear as Amy responded. When June read the words *okay, where?* she felt victorious. Like she had received a sliver of her power back.

And now, any minute, her ex–best friend would walk through the door, and then what? How were they going to unpack years of emotional baggage over lattes? June looked down at the plate she'd placed squarely in the center of the table.

And scones.

June had bought two no-foam almond milk lattes and a maple *and* a blueberry scone, with the thought that she'd let

Amy choose which pastry she'd prefer. But as June walked to the table in the corner—the one where she'd have the best vantage point for seeing Amy when she arrived, so as to not be caught off guard—she'd laughed at herself. Why had she bought Amy anything at all? Shouldn't she want to shove one of the crumbly muffins down Amy's throat instead of debating whether she was gluten-free? (She'd done that too, deciding to buy the maple because it was made with almond flour.)

June didn't know what she was feeling anymore. She'd been angry. Nostalgic. Sad. Depressed. Numb. You name the feeling, she'd felt it. This morning she'd landed somewhere between guarded and hopeful and, apparently, hospitable.

She wasn't sure what to say to Amy today. Preparing something wasn't her style. If she tried, it would come out all wrong and she'd sound like an idiot. That wasn't a risk she was willing to take. She'd follow Amy's lead. June was expecting an apology, which she planned to accept this time—though it wouldn't mean she would forget how it felt like she'd been kicked in the gut when Troy told her Amy was pregnant, her breath sucked away, his lips moving but June unable to hear a word that came out of his mouth after *baby*. She'd refused to cry in front of him, waiting until after she made him leave, then sobbing for hours until her tear ducts broke down. But the hardest part of all was when it hit her that Troy's baby would be permanent while her future with him had been erased.

Going back there, to those raw feelings, wasn't something June was willing to do. That would give Amy too much power over her. After she called off the wedding, June had packed up the emotional baggage from her relationships with Troy and Amy and shipped it off somewhere with no return address. Then she plowed forward with her life, refusing to look back.

She eventually returned to San Diego State and graduated with an English degree. She then met and married William. She had her girls. She managed a local independent bookstore before opening her own. For years, she had succeeded in not thinking about Amy or Troy.

But now that they were back in her life (she still couldn't believe she was saying those words), it felt like those boxes had been returned to sender and were sitting on her front porch, begging to be brought inside the house. *Open me!* June couldn't help herself—she was curious after all these years what she would find inside.

In the past few days when June had allowed her brain to return to 1996, she hadn't ended up focusing on the bad parts of the story. Like the day Amy had confessed that she'd slept with Troy and June went back to her campus apartment and ate wedding cake and drank Captain Morgan's spiced rum until she puked. Or the heart-crushing process of spreading the news that it was over. The feeling of being punched in the gut when each person inevitably asked *why* had been emotionally crippling. She also hasn't allowed herself to relive maybe the worst memory of all: the conversation with her mother. The one where she'd smugly said, *I told you so.*

Those memories would kill her to play back.

So instead, her mind kept looping the good memories, especially with Troy. Because there were so many of those. Like early in their relationship, when she'd come down with a really bad flu and couldn't get out of bed for days.

"June? I know you're in there!" Troy had laughed.

June groaned and rolled over on the couch. She could picture Troy standing outside her front door, wide grin, blond floppy hair falling into his eyes, probably wearing a T-shirt and a pair of board shorts. And flip-flops. Always flip-flops. June glanced at the bucket on the floor, thankfully empty, but probably not for long.

"I look awful. You can't see me like this!" She'd mustered all her energy to call out to him.

"I doubt that. I'm sure you look gorgeous while you're barfing."

June smiled. She did *not* look gorgeous. She hadn't washed her hair in days. She'd sweated through her clothes and let them dry, never bothering to change out of them. Her face was as white as a piece of her college-ruled binder paper. And her breath. She'd gagged the first time she'd tried to brush her teeth. She hadn't attempted it again.

"I'm not leaving. Either you let me in, or I'm going to live out here until you do. I brought a case of beer and a sleeping bag."

June got up slowly, her stomach swirling at the sound of beer. She removed the chain and cracked the door. "I'm probably contagious, and—"

Troy pushed his way inside, giving her a once-over.

"You weren't lying. You do look like shit," he laughed.

June couldn't hold her smile back. "Shut up." The room started to spin, so she gingerly walked back to the sofa. "That's not beer." June pointed to the grocery bag he'd set on the floor.

Troy smiled. "I know. It's chicken soup, Gatorade, saltines, orange juice, 7UP—I wasn't sure what would sound good to you, so I brought everything my mom would give me when I was sick." He dug inside the bag. "Oh, and a thermometer. Here, put this under your tongue."

June obliged, drawing in a deep breath to hold back the nausea. She could not barf in front of this man—there would be no coming back from that.

Troy removed the thermometer after two of the longest minutes of June's life. "One hundred point one." He rooted around in the sack again, pulling out a bottle of Tylenol. "Looks like you're going to need this."

"I can't keep anything down. I can't—"

The vomit went everywhere. On Troy's bare legs, his feet, his flip-flops.

"So that's what they mean by projectile!" Troy somehow had a smile on his face.

June couldn't figure out why he was being so cool about it. Why wasn't he turned off by this? She was mortified. "I'm so sorry. I'll get you a towel."

"I got it, I got it. Let me help you get into the bathroom so you can take a shower. It's all over you too."

"You're just trying to see me naked," June said, feeling so much better after her latest release but knowing it was going to be short-lived.

Troy shook his head. They hadn't had sex yet, but June was ready. Not right-then ready, because vomit, but ready once she was back in fighting shape. It had been Troy who'd kept them from moving too fast. They'd been dating three weeks, and the most they'd done was make out. She knew he was attracted to her—that was hard to miss as their bodies pressed together—so he was clearly doing the whole gentleman thing. Which June appreciated, of course. She'd known Troy was one of the good ones from the moment they'd met at a party. He'd saved her from one of his drunk friends who was trying to pressure her into doing a beer bong. Troy had sidled up with a can of Coors Light and told the guy to move on, joking to June that she was smart to stand clear because there were more germs on the funnel than on the toilet seat in the frat house. June had found him funny and charming and accepted the beer. And he'd been like that—good-natured, down-to-earth, and nurturing—all the way through their relationship.

Until he wasn't.

* * *

"June?"

June looked up. Amy was standing in front of her. June forced a smile but inwardly berated herself. So much for not being caught off guard! Amy looked flawless in white pants, an olive-green blouse, and black patent-leather heels that probably cost more than June's monthly car payment.

"Hi." June stood, smoothing the maxi dress she'd felt cute in but now seemed dowdy. She motioned to the seat across from her. "How was the drive? Probably a ton of traffic, I'm sure." June had banked on this. Wanting Amy to sit in gridlock on the 110 South. More time to think about her apology.

"Actually, none. It was a smooth, breezy ride."

"Oh? That's good!" June feigned enthusiasm.

"The drive as you come over the bridge and down Ocean Avenue is beautiful. Pasadena is great, but I forget how much I love seeing the water."

June couldn't remember the last time she'd walked down to the beach. It was only blocks from her house. It was easy to take for granted.

"This for me?" Amy pointed at the latte.

"Yes. Olivia told me you like almond milk lattes. And I grabbed scones too—the maple is gluten-free."

"Scones? I can't remember the last time I had one—carbs and I are *not friends*." Amy stopped suddenly, clearly realizing her slip. She quickly regained her composure. "I'll try the gluten-free. It was very nice of you to get this. Thanks." She broke off a piece of the pastry and popped it into her mouth.

"No problem," June said. "So—"

"So here we are," Amy finished. "May I start?"

"Sure," June said, wondering how the apology was going to feel. If it was going to check some sort of box for her. If she'd leave this coffee feeling any lighter, different.

"When I found out Zach and Olivia were getting married, I wasn't sure it was a good idea. Honestly, I'm still not. Don't get me wrong, Olivia is lovely, but it feels so rushed."

June took a sip of her latte. "I felt the same way."

"And I thought that the brunch would be a way to gauge how 'the other parents' felt. I suspected I couldn't be alone in this. I mean, Troy has been all about it from day one. But that's so typical Troy . . ." Amy fiddled with the lid on her coffee. "This is so weird. I think of him as my annoying glass-is-always-half-full ex-husband, because he is, but he's also—"

"My ex-fiancé," June said simply.

"Right. That. And that's where I'm going with this. I had planned to try to align with one of Olivia's parents—maybe come up with a plan to get them to put on the brakes. But obviously that didn't happen and can't happen now. Because of our history." Amy's watch dinged, and she checked it.

June suppressed an eye roll.

"Sorry, work. I do PR for the Rose Parade, and . . ." Amy looked up from what she was reading. "But you don't want to hear about that. Let me respond to my assistant, and I will turn off my notifications."

June listened as Amy dictated a text into her watch and could still see the twenty-three-year-old version of her former friend. June had always known Amy would achieve any goal she strived for. That was Amy. A go-getter, a hard worker. Back then, whether it was for a sorority fund raiser or a class project, Amy gave everything 110 percent. She was the one on the top branch of the phone tree and had a desk drawer full of well-used clipboards. June wasn't surprised to find Amy had a career working with the world's most famous parade. She wondered if she still used her beloved clipboards or if they'd been replaced by an iPad.

"Sorry about that. And please let me know if you need to get over to the bookstore. I don't want to keep you," Amy said.

"It's fine." June glanced over Amy's shoulder and could see the storefront. "We don't open until ten."

"Oh, wow. That's like midday for me!" Amy waved her hand dismissively.

June pressed her lips together into a line. "So, you were saying?" *While you weren't apologizing.*

"That we have to make this right for them. Any chance of talking them into postponing the wedding has now been over-shadowed by *us*."

"I'm not sure I would have gone so far as to ask them to postpone. I was conflicted because it was—*is*—all happening so fast, but I trust Olivia's judgment. And at the end of the day she—*they*—are adults," June said, with more vigor than she possessed. She agreed with Amy but felt the urge to protect Olivia. From what exactly, she wasn't sure.

"Right, of course they are. It's water under the bridge now anyway." Amy tore off another corner of the scone, and a few crumbs dropped onto the plate, forming a fluffy little pile.

June didn't know how Amy was able to eat right now. June's stomach felt like one of the knotted pretzels she saw behind the glass by the cash register.

Amy finished chewing. "I think we need to put this rift behind us. We should do it for them." She took a drink of her coffee.

Rift? What a casual way to describe our lives being imploded because you slept with my fiancé!

"And probably the easiest way, instead of getting into the *she said, she said*, if we can do it, is to wipe the slate clean."

June searched for the apology in Amy's words, but she was damn sure she didn't hear one. Was there a *she said, she said*? June had always thought this story had only one side: *hers*.

She thought of Olivia. How Olivia had asked June to please put aside *this thing* with Amy so she could marry Zach. Olivia hadn't meant to, but she reminded June of Olivia's thirteen-year-old self when she'd borrowed and promptly lost June's cubic zirconia stud earrings. June had been bummed out for days, and finally, Olivia had asked her mom to please get over it because she already felt so bad—how many times could she say she was sorry? And anyway, they weren't real!

Olivia hadn't understood the earrings had significance. That Troy had given those to June on their one-year anniversary of dating. He'd promised real diamonds once he closed on his first real estate listing. There was no way for June to explain that they were the only thing she'd kept from her former fiancé. Olivia didn't know she'd been engaged before. She'd never heard of Troy.

June had had no choice but to get over it.

She had no choice now either.

She had to suck it up and agree to put this behind her. So she told Amy she would.

And then she waited. For an apology that never came. Not as they finished their coffees and Amy pulled out her tablet

(June had been right) and started making a list of the wedding tasks they should start working on. June said several times that they should probably check with Olivia first, but Amy shook her head.

"This is my wheelhouse. She will be relieved we're helping, I'm sure, with as busy as she is with law school." *How would you know?* June thought, then painfully realized she could know. Olivia might have told her. Or Zach.

June took a deep breath and forced herself to see Amy's list as helpful rather than controlling. She listened as Amy said the items out loud that she was also typing: *Engagement party. Invites. Flowers. Band or DJ? Harpist? Catering? Photographer? Guest list? Venue? Wedding dress for Olivia. Wedding band for Zach. Suit for Zach—not tux!*

June didn't know what that last one meant—why couldn't he wear a tuxedo? Her mind drifted to the wedding she was supposed to have had with Troy. She and Amy had lain on her bed and made a list for that too. Amy had written the items in her spiral notebook. She had placed a label on the front that read *Maid of Honor.*

June scoffed under her breath. Maid of dishonor was more like it.

Afterward, June walked Amy to the bookstore to show her around. She thought an apology might happen there, that Amy would warm up to her, be happy for her that she'd accomplished her goal of owning a bookstore, and remember when they used to whisper their dreams to each other. But there was only more wedding talk.

June was relieved Chloe had the day off, not knowing how she would have introduced Amy to her daughter. What words would she have used. Probably not nice ones.

Later, Amy texted June to say that Zach was relieved they'd made up. June wondered if that was really what they were going to call this. Making up? Hadn't they simply placed a piece of plywood over a gaping hole, hoping it would protect against someone falling in?

June reminded herself that Amy had technically apologized three times. She'd said she was sorry back when it happened, then again when she'd come to her apartment a year later, and she'd tried last week at the brunch.

All three times, June had shot her friend down. June wondered why she kept wanting the very thing she'd already received.

* * *

Later that night, June poured herself a glass of wine and thought back on her friendship with Amy. Amy had been her sister from another mister, as they'd called each other. She remembered the first time they'd used their fake IDs to buy beer. The clerk had eyed them suspiciously as they walked up to the cash register with a six-pack. They'd also grabbed a carton of eggs and a loaf of bread to seem older. When he asked for ID, it had been Amy who'd whipped hers out. It looked nothing like her, but she'd charmed the clerk so much he'd barely glanced at it. The entire time June kept a straight face, but her heart was hammering in her chest and she was sure they were going to get arrested.

After, June squealed in the parking lot, impressed and invigorated by Amy's confidence. Amy made June want to be more outgoing. Stronger. Braver. And when they were together, June was those things. She felt like the best version of herself.

She stared at her warped reflection in the stainless-steel goblet she was drinking from and wondered what had happened to that woman.

CHAPTER THIRTEEN

"You will not believe this wedding to-do list that Amy has made—and she keeps adding to it." June plopped down on a stool at the large butcher block table where Fiona was trimming long-stem roses, calla lilies, and snapdragons for an arrangement.

Fiona put her sheers down and walked to the front door of her floral shop. She flipped the sign from *open* to *closed* and locked the door. "You have my undivided attention," she said.

"Listen to this." June squinted at the Google Doc on her phone. The one Chloe had helped her figure out how to navigate last week when she'd first received it from Amy. Why they couldn't email, June didn't understand. June didn't get a lot of things when it came to Amy.

"Here, use mine." Fiona pulled off the reading glasses perched on the top of her head. "Your font is freakishly large and you still can't see. You should give in and get a pair. Look how cute mine are!" She showed off the tortoiseshell frames.

"Everything looks cute on you." June took them from her and started reading.

"There's a June column, an Amy column, and a June and Amy column—"

"You two are sharing a column?"

"Oh yeah."

"Well, isn't that cute."

June shook her head. "Okay, so there's a long list that she says must be accomplished quickly. We're on an accelerated timeline because the wedding is in less than six months and Amy also has a Rose Parade to plan. In case you haven't heard!"

"Oh, I've heard." Fiona rolled her eyes.

June started reading. "Here's what I have to do *this week*: set up a wedding website, interview videographers and narrow them down to two, find at least two places to do wedding invitations, start a guest list, get a bid from at least two florists—"

"Woah!" Fiona put up her hand. "At least two florists? You're using me, right? I was named the number-one florist in Long Beach two years in a row, after all. If you talk to George over at George's Geraniums, I don't think I'll be able to get over it." Fiona smiled.

"Of course we're using you!" June said. "That is nonnegotiable. Olivia wouldn't have it any other way, nor would I."

"Okay, because I could cut a bitch." She picked up her sheers.

June laughed. "Don't worry. It won't come to that. Okay, so there's more. By Friday, I also have to find my mother-of-the-bride dress or, at the very least, select the color and style—and there's a note to please not pick green because that's the shade Amy looks best in."

"It does *not* say that." Fiona grabbed June's phone. "Give me those back." She pulled the glasses off June's face, and her eyes grew wide. "It really says that."

"Told you." June blew out a long breath.

"What's in your shared column?"

"For starters, she wants us to do the wedding registry together. She asked if I could meet her at Crate & Barrel *in Pasadena* tomorrow."

"Of course. The fact that she traveled out of her little Pasadena bubble to have coffee with you seems nothing short of a miracle."

June cocked her head and shook it.

"So you'll meet Olivia or Zach there?" Fiona asked.

"Nope—she says Olivia has class and Zach has to work but has promised to text us a list of what they want."

"Want me to come? Like I said, I could be very helpful in the kitchen knife section."

"As much as I wouldn't mind you cutting this bitch, I think it's better if you stay home."

Fiona made a pouty face. "But that's so boring." She picked up some greenery and started layering it next to the roses. "Doesn't it kind of seem like Amy is acting like she's—"

"The one getting married?"

Fiona nodded. "Do you think it's because she never had a wedding? It was city hall when she was pregnant with Zach, right?"

"I think so. That's what she told me when she came to my door when Zach was about a year old. You know, wanting me to forgive her."

"With Troy's baby in her arms?" Fiona said, exasperated.

"I was pretty cold."

"Well, again, Troy's baby was *in her arms*. You were upset."

"I was. But I could have handled it better." June thought back to that day. She hadn't invited Amy inside. Zach was fussy, and Amy kept adjusting him from one hip to the other as she rambled on about never meaning to hurt June. June could barely look at her. Or at the baby that had Troy's enigmatic hazel eyes.

"You did the best you could. And you weren't the one who broke up a marriage and a friendship. That was a consequence she was going to have to learn to live with. She might have called first."

Now that June was a mother, she could understand how overwhelmed Amy must have been that day. How exhausted. It didn't excuse what Amy had done. But June did regret slamming the door in her face. Which she had finally done when she couldn't hear Amy's voice for one more second. She had wanted to forget.

"I still cannot believe you never told me the story."

"I didn't tell anyone."

"But I'm not anyone! I'm your best friend!"

June wasn't sure why she'd never confided in Fiona. Fiona was on her second marriage because her first husband had cheated. But June found it easier to pretend that what happened to her had actually happened to someone else. Someone she didn't know anymore. And in many ways, that was the truth. "It's not that I didn't trust you. Because I do, more than anyone. It's more that I buried it. And I never thought it would come up again."

Fiona placed her hand on top of June's. "Don't let her railroad you tomorrow. It's your daughter's wedding too. Remember that. And if you want the Vitamix and she wants the Nutribullet, you hold your ground, girl."

June smiled. "Thank you. I love you."

"I love you too," Fiona said. "And I'm taking you shopping for your mother-of-the bride dress. I have a strong feeling you're going to look amazing in green."

* * *

Amy sat in one of the leisure power recliners and found the control button on the inside arm. She popped her feet up on the footrest and scrolled through the Crate & Barrel app while she waited for June to arrive. Amy had already preselected the items she thought Zach and Olivia would want. She'd done extensive research on the must-haves for every bride and groom but also added her own ideas into the mix.

Amy checked her watch. She had a text from June that she was five minutes out. *Right on time*, Amy thought, then couldn't contain the catty thought that rolled in next. *After that brunch, I doubt she'll ever be tardy again. Not a good look.*

She glanced around the huge two-story store, excited to start scanning the items and adding them to the app. She hadn't been able to do this when she got married—after city hall, she and Troy had opened a frying pan from her mom and dad and a set of mixing bowls from his parents. Amy hadn't mixed or fried a thing for the first year. There were a lot of frozen pizzas and TV dinners. They used the little money they did have to buy formula and diapers for Zach. They had a Mr. Coffee they'd purchased at a garage sale, but to have had a Breville espresso maker like she'd just seen online? She couldn't imagine.

She saw June enter the store and took a deep breath. She hoped this went well and that June had a good attitude about it. June had seemed checked out when they talked about the wedding at the coffee shop and hadn't had much to offer in terms of planning. That surprised Amy. June was the mother of the bride! June also hadn't updated their Google Doc in days. Amy had no idea if June had done anything on her list. And they were running out of time.

"Hi, June," Amy said as she walked up, punching the button so her footrest would go down. "Thanks for coming up to

Pasadena. I figured this location would be easiest for Zach and Olivia to get to."

"Hi. Of course, I get it," June said brightly, but her taut face spoke a different language. "What's all this?" She motioned toward a group of couples mingling nearby.

Amy pointed to the sign. "It's an in-store wedding registry event."

"Hmm," June said.

"Hi, there," said a tall man with a mustache and hair so gelled that Amy was sure it wouldn't move if he did a hand-stand. His name tag read *Jerome*.

"Hi, Jerome," Amy said.

"Here for the event?"

"Yes, we are."

"Good, good," Jerome said. "Names?"

"Abbott and Carter," Amy said.

Jerome leaned in. "You know, I think it's wonderful that you two are here and want to be part of this. It's not only an event for first-time marriages. Or traditional marriages. Come one, come all, we say here at the Crate. When's your big day?"

Amy was stunned. To be married to June? No thank you. She'd go back to Troy first. "Oh no, we're not . . . it's our kids who are getting married. Her daughter and my son."

June jumped in. "Also, she is not my type!"

Amy's mouth fell open. She waited for June to laugh, but she didn't.

"Good, good. I hear that. To each his own. So where is the happy couple?" Jerome glanced around.

"They're not here. Left it up to us," Amy said proudly and pulled her tablet from her bag. "I've already started a list of ideas for the registry."

Amy thought she saw a flash of irritation in June's eyes.

Jerome nodded his head hard several times, his eyes popping.

Amy waited for a *Good, good*, but it didn't come. Instead, Jerome said, "The bride must really trust you. When I married my partner, we would *not* have been as trusting. Our mothers—well, let's just say, I'm sure we would have ended up with totally useless things like punch bowls and cake stands. No offense."

Amy didn't mention she had both of those things on her list.

"I have a question," June said. "I'm not techy at all—that's her department." She pointed at Amy like being techy was a crime. "But why can't this be handled online?"

"Oh, it totally could. We have an app, and you can click through and add on that. And"—he looked at Amy—"You probably saw that we have Wedding Wednesdays on Insta too. Really no need at all to come in. But I'm glad you did!"

"I did see all the online options," Amy said defensively, giving June a look. Was that another dig from June? So she *was* pissed she had to drive from Long Beach. "But I also thought it would be better to see all of the items in person. Like there are so many different juicers. How could I decide without touching them all?"

"Well, technically, it's not *you* deciding," June said, a little too sharply for Amy's liking.

Amy pinched her lips together. She'd done *a lot* of work prepping for this. She'd taken precious time away from planning the Rose Parade to curate this registry. "I beg to differ. Look at this." She pulled up Zach's list on her iPad and read it. "Four old fashioned glasses, four coffee mugs, and a bar tools set." She exhaled. "He's going to live on that?"

"I've seen straight men get by on worse," Jerome offered.

Amy frowned at him.

"He probably let Olivia decide. What's on her list?" June asked.

"Hers isn't much better. Stemless wineglasses, a cast-iron skillet, one queen sheet set, and an ice cream scoop?" Amy huffed.

"Random. Maybe she eats ice cream in bed," Jerome piped in.

June laughed.

Amy didn't see the humor in any of this. "Well, we're here now, so we should probably get started," she said, deciding she wouldn't let June *or Jerome* get to her. "I have several suggestions."

"I'm sure you do," June said.

"Good, good," Jerome said, but his eyes said, *Bad, bad.* "So, I will be your personal liaison tonight. I will guide you around the store to answer any questions you might have. Shall we start over in housewares?"

"Oh, yes, let's start in housewares," June echoed, and gave Amy a death stare before following Jerome down the large aisle.

CHAPTER FOURTEEN

"Will you please stop reading that? You're giving off major stress vibes and threatening to undo my meditation from this morning," Chloe teased.

Olivia looked up from her phone and frowned at her sister. "Says she who probably snapped through her entire meditation!"

"Not true! I turned off the notifications on my phone for fifteen whole minutes!"

Olivia stuck her tongue out at Chloe and went back to reading the text exchange between her mom and Amy in the thread June had named *V & Z's Big Day*. Which would be a cute name if it were true. Olivia was starting to think she should change the name to *June & Amy's Big Day* instead. So much for their coffee date that was supposed to wipe the slate clean. Things had only gone from bad to worse after the wedding registry disaster. Her mom and Amy had gone to some engaged couples' event at Crate & Barrel—which still confused Olivia—and the text claws had been out in full force since.

Her mom and Amy traded barbs about useful kitchen items versus trendy ones. Amy argued that an air fryer with rapid air technology was the way to go. It held four dinner portions and could be operated by Alexa! June retorted that Alexa would be watching their every move and gathering data to take back to Amazon. They went back and forth about towel warmers, outdoor pizza ovens, and pasta-drying racks. They went three rounds over eight place settings versus ten. Neither of them seemed to notice that Olivia couldn't care less about any of it. And now, somehow, both Amy and her mom had purchased floor-length emerald-green dresses to wear to the wedding. And neither was willing to find something else. Olivia didn't care if they both wore green, but they were adamant that they should not match. June had sent a link to an article on etiquette that seemed to indicate the MOB had first dibs.

And it didn't stop there. Apparently there was also a shared Google Doc that was causing major drama. Olivia had never seen it. She didn't want to. Not that her mom hadn't tried to show her. The other day, as they had been discussing Fiona's ideas for Olivia's bouquet and the table centerpieces, June had ruined the moment by bringing it up. Waving her phone in Olivia's face. Murmuring about how if Amy tried to go with another florist, she'd let Fi cut her?

Olivia glanced at her mom now. June was standing on the opposite end of the LA Pacifica Ballroom at the Four Seasons Hotel in Santa Barbara, where they were waiting to meet with the wedding coordinator. June had sent a text about a wedding photographer she thought Olivia should consider. As Olivia was clicking on the link to check out the pictures, a reply came in from Amy. It was a link to a negative Yelp review followed by the screaming emoji. Olivia ran her hand through her hair. Her mom and Amy couldn't agree on anything. So much for their *truce*.

"Do you seriously meditate?" she asked Chloe.

Chloe shrugged. "What? If Bella Hadid can do it, so can I."

"Does it work? I feel like there's no way I could empty my mind of the things that stress me out." Olivia flicked her eyes over her shoulder to make sure her mom wasn't listening. Olivia lowered her voice, in case. "Like the Momzillas. I swear I'm this close to eloping."

Chloe leaned in toward Olivia. "Remember, this is *your* day, not theirs. You get to decide what kind of wedding you're going to have." She grabbed Olivia's phone and read. "And it's your choice who you want to take your pictures. And anyway, didn't they lose their vote after they played musical sexual partners?"

"Gross—don't make me think about that. Zach already makes enough terrible jokes about it." Olivia groaned, then considered Chloe's point. She did want to get married here. She could envision the wedding she'd been planning in her Zola app. The tables dressed with rose petals and elegant tiered candles. The dance floor with the DJ who would play all of Olivia's favorite nineties songs—especially "Tootsie Roll." The open bar in the corner where they would serve their signature drink—Aperol spritzes, in honor of where she and Zach had met. She imagined her guests walking the tree-lined property at sunset and taking pictures with the Pacific Ocean lurking in the background.

Olivia's screen lit up. It was a text from Amy. She huffed. "Look at this!" She thrust her phone into Chloe's face.

Chloe read, "*We should take another look at the guest list. Smaller and more intimate might be the way to go. I'm willing to make some cuts—like my work colleagues—if June is?*" Chloe stopped and narrowed her eyes at Olivia. "I love her use of the word *we*, as if this wedding planning really is a team effort."

"There is no *we* in Team Amy." Olivia shook her head. "Or Team June."

Chloe continued. "I personally think bigger is better—"

"That's what she said," Chloe and Olivia said in unison, then giggled.

"A text is coming in from Mom," Chloe said.

June: *While I agree that small weddings are nice, I'm not sure I want to tell people that have been in our lives a long time that they aren't invited. Everyone on our list is IMPORTANT.*

Olivia looked over at her mom again, passive-aggressively text fighting as if she weren't standing seven feet away from her daughter, *the bride*. Olivia could see the folding of the skin between her mom's eyes, the reddening of her cheeks.

Why can't she play nice? Did she really have to put *important* in all caps?

Olivia read the response from Amy: *Of course everyone is important! But so is the memory of your daughter's big day. We wouldn't want to have extra people instead of other things Olivia might want instead. Like a harpist! We wouldn't want her to have regrets later. (Sent from Siri)*

Olivia didn't want a harpist. She also didn't think her dad's friends from the hospital needed to be there. But she wasn't the one paying for the wedding. And neither was Amy! Her mom and Amy had been arguing so much that Olivia had to struggle to remember the wedding she'd imagined back in Positano. She looked over to see how her mom was reacting to Amy's jab. June shook her head at her phone.

Oh, you're frustrated? Olivia wanted to scream. *What about me? Does anyone care how many people I'd like to invite?*

Olivia's phone buzzed. It was another text from Amy.

Amy: *Hey guys—I'll be there in five and we can talk guest lists and themes! What do you guys think of fairy lights? We could pick wildflowers and put them in jam jars! I read about it in Buzzfeed. By the way, Santa Barbara is really far—was I supposed to bring my passport? Lol! Going to be a long way for wedding guests to travel . . . Something to consider! Might want to revisit the Pasadena idea again? LOL (sent from Siri)*

Olivia had quickly discovered that her mom and Amy overused *LOL* to soften their digs. Olivia saw her mom frowning at her phone, probably reading the same text—deciding on her best passive-aggressive comeback. The Momzillas had hijacked the text thread, both conveniently forgetting that Olivia was on the chain at all. It had become a platform to debate *everything* about weddings—down to whether photo booths were still in. They weren't, but it wasn't like anyone was asking Olivia.

The biggest issue had been *where* to have the wedding. Amy had been campaigning for a high-end ceremony in Pasadena, because she had connections at every five-star hotel within ten miles—hadn't they heard? She worked for the Rose Parade! Not to mention Zach had grown up there! June had been lobbying for Long Beach—for its laid-back beach vibe, not to mention Olivia had grown up there!

Olivia had let them go back and forth for a while on the location without interjecting. But after they'd blown up her phone for an hour one night as she tried to study for her test on torts, Olivia turned to Zach and asked him where he thought they should get married. He shrugged. "You know I don't care—I'd become your husband in that dirt lot off Alder that my dad listed the other day, if it meant you were going to be my wife."

Then Olivia said, "Aside from the dirt-lot part, that would make your mom happy—she thinks we should get married here in Pasadena."

She watched his face, wondering if he was going to disagree with his mom. Since moving in with Zach, she'd found out Amy had a lot more influence over his decisions than she'd realized. Even after their conversation about Amy, some of her behavior still caught Olivia off guard. Recently, Olivia had come home after a long day on campus with takeout from their favorite Thai restaurant. She opened the silverware drawer to grab forks, only to discover dish towels instead. She asked Zach what was going on. And he answered, with obvious embarrassment, that his mom thought the knives and forks made more sense next to the plates. When he saw the horrified look on Olivia's face, he promised he would be picking his battles but didn't think it mattered where the cutlery was stored. It had taken every bone in Olivia's body not to scream, *Control freak much?* But Olivia knew it was Amy—and her mom's—desire to control her wedding that was really getting to her. "I'll be right back," Olivia said to Chloe. "I'm going to the bathroom."

"Tell Zach I said hi," Chloe called after her.

Olivia smiled. "I will."

"Hey!" Zach answered. "Aren't you at the hotel doing a walk-through?"

"Your mom . . ."

"What now?"

"She's bringing up Santa Barbara being far away before she's arrived. I think she's going to try to make a case for Pasadena again. I'm not sure I can fight it anymore. I already told them it's what we wanted. Maybe we should have it in Pasadena. It is closer to most of our friends and family."

"Don't let them get in your head. *You* are the bride. *You* decide."

"Easier said than done."

"You can do it. I can also call my mom right now and remind her it's what we want—"

"No, that's okay. I should do it." She paused. "I'm so tired of the conflict, you know?"

"I know you are. I'm sorry. I wish they'd grow up."

"I do want it here, Z. I know it's far, but it feels like home."

"I know. I love the stories you've told me."

Olivia had shared memories of skipping rocks with her dad under the pier, her jeans rolled up to her knees and the water still soaking her pants anyway. And how her mom had taken her to watch the gray whales as they migrated down the coast to Baja. The ocean had always centered her, but it was the portion of the Pacific that hugged Santa Barbara that felt most like *home*. Not to mention it was also neutral territory—a place that wasn't on Amy or her mom's list.

"Stay strong, V. If you want it to be in Santa Barbara, that's where it will be."

"I love you."

"Love you too."

After they hung up, Olivia texted the Momzillas—using punctuation, so they would know she was serious.

I know Santa Barbara is far, and we haven't made an official final decision yet, but it's where Z and I hope to get married. Let's all keep an open mind today? Maybe we can look into a charter bus to bring some people up?

Despite her general rule *not* to use emojis, she made sure to follow it up with a bride, an engagement ring, and a bus.

Emojis, Olivia had learned, were the Momzillas' way of thinking they were connecting with her.

June hadn't said it, but Chloe and Olivia had speculated that their mom must have conflicting thoughts about Santa Barbara. She'd grown up there, but Olivia's grandfather had also died there. Olivia's grandmother, whom June had a complicated relationship with, still lived in the area.

Olivia waited to see who would respond first.

Finally, a thumbs-up came in from June.

Shortly after, Amy liked June's thumbs-up.

Olivia smiled. They both clearly still hated the idea.

Those women still wanted to kill each other.

And Olivia was ready to hand them each a knife.

* * *

When Olivia returned from the bathroom, Chloe nudged her. "Amy's here."

Olivia's grandmother, Eileen, also arrived as Amy walked into the room. Eileen's gray hair was pulled tight into a low bun, and she was wearing her signature strand of pearls and a full-skirted dress that was tight in the torso and looked to Olivia like it was from the fifties. Olivia and Zach had FaceTimed Eileen to tell her they had decided to get married in Santa Barbara. Eileen had been thrilled and asked to come on the tour of the Four Seasons—she only lived a few miles away. Olivia had asked her grandmother if she was sure she wanted to do that, reminding her that Amy would be there.

Remember her? The woman who broke your daughter's heart? she wanted to say. Eileen had pursed her lips and twisted her pearls. Surely her grandmother would come back with something sharp witted, something protective of June, Olivia thought. But instead, Eileen offered something cavalier, and Olivia's heart broke a little for her mom.

"Oh, honey, that was decades ago. Even your mother seems to be over it."

Olivia had nodded, but thought, *If only you could see the text thread I'm on.*

Olivia slid her phone into her back pocket and greeted Amy.

"I'm sorry I'm just getting here," Amy said as she hugged Olivia.

"You're ten minutes early." Olivia breathed in Amy's perfume. It was strong and musky—not surprisingly, the opposite of what her mom wore, soft and floral.

"I'm a wrinkly mess from being in the car for so long." Amy smoothed the nonexistent wrinkles in her chic black ankle-length dress.

Olivia watched her grandmother approach Amy, her face hard to read. "Amy, it's been a long time," she said as she gave her a once-over. "How are you?"

Olivia wasn't sure, but she thought she saw Amy stand up a little taller. "I'm well, you know, considering, you know, everything," she said, her voice catching.

Olivia knew her grandmother could be intimidating, but so could Amy. She'd never seen her future mother-in-law act nervous.

Eileen didn't respond. Instead, she stared at Amy. Olivia remembered reading something in undergrad about how this was an interrogation tactic of the CIA or FBI or some government organization.

Amy's chest expanded as she sucked in a deep breath. "I want to say I'm sorry . . . for everything."

"Sorry?" Eileen's blue eyes popped. "My dear, you don't need to apologize to me. You did me a favor. You are aware I didn't want my daughter to marry that man—well, he was a boy back then. When I found out what the two of you did, I was relieved. And it turns out I was right about him, clearly."

Olivia watched Amy's face go slack. Olivia wanted to say something, but what? If she defended her mother, she would be going against Amy. If she defended Amy, she would be going against her grandmother and maybe her mother too.

June walked over. "Why is everyone so quiet?"

"Just catching up." Eileen's eyes flashed, and then she smiled.

A tall, rail-thin woman with a pinched expression and a tight grip on an iPad hurried into the room. "Olivia Abbott?"

"That's me." Olivia stepped forward.

The woman extended her hand, and Olivia shook it. "Hi. Nice to meet you. I'm Ariel. Ready for the tour?"

Thirty minutes later, Olivia could hardly contain her excitement. This was an awesome location. She'd already snapped pics of the grounds to a dozen friends and uploaded several stories to Instagram.

"So, you said you and your fiancé are getting married on Valentine's Day?"

"Yes."

"They're super cheesy like that," Chloe chimed in. Olivia elbowed her.

Ariel tapped her iPad. "How does evening work for you? Four PM cocktail hour, five PM wedding, pictures six o'clock, six thirty to midnight reception?"

"That's great—thank you so much." Olivia squeezed Chloe's hand. "I can't believe you have an opening. The other hotels I called thought I was crazy to think there would be availability."

"I think giving yourself over a year is smart. I mean, some plan farther in advance. We're booked out for the next two years, but like I told you on the phone, we had a cancellation for next year," Ariel said. "Let's talk about the deposit."

Olivia felt as if the floor had dropped out from under her.

"Over a year out? No, we wanted to get married this February. In four months."

Ariel's face flushed. "That date is booked. I think we had a miscommunication. I'm so sorry."

Olivia's eyes began to water, but she sucked in a deep breath to stop herself from crying.

Chloe squeezed Olivia's hand again and gave Olivia a reassuring nod. "It's okay. We'll figure something out."

Ariel cocked her head at Olivia. "If you decide to wait, I can hold Valentine's Day for twenty-four hours. But then I'll have to give it to the first bride on the waiting list. Now if you'll excuse me, I have another appointment."

"Maybe waiting a year isn't the worst idea?" Amy offered as Ariel strode off.

Olivia knew the easy answer was to say she'd get married in a year. She wasn't an idiot. She knew all of their parents—well, maybe not Troy, but the others—thought she and Zach were rushing this. But what they didn't get was that nothing was going to change in 365 days; she was still going to love Zach more than she'd ever loved anyone, she was still going to want to be his wife more than anything. So why not do it sooner rather than later?

"Olivia and Zach have made it pretty clear they don't want to wait," June said, a sharpness to her voice that rattled Olivia.

Olivia shot her mom a look that she hoped conveyed, *I'm not six years old. I can speak for my damn self!*

June's eyes popped open wider and she shrugged slightly, clearly not getting the message.

Olivia flashed her mom a hard smile.

"Well, if they want to get married *here*, it sounds like that's what they're going to have to do," Amy said matter-of-factly.

"Well, I—" Olivia tried to jump in, but June's voice stampeded over hers.

"It doesn't have to be *here*—there are plenty of other locations."

"You mean Long Beach." Amy frowned.

"Well, it is Olivia's hometown," June reminded everyone, as if they didn't know.

Olivia listened as her mom and Amy went back and forth, talking as if she weren't standing right there. She looked at Chloe, who rolled her eyes as if they were watching a reality show, not their family. Although maybe it was the same thing. The tension between her mom and Amy was as thick as the carpeting in the room, and Olivia had lost her desire to speak up. At this point she'd rather marry Zach in that dirt lot he'd mentioned instead of dealing with these Momzillas for another year. Maybe city hall was the answer. Olivia scoffed under her breath. *Isn't that what Amy and Troy did? Maybe she can give me some pointers?*

"We can have it at my house—in the backyard," Eileen piped in.

June and Amy swiveled their heads in her direction. June's eyebrows shot up. Amy's face drained of its color.

"I can't believe I didn't think of it sooner. Why should William spend a fortune on this place anyway? It's a little stuffy for me. I can save him a bundle!" Eileen started waving her arms excitedly, talking about where to put the dance floor and how to arrange the chairs for the ceremony. Where they could put one of those fancy porta potties—the ones with the sinks inside!

Olivia watched her grandmother, trying to remember a time she'd seen her this animated. She was about to agree, to tell her *Yes, yes, yes!* Although maybe *no* to the part about the pigs in a blanket.

The Momzillas were both uncharacteristically quiet. Olivia looked at her mom—June's face had crumpled, and Olivia thought she could see tears pooling in the corners of her eyes. Amy's expression reminded Olivia of one of those pictures snapped as a passenger descended over the sharp drop on Splash Mountain at Disneyland. As the flash went off, the person's face screamed, *Holy shit!*

Olivia swallowed her excitement—especially the part about telling her dad he was about to save some serious cash. He'd been lukewarm on all the wedding planning, and Olivia hadn't been able to decide if it was the wedding budget or the marriage itself or a little bit of both that had him acting so standoffish. Either way, she wanted to make him happy. She took a deep breath and decided she would start planning for a simple ceremony at the courthouse. "That's such a nice offer, Grandma, but I can't let you do that—it will be too much for you to deal with. Maybe a big wedding isn't necessary—"

"Nonsense. I insist!" Eileen clapped.

Clapped? Olivia watched her grandmother, stunned. This normally stoic woman had come to life. She stole a look at her mom, who was watching Eileen with the same confused stare.

"It will be fun. We can look on Pinterest for ideas!"

"You're on Pinterest?" Olivia smiled at the thought.

"Sure! Who isn't?"

"Wow, Mom, you're full of surprises today." June found her voice, stiffer than the last time she'd spoken.

Eileen ignored her daughter's comment and the palpable tension in the group. "Shall we go over and see it?"

Olivia avoided looking at her mom and Amy and said, "Yes." She'd already declined once, but her grandmother had insisted. And you typically didn't tell Eileen no. At least that was how Olivia was going to rationalize this decision.

As they all walked toward the valet, Olivia could feel her mom's and Amy's eyes boring into her back. She wondered about the thoughts rolling through each of their minds right now. She knew they used to come to Eileen's house a lot together when they were friends. They must have so many memories there.

The caption on the Instagram story would be *Here we go! Back to the scene of the crime!*

Olivia also contemplated her grandmother's motivation. Had she thought of her daughter and Amy's shared past when she offered her home for the wedding? Were her intentions pure; did she simply want to help Olivia to make up for the way she hadn't been there for her own daughter? Or was she getting pleasure out of watching June and Amy squirm?

Either way, Olivia decided she wasn't going to let it be her problem.

CHAPTER FIFTEEN

As Amy walked up the path to Eileen's house, a chill pricked her arms. It was like she'd traveled through time and landed squarely back in 1996. The front porch floorboards still had the same white chipped paint. A canary-yellow bird feeder still hung from a pergola warped by the sea air. That might be the same potted plant resting next to the front door.

She glanced at June, who had been visibly upset since they'd left the Four Seasons, her lips frozen in a tight line. She understood how conflicting this must be for June—to have watched Eileen be so supportive of her granddaughter, knowing she hadn't been there for June. Amy wanted to lean over, to say something to June to let her know she understood—maybe make a crack about Eileen's dress looking like it was made from curtains, the neckline so high Amy wasn't sure how she wasn't choking—but June's shoulders were hunched, her chin tucked; she was definitely not open to chatting. And considering the text war they'd been in over the wedding, she couldn't blame her.

She had seen June's face go slack when Eileen offered her home to Olivia. June recovered quickly with a smile, but the disappointment that had flickered in June's eyes sent Amy's memory back to two decades before. Amy remembered listening to June on the phone with her mom—Eileen trampling over Amy's engagement news yet again. Amy's throat had burned with anger as she watched June bite her lip at her mom's lecture, Eileen's voice so shrill that Amy could hear every single hateful word: Troy wasn't husband material! The ring was a trinket! Why was she in such a hurry, anyway? Did she think he was the best she could do? Amy had reached over and held her friend's hand until she hung up and burst into tears, and Amy had held her, saying nothing but understanding everything.

Yet now, Eileen was embracing Amy's son—*Troy's son*—with open arms?

Amy decided to try talking to June. She touched June's shoulder and whispered, "I bet part of you wants to shove those stuffy pearls down her throat, right?" And then she offered a conspiratorial smile.

June's eyes softened, and Amy thought she might laugh. But June's features hardened like clay and she moved away from Amy without responding. Amy's face fell in defeat, her spirit crushed. It had been stupid of her to think they could transform back into the girls they used to be. She wouldn't make that mistake again. Despite Amy's emotional muscle memory telling her otherwise, they weren't those people anymore.

June had been shut down when they'd met for coffee. It had thrown Amy off, made her lose her focus. She'd hoped they could talk—*really* talk—about things, the way Zach had suggested. She'd brought a picture to show June. She'd dug through a box from college until she found one of the only photos of the two of them that she'd saved. They were at Disneyland, standing between Belle and the Beast from *Beauty and the Beast*. June had loved Belle because of their shared love of books. Her favorite scene in the movie was when Belle discovered the Beast's vast library. Amy had thought that the picture might be a good icebreaker, because she knew June had a bookstore now. That the image might start a conversation. But June had been so formal—it had all felt so tense, like a job interview, Amy the one applying—and Amy had lost her nerve to bring it out of her purse and rambled about being gluten-free instead. Which wasn't true; she consumed wheat with reckless abandon. May the box of sea-salt-flavored Triscuits she'd stress-eaten the night before be her witness!

After she and June agreed to put aside their differences—if you could trivialize the definition of what had happened between them with that word—Amy had thought they might hug. But June's body language screamed, *Don't come close, or I'll stab you with the wooden coffee stirrer.* When June gave her a tour of her bookstore, Amy wanted to tell her how proud of her she was, but she worried it would come out sounding condescending, so she complimented the decor instead. By the time she drove home, Amy had convinced herself this bizzarro universe version of them was better. There would be no risk of either of them getting hurt again. Amy put her guard back up and forged ahead.

But today, her heart had its own agenda. Her instinct to protect June—as hypocritical as she knew that sounded—was in full force.

Amy didn't think the wedding should happen at Eileen's. Sure, her home was beautiful. Romantic, with its impressive rose garden. Amy recognized Mr. Lincolns, Julia Childs, and Gertrude Jekylls, to name a few. She knew that roses had lengthy blooming cycles in Santa Barbara—up to nine months a year—and that many of her rose vendors would be impressed with the expert pruning and high-quality water filtration system she had spotted. But she would keep these observations to herself and not give Eileen the satisfaction. It had been obvious in the ballroom of the hotel that Eileen's icy demeanor and holier-than-thou attitude had not changed.

As they toured Eileen's property, Olivia mentioned that it had *Amalfi vibes*. Amy took in the lemon trees framing the side of the house and could see Olivia's point. But hosting the wedding here would bring up the past, something they were all trying very hard to pretend never happened. As they walked inside, Amy tried to imagine Troy being in this house again. (If Eileen would let him in!) What would it be like for him to be catapulted back to when Eileen rejected him? He'd pleaded with Eileen to give him a chance, to accept him into their family. Amy was pretty sure that conversation—if you could call it that—had happened right over there on that paisley couch.

A chill pricked Amy's arm again. What if Eileen had agreed? Troy wouldn't have driven back to school upset. He wouldn't have fought with June about Eileen's reaction. He wouldn't have called Amy. There would be no Zach.

Amy couldn't think like that. She forced the thought away and snapped a photo of the couch and sent it to Troy along with one of her favorite emojis, the guy with a straight line for a mouth. *Do you recognize this? You could be sitting on it at your son's reception.*

In typical Troy style, he wrote back that he'd be fine. That he'd been rejected on much uglier couches since then, and he gently reminded Amy that they both needed to go with the flow on this one—*ride the wave*, he added. She sent back a gif of a dog surfing and tossed her phone in her purse. Texting with Troy was dredging up more conflicting memories than standing in this living room.

Amy realized everyone had moved back outside.

"I think we set up the DJ over there," Eileen was saying to Olivia as she pointed to the corner of her yard, next to a bed of robust Rosa Queen Elizabeth roses. Not far from where Amy and June had sneaked more than one blunt back in the day. "Unless you want a band?" Eileen added.

Amy observed Olivia, her blue eyes so bright they matched the cloudless sky. Amy still couldn't completely wrap her head around the fact that this young woman was going to be her daughter-in-law. Twenty-six years ago when she was in labor with Zach, she could never have imagined that one day he'd be marrying June's daughter.

There was a part of her that liked having June back in her life—who thought that this knock-off version of her old friend wasn't all bad. The terms weren't ideal, but June's presence had made Amy feel more complete than she had in a long time.

But perhaps she was addicted to the drama. Maybe it was time to get a therapist. Troy had encouraged her to see one for years. He worried that she'd become too shut down, that she should figure out why she didn't want to find love again. Amy only smiled when he said this—when he bragged about his psychologist, who had worked wonders for his addiction to work. She knew she'd never fully open her heart again; the risk of getting it broken was too high.

"Zach and I have talked about a DJ; hopefully we can find one on such short notice. And maybe we can fit a dance floor there," Olivia said, pulling Amy from her thoughts. Olivia pointed to the corner of the yard with a view of the ocean.

"Do you think DJ Nice would be available?" Eileen asked. "I've seen him on Instagram!"

Olivia laughed. "Probably not, Grandma. But I like where your head's at."

Eileen smiled proudly. "I'll be right back—I have something for you," she said, and headed toward the house.

Amy took note of the change in Olivia since they'd left the Four Seasons. First, she'd texted the thread and asserted herself about wanting to get married in Santa Barbara. And now she seemed more vocal, emboldened to make her opinions clear. Amy wondered what had changed—and felt a twist in her stomach.

It had to be the text fighting between her and June. While it was mostly passive-aggressive at best, it had been hard to ignore the fact that Olivia hadn't been responding to most of the messages on that thread. And she hadn't responded to any from Amy in days. Although, Amy reasoned, she experienced that a lot with Zach too—and according to some of Amy's coworkers, getting ghosted by your kid wasn't unusual.

"This is where we should get married. What do you think, Mom?" Olivia looked to June, who seemed lost in her own thoughts. "Mom?" Olivia prompted.

June snapped to attention. "Sure, honey, yes," she said quickly.

Amy wondered if she'd heard Olivia.

Eileen bustled outside with the intensity of an Energizer Bunny. She bounced with every step. What was she so excited about? Amy's mouth fell open when she realized what was draped over Eileen's arm. June's back was to her mom, and Amy willed her not to turn around. She silently pleaded with Eileen to return to the house. But she was like a locomotive, and Amy couldn't look away. She knew she was about to witness a colossal train wreck.

"Olivia, darling, there is no pressure, but believe it or not"—Eileen laughed as she approached—"there was a time I was the same size as you." She stopped. "And I thought you might want to try this on. I haven't brought this out of the closet in a long time."

Olivia froze as her mom turned around. "Is that your—" Olivia started.

Amy's heart was pounding. She wanted to save June somehow, but there was nothing she could do. She shot Eileen a look: *Why?* But Eileen was oblivious.

"My wedding dress? Yes." Eileen fingered the fabric. "I married your grandfather in this. I thought it might be retro chic?"

June's jaw tightened. Amy's heart broke as she watched her. After June and Troy had gotten engaged, one of the first things June had said to Amy was that she hoped to wear her mom's dress. But June had never gotten the chance to ask her—because Eileen hated the idea of the engagement. And Amy could tell by the look on June's face that she also hadn't worn it when she'd married William.

To Amy's surprise, June didn't say a word now. Instead, she turned and stared at the ocean again.

"Come, come, let's try this on you!" Eileen grabbed Olivia's elbow and shepherded her toward the house. Amy heard Eileen suggest a seamstress in the area.

June kept her eyes trained on the sea as the sun started to set, soon to disappear into the horizon. Amy could see the slight quiver of June's jaw. The pain etched across June's face was too much for Amy to bear.

"Eileen," Amy called after her. "Choosing a dress, heirloom or not, is a huge decision. Why don't we table this until we finalize some of the other details?"

Eileen stopped abruptly and gave Amy a death stare, then looked to Olivia, who nodded in agreement. "Let's wait, Grandma," she said tactfully.

"Fine," Eileen conceded, and walked inside.

Amy thought for a moment. Eileen still seemed so insensitive. Borderline cruel. Did this mean she hadn't changed at all? What would be her reaction to seeing Troy again? And would she ever accept Zach into the family?

Amy followed Eileen. "So," she began, trying to sound casual as Eileen rehung the gown in the closet. "What do you think of the news? Pretty crazy, right? What are the odds of my son and June's daughter meeting and falling in love?"

Eileen gave Amy a long once-over. Amy self-consciously adjusted her dress. "I admit, it was a bit shocking," Eileen looked out the window at Olivia, who was taking a selfie with Chloe. "But Olivia is a smart girl. If she thinks Zach is the one, that's good enough for me."

Amy's emotions fought each other. She felt a relief that Eileen was being so accepting of Olivia's choice, but also an anger bubbling in her chest because she hadn't trusted June's. "But Troy wasn't good enough?"

Eileen smiled tightly. "I wasn't the only one who didn't think Troy was good enough. Didn't you divorce him?"

Amy froze. "That's not the same thing."

"Isn't it, though?" Eileen gave Amy another hard smile.

Amy balled her hands into fists, her fingernails digging into her palms so she wouldn't blow up. Amy had given Troy a shot, a chance. For Zach.

"Are you going to accept Troy now? He is Zach's father."

"I'm aware. I don't think we need to go over how we all know each other again, do we?" Eileen released a brittle laugh.

Amy's skin flushed.

"As for my granddaughter, you'll discover one day, if Zach and Olivia have children, that you get to recreate yourself for them." Eileen turned on her heel and walked out of the room. Amy trailed her like a puppy.

"I suppose I'm relieved you aren't going to tear Olivia and Zach apart with your negativity, like you did June and Troy," Amy found the courage to say to Eileen's back.

Eileen half turned, one hand on the door that led to the backyard. "You should have your memory checked. I think it was *you* who tore them apart." She pulled it open and gestured to Amy. "Now, come check out the sunset. It's breathtaking."

Amy felt as if the air had been sucked out of her. "I'll meet you out there," she said, and leaned against the wall to calm herself. Eileen had been cruel, but she wasn't wrong.

Amy stepped outside and made a beeline for June. Eileen's words made her more intent on getting back on the right path. And Eileen had been right about one thing—the sunset was spectacular. Hues of pink and orange lit up the sky like fire. Maybe having the wedding here wouldn't be so bad.

"I'm so sorry, June—I know how much you wanted to wear that dress," Amy burst out when she reached her.

June didn't acknowledge her. Maybe Amy hadn't said the words out loud. But she wanted June to know how she felt, to know that it had been hard to watch her wrestle with her past, to deal with her mom's lack of a sensitivity chip. She wanted to tell June how, after all these years, her empathy for her old friend still lay latent in her heart, like a time capsule that has been unearthed.

"You don't need to worry about me," June said, her words pointed. "I can take care of myself. But you can rest assured I'll get that wedding website handled and all the other things on your list. Isn't that all you care about?"

"No. I care about you. I was only trying to—"

June looked Amy in the eye for the first time today. Her stare was as hard as the rocks along the shoreline. "I know what you were trying to do," she said, then added, her words softer, "And I do appreciate it. But please, stay out of it. Let's not pretend we're friends. That we know each other anymore. I'll be your wedding assistant, and we can leave it at that. On that note, I will not be getting two bids for florists. We will be using my best friend, Fiona. And that is nonnegotiable."

Amy felt stung. The shard of empathy she'd had for June moments ago was replaced by the memory of a stone-cold June barely opening her front door when Amy tracked her down, cradling two-month-old Zach in her arms. She'd pleaded with June to forgive her. She'd said she needed her. But June told her to leave, refusing to look at the baby. To allow her heart to soften. Amy might have screwed up big-time, but June didn't have to be so harsh. She could have given their friendship another chance. And she could have at least pretended to give her another chance now. It'd been twenty-six years. Their children were getting married!

Amy swallowed the hot tears burning the back of her throat and stormed inside. She ducked into the half bathroom off the kitchen to catch her breath. She flicked on the light, prepared to let the tears fall. But when she saw the pink fluffy toilet seat cover, she laughed instead. She remembered Eileen had had one like it when she and June were in college. Amy sat down, hoping it wasn't the same one, and devised a two-prong plan. Just as she would in her job.

Number one: Amy would rebury her past with June. Now, per June's chilly request, she and Amy would be nothing more than two women whose kids happened to be marrying each other.

Number two: Amy would get the wedding venue moved from Eileen's house to the Four Seasons in Pasadena. She knew what to say to Zach to make that happen, and she had the connections to secure the space for *this* Valentine's Day. Because if they moved forward with having the wedding here, it would be an emotional shitstorm that Olivia and Zach did not deserve. Eileen was definitely on a mission to undermine June. And June was definitely on a mission to make Amy pay for her sins in perpetuity. If Eileen hosted, Amy might as well be hiring Eileen's seamstress to sew a scarlet *A* on the chest of the YSL gown she planned to buy.

Amy stood up and looked in the mirror. She reminded herself that she was the woman who once, in under five minutes, armed with nothing more than Morton's table salt and a Magic Eraser, had single-handedly brought her couch back to pristine white after an entire bottle of red wine was spilled on it. If she could do that, she could regain some of her pride and move the wedding to Pasadena.

CHAPTER SIXTEEN

June stared at her screen in disbelief. Amy could not be serious.

June tossed her phone aside and gritted her teeth as she unboxed the last of the books she'd ordered for the New Year's window display. She stopped at the one titled *New Year, New You! How to Forget the Past So You Can Have a Future.* The image of the author, a sixty-something woman in a smart navy-blue suit with a golden bob and gleaming white veneers, stared at June mockingly.

June scoffed at the woman—her name was Dr. Emma Thornberry—plastered across the cover in bold lettering that matched her hair. *You think it's so simple, Dr. Thornberry. I doubt you have a chapter on "I buried my past, but my daughter accidentally found it, and now I guess I have no future!"*

She picked up her phone and read Amy's text again. *Great news! I pulled some strings and the Four Seasons in Pasadena is available for V-day!*

June didn't want the wedding to take place at her mom's, but she would *never* tell anyone that. Especially not Amy. June stared at the text message until it blurred. She had a million things she wanted to write back, but none of them would be very nice. She would let Olivia respond, knowing she would politely decline. Her decision was already made.

June looked at the message again. It had only been sent to her! Why didn't Amy send this to the group thread? Was Amy trying to feel out June before she took the information to Olivia and Zach?

When June had walked through her mom's house last weekend, Olivia and Eileen were talking about famous DJs and high-end portable toilets as if June weren't there. It felt as if each room had taken its big, fat hands and slapped her across the face with a memory. But not any memory. Only those involving Amy and Troy.

When June entered into her old bedroom, she could practically hear Boyz II Men blaring from the radio; she could see herself and Amy swigging Goldschläger from a flask while getting ready to go out to the dive bars on State Street on the weekends when June made the trip home to Santa Barbara, Amy always game to tag along to be a buffer. In her bathroom, she saw them primping—June sitting on the toilet seat as Amy created her smoky eye, June admiring the finished product after, wishing she could show Troy. In the living room, she saw her mom sucking the wind out of her engagement news in one fell swoop. June could still feel the sharp pangs in her heart as she stormed out of the house. By the time June had made it to the backyard and saw the tree she and Amy would hide behind to smoke pot from the orange-colored glass pipe Amy loved so much, she felt like she'd been beaten.

And that was before Eileen offered her wedding dress to Olivia.

That had knocked the last breath June had out of her.

Then Amy had told June she knew how hard it must be for her. When Amy had spoken the words, June had felt an instant pain in her heart; there had never been anyone else who knew her the way Amy had. And in that moment, it felt like Amy still did. June had fought the urge to let her guard down—to tell Amy that yes, it was painful. But she hated herself for feeling hurt. She hated that she was jealous of her daughter. She hated that she didn't want her daughter to wear the dress, that she didn't think she could emotionally handle seeing Olivia walk down the aisle in it. June would be forced to face that, for Eileen, it hadn't been about the dress; it had been about who was good enough to wear it. And that person had never been June.

June had accepted that her mom would have never let her wear the dress if she married Troy. But when she got engaged to William, June had thought for sure that her mom might pull it out of the closet, where it had been since she'd shown it to June when June was in high school. But when June brought up wedding dress shopping, Eileen had suggested several boutiques where June might find *the one*, and June had had too much pride to say, *But the one I want is in your closet.*

While they were still at Eileen's house the other day, June had pulled Olivia aside and told her that she should try on her grandmother's dress. That she was sorry about her reaction and wanted her to have the opportunity to wear it if that's what she wanted. Relief had flooded her daughter's face.

When the dress didn't fit Olivia—it was too tight across the bust and hips, and Eileen had said there was likely nothing her expert seamstress could do about that—June had been relieved.

Relieved!

And then she'd felt awful—gut-wrenchingly I-might-throw-up awful. What mother felt relieved when a gorgeous wedding dress being passed down by her own mother didn't fit her daughter? A bad, selfish mother, that's who. June had glanced at Amy, who had stayed silent as Olivia walked into the room wearing the dress, Olivia trying her best to stay positive, though June could see how disappointed she was that it didn't fit. June had been tempted to ask Amy if her internal thoughts made her a shitty mom, but June had been so rude to Amy about being her wedding assistant that she was too embarrassed.

She'd felt bad for being so harsh. But June didn't know if she could trust Amy's intentions. Had she been trying to be empathetic about the dress when she suggested Eileen put it away? Because that was something the old Amy would have said. Or was this a different Amy, trying to manipulate June so she could take control of the wedding?

The Amy that June had shared coffee with—that Amy hadn't seemed like a caring friend. That Amy hadn't displayed so much as a hint of her pre–*I slept with Troy* 1996 self. She hadn't seemed sorry. She hadn't said anything remotely empathetic between sips of the latte June had *bought for her!* That Amy was all business; June could imagine her barking orders at her Rose parade staff. That Amy clearly wanted nothing more than to get the wedding back on track—the wedding she'd admitted she thought was happening too soon.

June reread the text, looking for new information she wouldn't find.

Nope. This Amy was nothing more than a master manipulator. Her end game was to get the wedding on her turf, and she would clearly stop at nothing to make that happen. June was fuming. She could feel the heat radiating off her body.

"Are you okay?" Chloe asked.

June jerked her head up from her phone.

"I'm fine," June lied. "Will you start on the window display? I need to take care of something."

"Okay. I have an idea. I thought maybe we could—"

"Sure, fine, whatever you think." June waved at her and headed to her office in the back of the store. She felt bad. "Sorry, Chlo," she called after her. "I'm a little distracted."

"Mom," Chloe said. "You want to talk about it?"

"No, honey. I don't," June responded as she slumped into her chair. Only then did she realize she was still holding Dr. Thornberry's book. She let out a frustrated sigh and chucked it into a pile of books in the corner.

June picked up a framed photo off her desk. It was from her fortieth birthday. June's arms were wrapped around fourteen-year-old Olivia and twelve-year-old Chloe, who, with William's help, had surprised her with a party at her bookstore. June took in her flushed cheeks, the faint beginnings of lines forming around her eyes. Where had the time gone? She'd be fifty in less than a year.

Fifty.

This fifty was different from the fifty she'd thought she'd be facing. This fifty involved a version of Amy she no longer recognized. This fifty involved her daughter's wedding. To Amy's son. This fifty involved conflicting feelings about Troy. Troy! She'd never thought she'd see him again. And now, here he was. June wondered if it meant something. If the universe had a master plan that was bigger than Olivia and Zach. Could it involve June and Troy?

June drove the thought away. Troy didn't have feelings for her anymore. He'd had years to get in touch, and she'd never heard from him. But seeing him again had sparked something deep within June. Although that was typical, right? To feel a flutter when you saw your first love?

June had thought of Troy after her divorce with William was final. Starting over had made her reflect on her past. But she'd told herself she was only lonely. That Troy had made his choice a long time ago, as had she. June fired off a response to Amy before she lost her nerve.

That was nice of you, and I hope it wasn't too much work on your part, but Olivia wants to get married at her grandmother's. She added the emoji with the hearts around its head.

She could see Amy responding. June looked at the photo again and wondered how Amy spent her fortieth. Had she been with Zach? Friends? She had clearly stayed friendly with Troy after their divorce. Had he planned something? June shook her head. Why did she care?

Actually, I told Olivia and Zach last night at dinner and they want to go see the place today! The appointment is at 11:30 A.M. if you want to come.

June glanced at her watch. 11:05! There was no way she could make it to Pasadena in twenty-five minutes. And she was positive Amy knew this. Why hadn't she texted June sooner?

Because she didn't want June to be there.

"Ugh!" June yelled to her empty office.

She called Olivia.

"Hey, Mom!" her daughter answered on the first ring, her voice bright.

June wondered if Amy was bluffing.

"I got a text from Amy—something about looking at the Four Seasons in Pasadena?" June made her voice sound as casual as possible.

"Yeah, she told us it was an option last night—I guess she called in like a billion favors. I got a text from her that the appointment is at eleven thirty, so Zach and I are going to head over and see it. After all she's done, I have to at least look at it."

After she coldly calculated this so she could manipulate you! And cut me out in the process! I could have called in some favors at venues in Long Beach, but I didn't want to undermine what you wanted!

"I thought you were doing it at Grandma's?"

Olivia's voice quaked. "I don't know. I wanted to. And I got really excited about it. But Amy brought up some good points last night. Pasadena is a lot more convenient for our guests. Santa Barbara is pretty far. And where would anyone park at Grandma's?"

June pictured the narrow street that ran in front of Eileen's house. It would be difficult, but still doable. They could hire valet drivers. She pressed her fingernails into her palm. She didn't want the wedding in Pasadena, but she could hear the strain in her daughter's words. She knew Olivia felt caught in the middle. Especially because of the text fighting that had been going on between her and Amy.

Olivia went on, "I loved the idea of having it at Grandma's house, but Amy mentioned how much work it's going to be— the dance floor, the bathrooms, moving out all of the furniture. There's so much more than I realized that Grandma will have to do to get the house ready. I don't want to put that on her. And Zach and I really don't have the time to help with a lot of it."

June couldn't argue any of these points—as much as she wanted to. She bit her tongue and said what she was supposed to say.

"Okay, whatever you want."

"Really?" Olivia asked.

"Really." June thought of the beach near her home where she wanted to see her daughter get married. She and the girls had so many good memories there. June still had the old red wagon she'd cart them and their boogie boards in every weekend stashed in her garage. Chloe had accused her of being a hoarder when she spied it a few months ago, tucked behind a light-blue beach cruiser June had overpaid for and never used. And sure, June wasn't able to park her car in the garage because she had a *slight* problem letting go of things. But the truth was, the faded red wagon represented a time when June was deeply needed, and she wasn't quite ready to let go of that feeling. She had even speculated that having Olivia's wedding on that same beach might help her move forward.

Olivia seemed to read her mind. "Mom, I'm sorry. I know you wanted it in Long Beach—"

That was June's opening. She could make a pitch for *their beach*. But she could tell by Olivia's voice that the decision to have the wedding in Pasadena was as good as made. "It's fine. The wedding should be where *you* want. Make sure it's *you* who is making the choice, okay?"

"You mean don't let Amy make it for me," Olivia snapped.

"That's not what I said."

"You didn't have to." Olivia's voice held a bitter note.

"I want what's best for you, that's all," June said.

Great. Now Olivia was annoyed with her on top of everything else.

"Okay," Olivia said, sounding tired. "I have to go. I'll let you know how it goes. Bye, Mom."

June hung up, and tears sprang to her eyes. She felt left out. She was the mother. She should be there. She could still go. Be late. But her pride wouldn't let her move from her desk chair.

June pictured Amy in her office in Pasadena, a smug look on her face as she marinated over the fact that she'd won. She could hear Amy telling her Rose Parade colleagues that the wedding would now be around the corner, not far from where Zach grew up! She'd lean in and roll her eyes. *It was almost all the way up in Santa Barbara. Could you imagine?*

A thought crystalized. June might have lost the battle, but she hadn't lost the war.

CHAPTER SEVENTEEN

V & Z's Big Day text thread:

> **Olivia:** *Omg!!!!!*
> **June:** *What? Are you okay?*
> **Amy:** *What happened?*

June took a deep breath as she waited for Olivia to finish typing. After Amy had gone behind June's back and taken Zach and Olivia to the Four Seasons in Pasadena without her, June wasn't sure she could handle another last-minute change. Thankfully, Olivia didn't love the property, so it had been decided officially that the wedding would take place at Eileen's. June had arranged to charter a bus for the guests who didn't want to make the drive and, to William's delight, discovered that the fancier porta potties Eileen wanted were in the budget. Not that June was keeping score, but June 1, Amy 0!

> **Olivia:** *The plush sharks i want to give as wedding favors are out of stock at the Party City by our house! and they are*

*completely sold out online I have class all day and don't have
time to drive around to the other locations!*

Olivia texted the group a picture of the shark.

June laughed under her breath at the three-inch plush shark
with *I chews you* written on its fin and a mischievous grin on
his face.

June: *I'm sure there are similar sharks you can get if this one
is sold out.*

Olivia: *It has to be these they were featured on the today show
Kaia Gerber gave them out at her wedding in the Bahamas
everyone is going to want them she's a huge influencer on
Instagram*

June still wasn't used to her daughter's grammatically incor-
rect text messages. How she could be a law student and not
consistently punctuate or capitalize in her texts baffled June.
She also wasn't sure who Kaia Gerber was or how she and her
sharks were influencing people, but she couldn't believe these
smirking sharks could really be flying off the Party City shelves
because some celebrity said they were cute.

They were pretty cute, but still.

Amy: *Maybe this is a sign to change party favors? Cindy Crawford's daughter is kind of a big deal, right? I thought that
cassette tape box idea I mentioned was cute. You guys could
fill them with Hershey's kisses and write Zach & Olivia are a
great mix on them! Also-we still need to confirm the photographer. I'm so glad you went with my choice! She's amazing!*

June felt anger rising in her throat. Amy had been relentless
about this photographer. She'd done Amy's friend's daughter's

wedding, and Amy had written fifteen texts describing the ambience she created in her pictures. Like she was some wedding expert. Now she was inserting the photographer into a totally different conversation.

June pulled up the email thread she'd had with the photographer. June thought the woman arrogant and overpriced. Asking for her own room to *set her intention* for the day—who did that? In a burst of anger, June shot off an email, saying she'd no longer be needed.

That felt good. She smiled and turned back to the text thread and the unfolding shark dilemma. How did Amy know Kaia was related to Cindy Crawford? Olivia had already told Amy she didn't want to give boxes shaped like cassette tapes— that the whole retro thing wasn't her and Zach's vibe. June would take a shark with a smirk over Amy's lame idea any day.

> **Olivia:** *I want these they are soooo perfect for us Z told me this shark joke while we were in Italy and I laughed so hard I cried it's kismet*
> **Troy:** *I'll BITE. What was the joke?*

June couldn't help but smile at that. She was happy they'd added William and Troy to the thread. It made it a lot more fun.

> **Olivia:** *what does it cost to swim with sharks?*
> **Troy:** *?*
> **Olivia:** *an arm and a leg*
> **Troy:** *Ha!*

June haha'd Olivia's punchline.

Amy emphasized her own comment about the cassette tapes, wanting Olivia to respond. June groaned. You would think *she* was the one getting married.

William: *Olivia, don't take this the wrong way but I'm at work and this is a distraction. I hope it all works out with the sharks though.*

William has left the conversation.

June sucked her teeth. You didn't have to officially leave a conversation. You could mute the alerts for a text chain. She'd explain it to him later and add him back in.

Troy: *What happened to those sharks at the Pasadena Party City? Did they vanish into FIN air?*

June laughed out loud at that one.
Olivia replied to Amy's comment.

Olivia: *I have faith we can get the sharks did I tell you we are also going to tie ribbons around their necks that say Z&V's Wedding Day?*

Amy: *You should have a backup plan in case you can't get them . . . Let me know if you want me to put the cassette tape boxes on hold or something else in case . . .*

June grimaced. Amy loved to type *dot, dot, dot* after every passive-aggressive thing she wrote. She was relentless! And such a control freak. June agreed that a backup plan was a good idea, but she would never chime in and say that. Or make a suggestion as to what the backup item should be. June wouldn't agree with Amy even if June was about to be attacked by a shark and the truth was the only thing that could save her. Well, maybe then she would.

Olivia: *let's wait and see what happens with the sharks but crossing fingers we will*
Olivia: *can anyone help*
Olivia: *I'm so sorry to ask but Zach can't do it either*

June's day was open. She had been planning to do inventory at the store, but these sharks were important to Olivia—and apparently Cindy Crawford's daughter?—so she'd do it. It would also give June a huge amount of satisfaction to save the day. June wrote back as much (not the save-the-day part) and hit send. As she did, a text came in from Troy.

He said he'd help too.

Shit. June hadn't seen Troy since the brunch and certainly didn't want to get reacquainted with him while hunting down plush toys. Now what should she do? If she backed out, she'd look like the jerk who couldn't put her past behind her for the sake of her daughter.

> **Olivia:** *thank you both so much I tried calling some Party Cities to see what inventory they had but no one answered the phone we need 125 total you might have to go to more than one hope that's okay.*

June had an idea. She would suggest that she and Troy divide and conquer. Troy would take half of the stores; she'd take the other.

June watched her screen. Troy was typing. She rubbed the skin between her eyes as she waited.

> **Troy:** *No problem at all. Happy to help. June and I are on it!*

Then he added a gif of the Baby Shark cartoon video—with the lyrics *Do do do do do do* floating in the sea.

June squeezed her lips together so she wouldn't smile.

It was settled. She would be shark shopping with her ex-fiancé. June smoothed her greasy hair in the hallway mirror—and wondered how old she'd appeared to Troy when he'd seen her at the brunch. The last time they were together, June had been twenty-three. And now? She tried to evaluate her reflection as if she were seeing herself for the first time in over two decades. She couldn't imagine what his impression of her had been.

She inhaled deeply. She could do this. What was one day of tracking down plush toys with Troy?

So what if they hadn't spoken in twenty-six years?

So what if the last time they did talk, she'd called him a worthless prick whom she wouldn't marry if he was the last man on earth?

So what if they would be shopping for party favors for the wedding of the love child he had with her best friend!

June: *Happy to help! 125 plush sharks here we come!*
Olivia: *thanks sm Gtg I have class in ten*

Forty-five minutes later, June's hand was shaking as she hurried to blow-dry her hair. After Troy side-texted June to offer to pick her up—saying he had a plan for how to catch the most sharks in the least amount of time and that he wanted to *cast their net wide*—she'd wasted precious minutes trying to salvage her four-days-unwashed hair with dry shampoo. But she sprayed so much on her roots that the top of her head looked like a powder wig. She'd FaceTimed Fiona in a panic, who'd confirmed that yes, she'd need to wash her hair.

She wrapped her hair around a brush and blasted the heat. When she tried to pull the brush free, it tangled in her half-wet locks. She yanked at it, but the hair only seemed to wrap itself tighter. She stopped, the brush dangling from her strands, and stared at herself in the mirror. *Pull yourself together, June.* She grabbed the edge of the sink and breathed deeply. *You can do this. Carefully unwrap the hair from the bristles. Don't make any sudden moves.*

Finally, the brush broke free, but so did a large chunk of her hair. June rubbed her sore scalp and tossed the brush aside. She rough-dried her hair, ran some product through it, and decided it would have to do. She threw on jeans and a sweater, hoping less really *was* more.

The doorbell rang. She grabbed her purse. What if Troy wanted to talk about *them* today? What would June say? She wasn't ready for this—to open the box she'd sealed so tight the *jaws* of life would be required. She laughed to herself. *See what I did there?*

She blew out a long stream of air and opened the door.

Troy smiled so wide the corners of his mouth practically stretched to his ears. "Hi."

"Hi," June said.

"You look great!" Troy said. "Sorry, maybe that's not what I should be saying right out of the gate, but you do. I would have told you at the brunch, but—well—we were a little busy with other things. Anyway, you haven't aged."

A smile escaped from June's lips. She took him in. There was a nick on his chin from shaving. His hair was still a little wet—probably from a recent shower. He smelled like some sort of man soap. "Thanks. You look good too."

"You kind of have to say that now. After my verbal throw-up."

"I don't, actually," June said, a little twist to her lips. Maybe this day wouldn't be so bad.

June pulled out her phone and texted the sentiment to Fiona, who replied with a *you've got this* Bitmoji.

June studied Troy again and suddenly saw him as his younger self, standing on the doorstep of her apartment with chicken soup, Gatorade, 7UP, and saltines, ready to help her recover from a terrible stomach flu. His face was thinner and covered in a deep tan from surfing almost every day, his hair sun bleached and long, curled around his ears. He looked twenty-three again. She blinked several times. "I can't believe we're almost fifty," June burst out, then felt her cheeks heat up.

"I know. I can't believe how fast and slow time has gone. I still feel like that college kid, but also like a grown man. I'm probably not making sense."

It one hundred percent resonated with June, especially given the past few days, but she didn't know how to articulate it. How seeing Troy and Amy had reconnected her with her twenty-something self. A person she'd turned her back on so long ago. An awkward silence settled over them. June finally located her voice. "We should probably go get those sharks," she said as she pulled the seat belt across her body. "So, what's the game plan?"

Troy reached into the back seat and handed her a stack of papers. "I printed the locations of the Party Citys from here to Van Nuys. I figure we will stay close to the 405 so we can get on and off the freeway easily as we check them off our list. I also thought we could try calling them and asking if they have the sharks so we don't waste our time—maybe we can get someone to answer."

"Sorry, you lost me at Van Nuys." June's eyes popped. "That's horrifying. The 405 is terrible after you get north of the South Bay."

"Do it for the sharks." Troy smiled and pulled away from the curb.

They struck out at the first four Party City locations; the shelves were empty where the plush toys should have been. One pimply-faced employee after the next thrust their phones in

June's and Troy's faces to show them the craze the sharks had created on social media. June slumped into the passenger seat. "You know I laughed when Olivia said she was worried they might sell out?"

"I laughed too—thought she was kidding at first. I hadn't heard about the whole inside joke." Troy leaned against the headrest.

June looked through the stack of papers. "Next up, Culver City?" When Troy didn't respond, she looked over.

Troy was staring at her.

"What?" June asked. June wasn't sure why, but her heart started to thud so hard she was sure her sweater was moving. She adjusted her position so Troy couldn't see it.

"She looks so much like you did."

"Who?"

"Olivia."

"Oh, yeah, I know. My mini me."

"June, I have something to say . . ."

June's mouth went dry. Was he going to tell her something about *them*? As they'd driven around this morning, June had been thinking a lot about their wedding that never was, wondering what they would have planned had they gotten this far. She was sure it had probably brought things up for him too. But there, trapped in Troy's bright-red Tesla, her hands gripped tightly in her lap and her giant purse at her feet, she felt almost claustrophobic. Maybe because the mere thought of discussing the past with Troy made June's throat close up. She wasn't ready.

June's phone buzzed. She frowned at the screen. It was a text from her mom. Eileen had started a group text with Amy. And she'd titled it *No sharks in this sea! WTF?*

"What is it?" Troy asked.

"It's Eileen." She made a face she knew he'd still understand.

"Still the same old . . ." Troy paused, as if trying to decide how far to take it. "Crotchety Eileen?"

June nodded.

"Still wearing the pearls?"

June laughed. "I think they're fused to her neck at this point. She'll want to be buried in that necklace." She read the text and groaned. "Oh my god, this woman!"

"What is it?"

"You really want to know?"

"Oh, I'm all in at this point."

"Well, first off, it's to me and Amy."

"Okay."

"I'll read it to you." She squinted at the screen.

"Avoiding getting readers?"

"Like the plague! I keep increasing the font on my phone to fight it."

"Don't tell me you buy large-print books?"

"God no! I wear my reading glasses in the privacy of my home or my office at work. But in public? No way! I'm magnified font and flashlight app all the way."

"I have the ones you perch on your nose." Troy reached into his pocket and put them on.

"No!" June exclaimed. "I'm sorry, but no. Take those off!"

"Amy told me the same thing." Troy stopped, clearly realizing his mistake. "Sorry—I . . ."

"It's okay, you were married to her. She is the mother of your son." June's throat tightened as she said the words, a pinch of regret tinged with a teaspoon of jealousy.

They fell into another awkward silence. Finally, Troy broke it.

"So what does the text say?"

June started reading. *"June—talk some sense into your daughter. Olivia told me about these sharks. She asked if I could go to my local Party City and see if they are in stock? Kaia Gerber is certainly a big deal with her modeling career and all but—"*

Troy interrupted. "Your mom knows who Kaia Gerber is?"

"Apparently." June continued reading. *"Kaia is certainly a big deal but those sharks are corny—did you see the smirks on their faces?—so you need to tell Olivia as much. Suggest she goes with something classy, that everyone can use, like a candle or a bar of soap. She will regret this in a few years when she looks back on it."*

"Why doesn't *she* suggest it to Olivia? Why is she putting it on you?"

June sighed. "I have no idea. But there is no way I'm going to break Olivia's spirit over this. I'm typing no right now."

June: *Mom, Olivia wants the sharks so I'm going to support her in this. It's her big day.*

"I think they're cute." Troy grinned, and pulled up the image on his phone.

"Me too," June agreed, and pointed to the picture. "His expression makes it look like he has a secret."

"Maybe he does—the secret to a lasting marriage."

"Then this guy's about ten years too late for me!" June snorted.

"I saw William left the conversation. He's a pretty serious guy, huh?"

June wasn't sure she was ready to talk about her ex with her ex. It felt wrong. William hadn't been the best husband, but he'd been loyal.

"If you don't mind me asking, what happened with you guys?" Troy asked.

He wasn't you. June was surprised that was the first thought that popped into her head. No, no, no. She would not give Troy that much credit. She was feeling nostalgic today, that was all. She and William had their own issues that had nothing to do with him.

June's phone buzzed, and she'd never been more thankful to hear from her mom. "My mom responded." June frowned.

"Dare I ask?"

"*June . . .*" June turned to Troy. "She uses my name when she texts." She shook her head. "Even when it's only me. Anyway, she wrote, *June, you are her mother, and she will listen to you. No respectable bride gives a plush toy as a gift at her wedding.*"

"Now Amy is typing something," June exclaimed. "Great. This is all I need. She's probably going to agree with her. As you saw on the other thread, she wants those cassette tape boxes."

"Lame idea, if you ask me."

"Right?"

"What's she saying?"

"We'll see," June said, as she screenshotted the thread and sent it off to Fiona for dissection. She was instantly rewarded with Fiona's angry Bitmoji—the one with her arms folded tightly across her chest.

June turned to Troy. "You know my mom is probably more worried about how *she's* going to look. How her pickleball friends are going to react. Since it's at her house now—which don't get me wrong, I'm happy about it. Make that ecstatic."

"Yeah, I heard about the whole trying-to-get-it-switched-to-Pasadena thing. Amy means well, but she sometimes doesn't know when enough is enough."

June didn't agree with Troy's assessment that Amy had meant well, but she stayed silent. She didn't want to get into it. "Oh! Amy's text is in. Wow."

June reread it to be sure she was understanding it right. "I can't believe it."

"What? What did she write?"

"She's defending me. Well, me and the sharks." June smiled, then read it to Troy. "*I agree with June. It's Olivia's big day. If she wants sharks, then I say she should have sharks. She knows they're campy. She's owning that. But they mean something to her and Zach so we should stay out of it.*" June was silent for a few moments. "I'm surprised she did this."

"You shouldn't be."

"Really?"

"I know you guys have a complicated history—we all do—but Amy has a good heart. She always has. And she's loyal."

June started to remind Troy that Amy had not been very loyal when they were together, but he stopped her before she could.

"I know she made a huge mistake—obviously, we both did—but she's grown, June. Trust me."

"Aren't you drinking the Amy Kool-Aid?"

"I have raised a son with her, so I think of anyone, I would know," he said, not unkindly, and June again felt a prick of envy, wondering what it might have been like to share a life with Troy.

"You should taste the Kool-Aid," Troy continued. "It's not as bad as you think. And neither is Amy." He started the car. "Shall we?"

June let Troy's comment settle into her thoughts as he pulled out of the parking lot. While she and Amy might be butting heads over wedding planning and Amy had annoyed June to no end with her control-freak ways, June had heard Amy strongly suggest to Eileen that Olivia wait to try on her wedding dress. That had meant a lot. And now she'd had June's back again today. Maybe Troy was right. Maybe grown-up June should give grown-up Amy a chance.

June sent Amy a text before she could change her mind.

June: *Thank you.*

Amy responded right away.

Amy: *You're welcome. Eileen can be such a . . .*

June didn't mind Amy's *dot, dot, dot* this time. And June wasn't sure how Amy found the graphic, but the next text she sent June was a picture of Jaws with a strand of pearls around his neck.

June snorted.

"What's so funny?" Troy asked as he navigated the gridlock on the freeway.

June wanted to keep this moment to herself. "Nothing. It's an inside joke."

Troy asked Siri to call the next Party City on their list, and June wondered if she and Amy would ever be real friends again. Then she remembered Troy had started to tell her something earlier.

"Hey, what were you going to say to me before?"

Troy kept his eyes on the road, but she watched his hands. The knuckles whitened as he gripped the steering wheel. "I can't remember," he said. But June could tell he was lying. Maybe, like her, Troy had decided he wanted to keep something to himself too.

CHAPTER EIGHTEEN

Amy had never imagined that in this lifetime she'd be at a second wedding cake tasting with June. The last time hadn't exactly ended well; her red velvet cake PTSD still resonated. She'd touched on it with Zach at the brunch, but there was no way to describe why she couldn't physically or emotionally stomach it. The cake represented it all—regret, pain, loss, punishment. She could still remember the way the spongy red velvet and the sweet vanilla frosting felt and tasted when it was smashed into her face, working its way into her eyes, her nose, her heart.

Amy slipped off her blazer and hung it over the back of the chair. Whether it was the stress of spending the next two hours confined to a bakery with June or hot flashes that had her perspiring, Amy couldn't be sure. Regardless, she was happy to be the first to arrive. She repeated her mantra in her head.

Today is not about you.

It was such a simple concept. One she'd come across last night during her Google search on repairing broken relationships.

Although she would never search the phrase *burying the hatchet* again. That had a lot of meanings that had nothing to do with forgiveness.

Since June had come back into Amy's life—or Amy into June's; who could be sure?—their constant attempts to one-up each other and to *win* had taken center stage. Ironically, it had been Eileen who had given Amy the wake-up call she needed. Eileen's text attack on June over sharks—*sharks!*—had made Amy face the fact that she and June had been acting like children and they needed to grow up. That Olivia, not either of them, was the bride, and if she wanted to give killer fish plush toys as gifts or eat sliders in a Santa Barbara backyard, then so be it.

"Hi! Are you here for the tasting?"

Amy startled at the sound of a bubbly voice. She looked up to see a young woman with scarlet hair that was shaved on one side of her head and a tattoo on her forearm that read *all the feels*.

"The wedding cake tasting?" Amy clarified. "Yes, I am. It's under Abbott."

The redhead lifted her eyebrows. "Technically, it's not a wedding cake tasting. Those are considered throwbacks, to, like, *the nineties*." She wrinkled her nose.

"Way back then? You probably weren't alive yet!"

The young woman chuckled. "I was born in 2002."

Amy instantly thought of Zach, who in 2002 had been five years old, a kindergartener with an unhealthy fixation on Tickle Me Elmo. Amy could still hear that doll's creepy laugh. "What will we be tasting today, then?"

The woman's heart-shaped face lit up. "Oh! We have it all. Cupcake towers, mini cupcakes, stacked cinnamon rolls—those are a personal favorite." She patted her chest. "There are wheels of cheese, donut towers, cake pops, pancake cakes, churro cakes, mini pies, Rice Krispie treats, cheesecake bites, a candy bar . . . or it's possible to taste slices of cake—if the bride wants to be retro."

Amy pulled out her iPad and stylus. "Can you say those again, more slowly? I'm going to make a spreadsheet so we can keep track of what we like."

The woman wrinkled her nose but listed them off obediently.

Once Amy had compiled the choices and assembled them into the five-star rating system she'd created earlier that week, she checked her watch. "The bride and her mom should be here soon, and then we can get started." The door chimed, and Amy tensed. She wasn't sure she was ready for this.

June waved awkwardly as she came inside. "Hey."

"Hey."

Amy was surprised by how much June still looked like her younger self. She was wearing a simple white T-shirt and jeans, her hair curled in loose waves that fell onto her shoulders, and there was a natural flush to her cheeks. She glowed. Amy yearned to tell her how youthful she looked, but she didn't want it to come off fake. Amy had been intimidated by June since she'd seen her at the brunch. Envious that June didn't seem to need Botox or filler or any of that.

June dropped her purse onto the table and slid into the chair across from Amy. Their eyes met, and Amy wondered if she was as nervous as Amy.

"Can I get you ladies started with some champagne?"

"Please!" they both exclaimed.

The redhead gave them each a deep pour of the Brut and a knowing smile, as if she was aware how much they needed it.

Amy held up her glass. "Cheers."

June clinked her flute against Amy's. They both took a long drink.

"This is weird, right?" June said.

"Weird doesn't begin to cover it." A playful smile formed on Amy's lips. "Although it can't be any stranger than shopping for stuffed sharks with Troy."

June's eyes twinkled. "True."

"How did you guys track down over a hundred of those?"

"On Nextdoor, if you can believe that."

"Seriously?"

"Turns out it's not only a place for angry people to rant politically." June took another sip. "After going to *thirteen* Party City stores, we had collected seven sharks. It was not looking good. I swear Troy would have pulled an all-nighter, but I was exhausted and ready to give up—there were these ugly hedgehogs overflowing from the shelves that started to look cute to me. I closed my eyes and was hugging one of the sharks. Troy took a picture of me and posted it. He begged for anyone who might have a connection to please help this poor mother of the bride."

That's so Troy, Amy thought.

"Turns out one of Troy's neighbors was an original investor in Rande Gerber and George Clooney's tequila company," June shrugged. "He sent a message to Rande, who messaged his daughter, and the next thing I know Troy and I are in Malibu at Kaia's assistant's house picking up bags of sharks."

"You can't make that shit up!"

"Right?" June said. "Olivia doesn't know yet. I'm going to tell her today." She pulled a shark out of her purse and handed it to Amy.

Amy flipped the stuffed animal over and read the inscription on its white belly. "*To everlasting love. Xoxo, Kaia.*" Amy smiled. "That's sweet. You did a great job.""

June waved off the compliment. "I still don't understand any of it, but Olivia will be happy. And that's all I care about."

Amy's heart pricked. Over the years, when she'd allowed herself to think of June, there had been so many questions. Had she found love? Had children? Was she a good mom? It was obvious the answer was yes to the last one. Regardless of their dubious past, Amy respected the hell out the way she had raised Olivia.

The young woman returned with the bottle of champagne. Her mouth fell open. "Is that one of *the Kaia Gerber sharks?*"

June stealthily rolled her eyes at Amy.

"Is one of you the mother of the bride?"

"I am," June said.

"I can't believe your daughter scored these. They are going for like fifty bucks apiece on eBay," she said as she refilled their glasses.

June thought of the 125 sharks they'd squeezed into the trunk of Troy's car. "Hopefully, Troy put the sharks somewhere safe where they won't get stolen. Who knew there was a black market?"

"After hearing that churro cakes are a thing, I think I'll believe anything at this point."

"Churro cakes?"

"You'll see."

"Those do sound kind of good," June mused. "You know I didn't have a cake? At my wedding with William. I couldn't. You know, after—" June didn't finish.

"Let me guess. You had a cheese wheel instead." Amy raised an eyebrow.

"A what?"

"Oh, get ready, girl. This isn't going to be your ordinary cake tasting today—apparently, you don't actually taste cake."

June cocked her head. "Does Olivia want a cheese wheel?"

"I have no idea, but I've been told, by *all the feels* over there, that wedding cakes are very 1990."

June drained her glass. "I'm going to need more of this."

"I'm sorry you didn't have a cake," Amy said.

"It's not your fault."

"Actually, it kind of is." Amy smiled sadly. "If it makes you feel better, we went to the courthouse and got Red Lobster after."

"Wow. That's sad. Was Chili's booked?" June wrinkled her nose.

Amy nodded. "I wore a plastic lobster bib."

June grinned. "If you have a picture, all will be forgiven!"

The word *forgiven* floated between them. Amy could practically see it. Reach out and touch it. She wondered if all could ever be forgiven.

June's phone beeped. Amy's vibrated. They both read the group text from Olivia.

"She's not coming." June looked up, her face twisted in confusion.

"And she's leaving the decision to us?" Amy read on.

"That's what she said."

"Pancake cake it is!" Amy clapped her hands in mock cheer. "Do you think she's avoiding us? Or doesn't want to taste a pancake cake?"

June cocked her head. "Maybe a little of both?"

All the feels interrupted them. "Can I bring you guys the look books so you can decide what you want to sample?"

"Why not?" June said. "And more of this." She pointed to her empty glass and then looked at Amy. "Thank you again for yesterday—with my mom," she said, tracing the rim of her flute.

"It's the least I can do. And I owe you an apology," Amy said. "A real one."

"No—" June started.

"Please, let me say this."

June sat back and folded her hands into her lap.

"I'm sorry for what I did to you. There are no words. But I need you to know that I understand how much I hurt you—how much I took from you." Amy's eyes watered. "I don't ever expect you to forgive me, but maybe we can try to forget, start over, something? Especially since your amazing daughter is marrying my son?"

"I'd like that. I'm so tired of the tension." June exhaled. "And for the record, Zach is pretty great too. Whatever you did with him, it worked."

Amy's cheeks warmed at the compliment. "Thank you for being so gracious," she said, taking another swig of champagne. "And by the way, your mom still sucks as much as I remember."

June smirked. "She really does, doesn't she?"

"When I saw her going after you about those sharks, it made me realize, I've been doing the same thing. I shouldn't have pushed so hard for Pasadena."

June held her gaze. "Let's be honest. This was never about Pasadena."

Amy looked down. "I know."

The woman dropped off the book and a full bottle of champagne.

"Speaking of things that we're sorry for, I have a confession. I'm the one who canceled the photographer," June offered, referencing the sudden dropout of Zoe Whitford, *elegant and amazing photographer*. Or at least that's what it had said on her website.

"No! I thought she had a death in the family?"

June blushed. "I lied! Then I had to bribe the new one with two first-class plane tickets and a suite at the Biltmore to get him to commit at the last minute. William was pissed!"

Amy opened her mouth in mock outrage. "I can top that. I had a plan to sabotage the engagement party venue. Was going to call the Department of Health to get the place closed down so I could get it moved to where I wanted to have it!"

"Low!"

"I know—I probably wouldn't have taken it that far—at least I hope not," Amy said, and wondered how she'd let everything get so out of control. How she'd lost sight of what a monumental day this was going to be for Zach. For Olivia.

"We really did lose our minds there for a while, didn't we?"

"We did." Amy thought about the past few weeks—how she and June had gone from sending each other passive-aggressive emojis to full-on wedding attack mode. She could see the montage in the movie: a three-minute sequence of the mothers of the bride and groom trying to take each other down. Only this wasn't their wedding. Their day. Their anything.

June started flipping through the book. "This looks good." She turned it around so Amy could see the picture of the donut tower.

"Let's try it. Why don't we sample everything? You know, to be sure we did our proper research for Olivia."

"Absolutely."

Amy slid her iPad out of her purse. "And I've developed a complex rating system so we can keep track of what we like."

She spun the tablet around to face June and began to explain the different categories. When she got to moisture level and density, she could see she was losing June. "What? You hate this, don't you?"

June took the iPad, closed it, and laid it on the table. "How about we do this old-school? Utilize our taste buds and some champagne?"

Amy shoved it back in her bag. "But I hadn't gotten to the texture and flavor components."

"And thank goodness for that!" June laughed. "Our kids are getting married. Let's enjoy the moment. That we get to be part of it."

Amy's insides warmed. "You're right." She grabbed her glass and took a large gulp. "I'll drink to that!"

"And one more toast," June said, holding her glass up. "To burying the hatchet."

Amy's eyes popped.

"What?" June asked.

"Long story. How about to starting over?"

"To starting over," June repeated. Amy swallowed the frizzy liquid, feeling lighter than she had in years.

*   *   *

Olivia smiled at her phone. "There's good news and bad news."

"Give me the good first," Zach said. He pushed pause on the remote and leaned his head against her shoulder. They were parked on the couch, binge-watching *Love Is Blind*. They had started the episode where the newly formed couples move in together. Olivia had joked that they were starring in their own version of a reality show. They'd decided that theirs would be called *Your Parents Have Something to Tell You!* and it would follow young couples whose parents hated each other because of something that had happened before they were born and they had zero control over.

"I think our plan worked," Olivia revealed. "Marni texted me from the bakery that she overheard some apologies being exchanged. And they're already on their second bottle of champagne."

Zach kissed her neck. "We're totally flexing right now."

Olivia smiled. "Well, we did learn from the best," she said, and planted a soft kiss on his cheek. "Ready for the bad?"

"Lay it on me."

"Marni is pretty sure they are leaning toward the donut tower."

"Tacky ass glazed donuts at our wedding is a small price to pay for peace," Zach asserted, before tilting Olivia's chin toward him and dotting her neck with his lips, sparking a fire in her chest. As she let him push her back on the bed, she decided that while she was happy their moms had gotten over themselves, at the end of the day this was her life to live with Zach and she was thrilled that fate had brought them together.

Later, when her future husband hit play to restart the show, she found herself rooting for all of the couples on the series who had met in such an unconventional manner. It was working for her and Zach. Maybe it would work for them too?

CHAPTER NINETEEN

Olivia and Zach's engagement party started off on such a high note.

"This view is spectacular," William conceded as he took a deep sip of his WhistlePig bourbon and pointed to the lights of the cargo freighters that were waiting for their turn to enter San Pedro Bay, which he remembered reading was known as America's Port because it was the busiest in the United States. He turned to June as he calculated the cargo that was likely to be on those ships—auto parts, electronics, furniture. "How did you get this place on such short notice?"

"I'm very well connected in Long Beach." June widened her eyes in amusement, but when she noticed William's arched eyebrow, she tilted her head toward Fiona, who was chatting with a portly man in a charcoal suit. "Fiona knows the GM and called in a favor."

"She's a good friend," William observed, as he caught Fiona's eye and waved. "Those are hard to come by."

"Believe me, I know that better than anyone," June said, before blowing Fiona a kiss.

"This place is perfect." Amy swooped in a moment later and hugged June. "Thank you for finding it. We were really screwed there for a minute."

"Karma really is a bitch," June said.

"And let's admit it, so were we." Amy smiled. "I'm glad we figured things out between us so nothing else wedding related can go wrong."

"I feel bad—I can't believe the other place had a hepatitis B breakout," June said. "Like somehow our wedding sabotage brought that onto them."

"I know," Amy said. "I feel the same way. I was so against that restaurant—gave you such a hard time about it—and you remember the horrible plan I had." She made eyes at June. "And then the place really did have to shut down."

"Horrible plan?" William inquired, then held up his hand. "Never mind. I don't want to know."

"Probably for the best," June said, and squeezed his arm. "It all worked out—we are where we're supposed to be."

"For what it's worth, I did send a huge care package to the restaurant from all of us— to balance out the karma, just in case."

"Thank you for doing that," June said. "I'm happy you and I are on the same team—*finally*." She glanced around Amy's back. "Wait, is that your iPad? You brought it here?"

"I can explain," Amy said sheepishly. "You see, I have this extensive party checklist—"

"Do you have a checklist for every single thing in your life?" June leaned in closer and whispered, "Did you have one for *us*?"

"No!" Amy stammered. "Well, maybe."

To William's surprise, June burst out laughing. "One day, I want to see that one."

"The only thing on it now is to be a good friend to you, if you'll let me."

June smiled. "I will."

William would have gagged at the lovey-dovey exchange he was witnessing if he weren't so happy the women were finally trading compliments instead of barbs. One minute they were at war over whether to stuff the mushroom appetizers with blue cheese or goat—yes, that was a real text argument he'd unfortunately had to bear witness to after June pressured him to rejoin the text group—and the next, they were practically serenading each other with love songs in public.

William didn't know what had triggered the makeup between the women—June had been cryptic when she announced they were friendly again; something about a pancake—but he honestly didn't care. He was simply happy to see that *his June* was back. The grounded and very adult-acting bookstore owner whose biggest problem was whether to turn in her Subaru at the end of its lease. He much preferred her to the heat-seeking wedding-planning missile that she had become.

June looked like herself again too. Tonight she was wearing a beautiful pale-pink silk dress, her long golden hair wrapped in a braid. The last few times he'd seen her, she'd had on too much makeup and her hair was pulled back into a severe bun or ponytail, as if she were playing the part of some corporate tycoon. He was happy that she was soft once more—inside and out. It suited her. She wasn't built to hold rage in her heart.

Her kind soul was one of the many things that had drawn him to her when they met. He knew he could be sharp like a dagger and June's pliability balanced his edges. But that hadn't been enough for them to find a common footing in their marriage. June was always slightly out of William's reach—like the name of an actor in a movie that you can't quite remember. The reentry of Amy and Troy into June's life had been the final dots in a pattern William had tried and failed to connect during his twelve-year marriage to June. He could now see the full picture. She'd never been truly his because she'd never fully let go of them, or their betrayal. As he watched her offer a genuine smile to Amy, he hoped that she could now.

"I'm glad to see you two getting along," William said, draining his glass and looking around for one of the servers. He had a rare night off and a hotel room one block away, and he intended to take advantage of it.

He caught Olivia's eye and winked at her. She looked beautiful—and so mature!—in a long red dress with a plunging neckline he wished weren't quite so deep. She was standing with her grandmother Eileen and laughing at something Zach had said. William had to admit that the kid had grown on him, and not only because when he'd spoken to him last week, Zach had asked William smart questions about anesthesiology. Although that didn't hurt. It was mostly because William could see how happy he made Olivia. William still thought the wedding was rushed and would prefer his daughter wait to get married until she was older, maybe thirty—wasn't that reasonable?—but he could see that Zach would make a good partner.

June often implied that William had learned nothing about women from his time married to her, but he had. His ex-wife and two daughters had taught him many times over that sometimes it was best to go against every single one of his natural instincts and say nothing. Case in point: how he'd listened to June and swallowed his misgivings about the wedding. It turned out that letting Olivia make her own decision had been the right thing to do. And he'd never been more sure of that than right now as he watched his daughter. She was smiling at Eileen and leaning her head back against Zach's chest. Zach glanced at her, his face lighting up with what could only be described as joy, before he kissed the top of her head. "Did you see that?" William asked June and Amy, wanting to share the moment.

June and Amy were oblivious to his question, deep in conversation. Fiona had now joined them, and Amy was telling a story about how June had forced her to put her iPad away at the cake tasting.

He turned his attention back to Olivia, who was now leading Zach to the small dance floor. Zach pulled her close, their bodies connecting as if they were custom fit.

Amy finally noticed them. "They look so happy."

"They do," June concurred. "Who would have thought . . ." She trailed off, letting each of the others find their own ending to the sentence. William considered what the rest of his thought would be. His would go something like this: *Who would have thought I'd be able to let go of my daughter and trust that she was making the best decision for herself?*

After the song ended, William found Olivia and Zach at the bar. "Beautiful place," William said.

Olivia's face lit up as she took in the room. Complete darkness blanketed the outside, making the city lights shine brighter. "Thank you, Dad, for all of this," Olivia said.

"Yes, thank you," Zach added, and shook William's hand before introducing him to a very tall young man named Logan.

Both of their grips were firm. William liked that. "You're both very welcome. But I didn't really do anything except hand over my credit card." He laughed at his own joke and looked at

Olivia. "It's your mom and Amy who pulled this engagement party off—and in record time, too."

"Don't be so modest!" Olivia teased. "But yes, Mom and Amy did a great job when the other place canceled on us. I had exams, so I couldn't help them at all when they were scrambling." She glanced at June and Amy, and William followed her gaze. They were talking to the bartender, who was holding two shot glasses. Amy was clapping and June was pointing to a bottle of tequila. "I'm happy they're getting along, but their rekindled friendship seems a little . . ." She paused to search for the right word and looked at Zach.

"Intense?" Zach filled in the blank.

They all laughed nervously.

"But hey, they aren't fighting, so this intensely happy version of them is better, right?" Zach offered.

"I hope it's sustainable." Olivia said this so quietly William almost missed it.

He'd had the same thought.

"It will be—I'll make sure of it," Zach promised, and Olivia's face relaxed. It had always been William's job to protect his daughter, and it surprised him how good it felt to watch Zach step into that role so easily.

Zach kissed Olivia on the cheek, and he and Logan excused themselves to say hello to another friend from high school. William tried to remember the last time he'd been alone with his daughter. He couldn't.

"I like him," William said. "He's a good guy. Solid handshake too. And I like his friend. They say you can judge a man by the company he keeps."

Olivia smiled. "Well, he hangs with me a lot, so he must be pretty amazing then?"

William laughed. "He's lucky to have you."

Olivia gave him a skeptical look. "So, you're not disappointed that I'm marrying a man I only met a few months ago?" she asked with a knowing smile.

For a moment William debated whether June had betrayed his confidence. But no; although she'd been acting totally out of character with all the wedding high jinks, she wouldn't have done that. He had always been able to count on June's discretion.

"No, I'm not. But if we're being honest, I would have appreciated hearing about it from you, not your sister." He winked to soften the accusation.

Olivia blushed. "I was so happy that I didn't think I could handle it if you weren't happy for me. I'm sorry. I know it was childish."

"I was caught off guard, sure. And worried about you, yes. But I would never let my own issues trump your happiness. Did you really think I would?" William frowned and felt a stab of something. Surprise? Sadness? He wasn't sure.

"This isn't an excuse, but mom wasn't exactly jumping up and down when we first told her—and I totally get that, I do—so then I was really scared to tell you, because . . ." Olivia touched his arm. "This isn't a bad thing. In fact, I love this about you. And I'm *usually* the same way." She laughed lightly. "But you're pragmatic, sometimes to a fault. And this time I didn't want pragmatism. I wanted blind faith."

William nodded. "I understand. I was twenty-three once too, you know."

"You were?" Olivia snorted. "I thought you came out of the womb like this."

William fiddled with the top of his bourbon glass. It was hard to remember when he'd been younger and more carefree.

Now blind faith was about as foreign to him as using those moving walkways at the airport. "For the record, I am. Happy for you. I only wanted to make sure you were keeping your eye on your future too."

"You mean law school? I hope you know I'd never give up law school for a *man*." She scrunched her face. "Besides, Zach is excited to have a lawyer wife," Olivia puffed out her chest. "He says it's super hot."

William chuckled. "Another reason to like him."

"Does this mean I have your official approval?"

"It does. But don't think I'm doing the Macarena dance at the wedding. My approval and happiness for you has limits."

"Damn!" she exclaimed, and even though it wasn't that funny, they both laughed hard. They laughed so deeply that William noticed a woman drinking a lemon drop martini look over, clearly wanting in on the joke. They laughed so hard that William wondered why he didn't make time to laugh with his daughters more often. Because it felt fucking fantastic.

Olivia wiped tears from the corners of her eyes and caught her breath. "I needed that. Thank you, Dad. I love you," she said as she threw herself against his chest, her head resting below his chin.

* * *

Troy hadn't been able to stop thinking about June since they'd gone shark shopping last week—he was still riding the *wave* of their success. He'd wanted to text her so many times, but after he'd sent her a shark joke, one he'd been sure she would love and would open the door to some serious under-the-sea banter, she'd only haha'd his text.

Who's the most famous shark writer?
William Sharkspear!

That one still made him laugh.

He'd been watching June since she arrived tonight, trying to work up the courage to talk to her, *really* talk to her, something he'd failed miserably at when they spent the entire day together. Sure, they'd exchanged pleasantries and complained about traffic, but that was it. They certainly hadn't acted like two people who had once been in love, who had once been engaged. He'd started to bring up the past—to tell her how sorry he was for everything. To let her know he'd always wondered about her. But he'd chickened out. And when he'd asked about William, she'd dodged his question.

But when Troy talked with his therapist, she'd encouraged him to take a risk—to tell June what was in his heart. So that's what he planned to do tonight. He wasn't sure what he was going to say. He'd let the moment decide it for him.

He glanced across the room. June was at the bar with Amy—she'd been practically attached to her hip all night. He'd never thought he'd have to pull June away from his ex-wife to get some time, but it looked like that's what he was going to have to do. Amy had called him the day after the cake tasting and told him they'd made up. Troy was relieved to hear that because they had been going at it for weeks, but he was also jealous that June had forgiven Amy and not him. And maybe that was his end game tonight. To try to get that forgiveness too.

He headed toward the bar, taking in how gorgeous June looked with her hair in a braid, the way she'd often worn it back in college. To ease his jumpiness, he grabbed another signature drink, the Amalfitini, from a tray. (He'd already had two.)

On the way to the bar, he chatted briefly with William. He could see William struggling to find a category to put him in. Was he the man who'd cheated on his wife? (Bad!) Or was he the man who'd paved the way for William to find June and create the family he loved so much? (Good!)

"Hello, ladies," Troy said to Amy and June.

"Hi," they chirped.

"June, can I steal you for a few minutes? I've got some serious shark business to discuss."

June widened her eyes at Troy. "Are we talking great whites? Hammerheads? Tigers?"

"I can't disclose that here. It's highly confidential."

"Above my shark pay grade. I get it," Amy said. "I have some official business of my own anyway. Good luck, you two. I hope you solve all of the world's shark problems."

She stood up from the barstool and made a straight line across the room for Eileen, of all people.

* * *

Amy drew her shoulders back and pressed forward. She'd rehearsed her speech in the shower earlier, but with every step toward Eileen, she felt her confidence waver. She glanced at June walking toward the outside terrace and reminded herself that this was for her.

Eileen was wearing a charcoal-gray dress, a pearl pendant pinned over her heart and her matching pearls around her neck, as usual. Amy had to admit she looked elegant. She was engaged in a conversation with a woman Amy had met earlier, one of Olivia's friends from college. "May I interrupt?" Amy asked.

"I believe you already have," Eileen answered, her lips tense around the words.

"It was nice talking to you. I'm going to find Olivia," the woman blurted and hurried off, wanting no part of the conversation that was about to happen.

Can I come with you? Amy wanted to say.

Amy eyed a server passing by with a tray of smoked-salmon-and-dill canapés. She grabbed two. "Want one?" she asked Eileen.

Eileen shook her head and looked at Amy's napkin as if it were overflowing with food.

Amy ignored it.

"So, Eileen, I was hoping we could talk."

"About?"

"June—"

Eileen cut in. "I don't want to get in the middle of what's going on with you two."

"Actually, we are in a good place right now," Amy said, and Eileen arched her brow. "But I didn't want to discuss June and myself. I was wondering if we could talk about June and *you*."

"And *me*?" Eileen put her hand over her heart.

Amy took a bite of the canapé, and some of it trickled onto her chin. She wiped it away quickly. "Yes. All of this." Amy swept her hand toward the engagement party guests standing nearby. "It has brought up a lot of emotion for me and I think June too. And—" Amy took another bite and chewed quickly.

Eileen's features tightened. "For the love, woman! Out with it! What are you trying to say?"

Amy wiped her mouth and balled up her napkin. "I'm trying to say that I think you might be missing what's happening with your daughter. What this wedding is dredging up for her. The complicated feelings around her engagement to Troy. Especially when it comes to you."

"Me?"

Eileen reminded Amy of one of her Rose Princesses involved in a scandal, defensive, refusing to be accountable. In denial. "Did you two ever talk after she called off the wedding?"

"Of course we did." Eileen crossed her arms over her chest.

"I mean, did you *really talk*? Did you know how badly she wanted your approval? How heartbroken she was when you wouldn't give it to her—or to Troy?"

"I knew she was upset, yes, but I think she understood why I couldn't support it. And anyway, I was right."

Amy treaded lightly, remembering a quote she'd read recently online that had resonated with her. "Yes, in many ways, you were right. But let me ask you something. Is it important to be right or important to be happy?"

Eileen blinked rapidly.

"Because sometimes, a child needs her mother. Whether she made a mistake or not, whether she was right or wrong. It was a really low point in her life, Eileen. So I'm asking, were you there for her?"

Eileen puckered her lips and walked away.

Amy exhaled hard and hailed the crab cake server, taking three off his platter and telling herself she deserved every single calorie.

* * *

"I'd love to get some air. You?" June asked.

"Please," Troy said as they walked out to the roof deck. "It's beautiful out here," he remarked. "What a view—I bet there's a shark or two out there." He pointed to the ocean.

"Or there." June extended her arm. "That's the Long Beach aquarium!"

Troy laughed. "Our sharks would be so proud—so well represented in the LBC."

June giggled. "It never gets old."

"You didn't seem to love my William Sharkspear joke, though."

"I did, but you know, I was trying to have boundaries."

"Boundaries?" Troy asked.

"Yeah, you know, those lines you draw to keep people out?"

"You're trying to keep me out?"

"No. Maybe. I don't know . . ." June didn't finish her thought. "But not tonight. Tonight I've had several glasses of champagne *and a tequila shot*. And champagne/tequila June knows no boundaries!" She set her drink on a table and put her arms in the air like Superman.

Troy laughed. "You and Amy seem to be doing well. No boundaries there either?" he asked, hoping he sounded lighthearted, that his jealousy didn't betray him.

June went quiet for a moment. "We needed to figure it out—for Zach and Olivia. We were going down a bad road."

"I know, I get that. I guess I was hoping that maybe we could figure things out too."

"It's complicated, Troy."

"What do you mean? Weren't there three of us involved? And now two of us are doing shots together, and by my count, there's still an odd man out."

So much for the jealousy not betraying him.

"It's complicated," June said again, and leaned against the railing.

"You mentioned that." Troy loosened his tie, which was suddenly choking him.

"What do you want from me?" June turned around, but continued before he could answer. "Look, the shark shopping

was fun. We went to the 'Bu and met Kaia Gerber's assistant."
She smiled sadly. "But at the end of the day, we were two parents helping our kids, nothing more. Can't that be enough?"

"I'm sorry for everything," Troy said, his throat tight.

"Please, don't. I know you're sorry. That everyone is *so sorry*.
And believe me, in the beginning of this I was desperate for
apologies, but now I feel like I'm drowning in them. There's no
need to retread this." June's eyes darkened.

"I think we do. You needed to figure it out with Amy. What
makes me, *us*, different?"

"Everything. Nothing. I don't know." June picked up her
glass and waved it, and some champagne spilled over the side.
"Maybe I'm exhausted and want to move forward without all
these deep emotional dives."

"There was another joke in there, you know."

June gave a brief laugh. "I know, damnit!" She broke off and
gazed at the skyline. "I understand what you're saying. I know
it's selfish, but I guess I need you to know how bad I felt—how
hard it was to lose you."

She drew a deep, audible breath. "You said it would always
be you and me against the world, and the minute things got
tough . . ."

"I left," Troy finished. "I know how much that must have
hurt you—"

"I'm sorry, but you don't," June interrupted, her voice shaking a little.

"You're right. I don't. But for what it's worth, I thought I was
doing the right thing. I wanted to be there for my child. And I
would make that same choice again. But it doesn't mean I don't
hate that you got hurt in the process. That *we* were destroyed."
Troy glanced inside, where Olivia was standing with Chloe.

Troy blinked several times. He could have been looking at a college-age June.

"As much as I hate what you did, I'm happy to have the life that I do. I wouldn't trade my girls for anything."

"Of course," Troy agreed. "I wanted to talk to you about this the other day, but—"

"There wasn't time in between shoving sharks in the trunk of your car and arguing with Party City employees about what may or may not be in their back stock?" June looked him straight in the eyes, and every nerve in his body seemed to cry out.

Did she feel that energy between them too?

They fell into a comfortable silence. Finally, Troy turned to her. "I'm happy for you, June. For the life you've built." He paused, gathering the courage to say the rest. "I've missed you."

June's mouth fell open. "You have?"

"Yes. Is that so hard to believe?"

"I don't know. Maybe. It was a long time ago."

"I guess I always wondered, *What if?*"

"That's a dangerous game to play."

"Have you—"

"Played it? With you in mind?"

"Of course," Troy admitted, his pulse quickening.

"I guess I have lately," June testified, a little reluctantly. "Since all this. But before, I couldn't go there. I had to bury it. It was how I coped."

"I had my own way of coping too—I tried the whole *Put it in a box* thing, but that didn't work at all. I needed to get my emotions out. I've been writing to you. Letters."

"What do they say?"

Troy rubbed the back of his neck as he thought of the years of material he'd shared in the pages of notebooks, typed into Word documents. Eventually graduating to unsent emails that flooded his drafts folder. When Zach said his first word—*hi*—Troy had spent six pages on that one. And when Zach almost said *commission* when he was barely two, Troy's heart had exploded as he wrote about his son following in his footsteps. Then there was the night he'd downed a Long Island iced tea after not touching the stuff for a decade and he'd poured out his heart and soul while drunk. And when he and Amy agreed it was over between them, both crying silently as they looked over Zach's bed, even that story he'd wanted to tell June. Because didn't he deserve to have that marriage fail? After what he'd done?

As he wrote, he'd pretended he was talking to June like they had when they were young—when she'd curl up on the twin bed beside him, their legs intertwined, and they'd share their hopes and dreams for the future. "I wrote so many things to you—about Zach, my career, the divorce. And a lot of them were about how much I missed you and hoped your life had turned out okay."

"Troy." June opened her mouth to speak, then closed it again.

"I still have them," Troy continued. "In a total cliché place: a cardboard box in the back of my closet. It's ripped so many times, I've duct taped it to hold it together. This is going to sound strange—"

"Stranger than the fact that you have a box of unsent letters to me in the back of your closet? Wonder what else is in there . . ." June rubbed her chin.

"A few dead bodies, my toenail collection . . ." A teasing smile crossed his face.

He didn't mention that Amy had found the letters once. Not long after Zach was born. There were maybe only two or three, but the look of devastation that clouded Amy's face would be forever etched in Troy's mind. Troy would always see that day as the beginning of the end. He'd promised Amy he'd stop writing to June—but he hadn't. He couldn't.

Troy had moved toward June without realizing it, like she was a gravitational pull he couldn't fight. He could see the freckles on her nose. The ones he used to count, tapping them lightly, one by one, before he kissed her. Now he put his hand under her chin and cradled it as he brought her lips to his. He wondered if he'd remember—if when they touched, it would send him back again. Or if it would be a new feeling.

"Well, well, well." Amy's voice cut through the air like a whip.

Troy swiveled around. Horror, shock, and sadness were streaked across Amy's face like an emotional finger-painting project.

June and Troy sprung back from each other. "It isn't what you think," June said unsteadily, but her cheeks were crimson, as if she'd committed a crime.

But had she? Troy wondered. Had they?

"Then why stop? Looks like I interrupted what was about to be something serious. Please, go right ahead, don't mind me. Should be like riding a bike for you two."

"Amy—" Troy stepped toward her.

"No! Do not come near me."

Troy dropped his eyes to his feet, hating to see Amy hurting. Knowing he was to blame.

"How could you?" She pointed to June. "I thought we were becoming friends again." Her eyes filled with tears. "I was so stupid to believe you actually cared about me."

"I do," June said.

"You have a very interesting way of showing it. By shoving your tongue down my ex-husband's throat at our children's engagement party."

"Don't you think you're being a little hard on June?" Troy tried again, wanting Amy to yell at him, not June. The women had figured things out. This was what June had been trying to tell him earlier—that things with him were too complicated. He wouldn't listen. "This is my fault. Be mad at me."

"Well, aren't you trying to be the white knight. Does June know who you've become? That your bedroom boasts a revolving door of girls that are around *Olivia's* age? I'm surprised you didn't bring Sloane tonight. The one I met a few weeks ago at Trader Joe's? You were kissing in the pasta aisle—planning the dinner you were going to make for her."

June looked at Troy in alarm. Troy inhaled sharply. He was losing June. Again.

Anger flashed in Amy's eyes as she glared at June. "Oops, sorry, I guess you didn't realize he's not available."

"Amy, come on—" Troy started.

"What would our son say if he saw you right now—out here kissing your ex?" Amy shook her head at Troy. "I always knew you were selfish, *especially as a father*. You couldn't manage to be the dad Zach needs on one of the most important nights of his life? When he gives *everything* to you? Even his career? He doesn't love it, you know. Real estate isn't his passion. He does it only to make *you* happy, which you would see clear as a bell if you ever took your head out of your own ass."

Troy felt like he'd been slammed in the stomach. Was that true? He would never want Zach to do something he didn't love. How had he not seen it? He locked eyes with Amy. Her barbs were below the belt, and he could tell by the look on her face that she knew it, but still, they hit him hard. She was right. He had put himself first yet again. "You're right, I'm sorry. But I didn't mean to hurt anyone."

Amy looked away, but not before he could see the pain in her eyes. Not only for Zach but for herself. There was a history between them that far outreached the parameters of this balcony. When she found the letters, she'd said out loud the thing that she'd tried to convince herself wasn't true since the day they got married. That she was second best. He denied it, saying the letters were only an outlet, that they meant nothing. But maybe she had been right.

Maybe June had always been his number-one.

"Always so sorry after you've hurt someone, aren't you? You take, take, take, and then you apologize."

Troy tried to gauge what June was thinking. Did she agree with Amy?

He wanted to remind Amy that she had also been present the night they slept together. That she had also apologized after the fact. But that was not the point. They were all so raw and exposed. There was no black and white to their situation. Only miles of emotional gray.

Amy scowled at them. "You know what? Forget it. Kiss away— have sex right here, for all I care. You two deserve each other," she hissed before storming back to the party, almost knocking over a server carrying a tray of feta and watermelon cubes.

Troy and June stood in silence for a while after Amy was gone, the air so thick with decades of regret that no words needed to be spoken. Finally, June met his eyes and gave him a cold stare. "I should get back inside."

"Wait." Troy grabbed her arm. "I'm sorry I screwed things up for you with Amy. I shouldn't have pushed you to talk to me about *us*. I was selfish. And I can't be that way anymore. I need to tell you something."

"There's more? Troy, I'm not sure I can handle *more*."

"Zach met Olivia because of me," Troy said anyway.

"What?" June asked.

"I knew Olivia was in Positano. I asked him to go there to find her."

June pressed her thumb between her eyes. "So it was a lie that they met by chance? *You* were the reason he was there? You sent him to stalk my daughter? This is a joke, right?" Red blotchy spots appeared on June's neck. "Tell me this is a joke, Troy."

"It's not a joke, but listen, it was all innocent, I promise you. He didn't stalk her. He was already on the Amalfi Coast, in Amalfi. When I saw on Instagram that Olivia was in Positano, they were so close—"

"What?" June's eyes flared with disgust. "Why were you following my daughter on Instagram?" June's voice was high. She covered her mouth with her hand. "Did *you* want to date her?"

Troy shook his head hard. "God. No! June," he said, and reached for her arm again, but she moved out of his reach. "It was because of you! I couldn't find you anywhere, so I did the next best thing—"

"You creeped on my daughter?"

"No, listen, please. I ran into someone we went to school with. Dana Strong. Remember her? Well, it's Dana Richards now—"

"I know who she is," June said sharply.

"Anyway, she told me you were single and that you had two daughters, but not much else. And you aren't on social media, so—"

"For this exact reason. Because I don't want to be slapped in the face by my past. Like this!"

"June—I meant well. Like I said, I missed you and wondered about you. So I followed Olivia. And Chloe. Their profiles were public . . ."

"What does that mean? Public?" June put her hand to her temple. "Did they know it was *you*?"

"No, I don't think so." Troy's throat pulsed. "I would go on to look. See what you might be up to."

"Why didn't you send them a message that you were trying to reach me?"

"In hindsight, maybe I should have. But I was afraid. And obviously didn't think any of this through."

June tried to push past him.

"Wait, please. Let me explain."

"You have thirty seconds, and then I'm done. I won't let you take up a moment more of *my daughter's*—and *your son's*—night."

"When I saw that Olivia and Zach were both in the same part of the world at the same time, I thought it was fate. For so long I wanted a way back into your life—"

"Well, congratulations. You got it."

"Look at it this way. We probably wouldn't be here now if I'd done this any other way. Olivia wouldn't have met Zach," he said. "And look how happy they are!"

"That's a convenient excuse for you to use now."

"I was desperate to have a connection to you. I had no idea that they'd fall in love."

"Does Olivia know about any of this?" June asked.

"I didn't, but I do now," Olivia said, Amalfitini in her hand, tears in her eyes. "So it wasn't fate that we met? You sent him there on some sick assignment?"

June moved toward Olivia, but her daughter backed away. "Honey," June started. "Does it really matter why he was there? He fell in love with you."

"If that's how you feel, why didn't you say that to Troy? I've been standing here for a while, Mom." She didn't wait for June to answer. "Zach lied to me." Olivia's voice was small. She looked at Troy, her eyes hard. "When all of the stuff from the past came out, Zach promised me he was nothing like you. That he'd never deceive me. But I guess that was the biggest lie of all," she said, before turning on her heel and storming toward the bar, where Zach was sipping a whiskey with Logan. June and Troy watched in horror as Olivia pulled him aside and confronted him, waving off Chloe when she attempted to step in and defuse the situation.

"Fuck," Troy muttered under his breath as he raced to the bar. June was close behind.

"Olivia, please," Zach was saying when they approached. "I didn't know how to tell you."

"Haven't you learned anything from our parents? We have to be honest with each other. You let me believe it was fate, when it was all a manipulation. How can we start off our life on a lie?"

Zach looked as if he'd been slapped. "I love you, Olivia. There's no lie in that."

"How can I believe a word you say?" Olivia was crying, tears splashing down her face. "We are doomed anyway. Look at our parents."

Troy's stomach dropped as he met Amy's eyes, who had also come to see what was wrong.

"The wedding is off," Olivia said.

"Olivia." Chloe grabbed her arm. "Give him a chance to explain."

"Not tonight. Maybe not ever," she said, then turned to Logan. "Were you in on this too?"

"No, I—" Logan started, but Olivia turned toward the door, not waiting for him to finish.

"You coming?" she called back to Chloe, who gave Zach a sad look before following her out of the room, as June chased after both of them. Zach stared after her, a mask of shock covering his face.

Troy set his hand on Zach's shoulder. "I'm sorry, son. This is all my fault."

Zach looked at Troy, his eyes blazing. "That's the first honest thing you've said in months." He turned to Logan. "Let's get out of here," he said, turning his back on Troy and fleeing the destruction.

CHAPTER TWENTY

Olivia sat in her childhood room and turned up the volume on her phone, "Dandelions" by Ruth B. blaring through her Air-Pods. She let the words of the song—*their* song—blanket her as she remembered. She and Zach had been hiking the Path of the Gods. They'd been debating music. When country music came up, Zach had mentioned Sam Hunt, of all people. He said he liked some of his songs; didn't she? When he saw her face, he flushed and said, "I have zero taste, obviously. I guess now's not the time to mention my secret love for Katy Perry."

Olivia gritted her teeth to hold off a smile now. Despite how angry she was, the memory of Zach breaking into a terrible rendition of "I Kissed a Girl" made her miss him. That was Zach, or who she'd *thought* Zach was—unassuming, quirky. She'd told him she preferred vibey music by women who had something to say. Like Ruth B. She'd scrolled through her phone until she'd found her favorite song—giving him one of her Air-Pods so they could listen to it together. As the lyrics danced in their ears, Olivia's heart bobbed up and down too—this was exactly how she felt about Zach. She'd never known anybody like him. This was a once-in-a-lifetime love. She'd never felt so happy. While he listened, he stared at her in a way that made her feel like he was born to give *her* that look.

She'd thought, *I love this man.*

Then she'd blurted it, her eyes popping in shock after the words dropped out of her mouth. She'd never said that to anyone romantically. Sure, she'd had boyfriends, like Jason, whose sleeve of tattoos and sexy smirk made her think she was in love, but that relationship and the others never progressed beyond infatuation.

It felt like an eternity before Zach responded. In those moments, she convinced herself she'd ruined everything. He thought she was too clingy. She was about to find out that, to him, they'd only been hooking up.

Finally, Zach responded.

He'd cupped her chin and said, "I love you too, V." Then he sang more Katy Perry in her ear.

Olivia heard a soft knock at the door. She removed her AirPods and tensed, hoping it wasn't her mom. Again. "Can I come in? I'm alone," Chloe said.

"Yes," Olivia said, relieved.

Chloe sat on the bed next to Olivia and took her phone from her.

"Are you trying to torture yourself?" Chloe asked as she looked at the picture Olivia had been staring at. It was a selfie of Zach and Olivia sitting on a rock, the sea in the distance.

"Yes. The answer is yes," Olivia replied dryly. "I want to be back there, on that hike with him. Back when I didn't know he was a stalker. A liar. A creep."

Olivia rubbed her bare ring finger—it felt as vacant as she did.

She replayed slamming the engagement ring on the bar and storming out of the party last night.

She saw her mom's face as she realized Olivia had overheard Troy.

Troy's expression as he understood the damage his words had done.

Zach's eyes when Olivia told him it was over.

Amy, as she watched her son lose his fiancée.

Logan's eyes when she accused him of being in on it.

She could feel her sister's tight grip around her hand as she guided her out of the building.

She heard her own voice echoing in her head. *The wedding is off.*

Her phone buzzed.

"It's Zach calling." Chloe offered a questioning gaze.

Olivia shook her head. "Don't give me that look, Chlo. He lied to me. He made me think it was a cosmic miracle that we'd met."

Chloe opened her mouth to say something, but closed it.

Olivia already knew what Chloe thought. That Olivia should hear him out. That there were two sides to every story. Troy's and Zach's. That even though he hadn't been truthful about *how* they'd met, he did love her and want to marry her.

Zach did seem desperate to talk to Olivia. He had texted, snapped, called, messaged her on Facebook, DM'd her on Insta—shown up at June's door! But Olivia had told her mom to send him away. She didn't want to hear his excuses. No matter what he'd say, it wouldn't change that he'd misled her. How could she ever trust him again?

Logan had sent her texts too, saying his best friend could be a dumbass but he wasn't a bad guy. He hadn't meant to hurt her. To please at least hear him out. But she hadn't replied.

She also hadn't been able to bring herself to block Zach—she was still checking his socials to see if he'd posted anything (he hadn't)—but she had blocked his dad and made all of her social media accounts private. She felt a chill snake up her arms. She could not believe that Troy had stalked her online. Then he'd sent his son to hunt her down in person. Every time Olivia replayed the moment she'd met Zach, her stomach twisted. To think he'd already known she was in Positano; that he'd followed her while she shopped, then pretended to see her for the first time outside of that boutique. Had the photography story he'd given her been a bunch of horseshit too? If so, he should get an Oscar for that performance.

Olivia's tears began to fall again, and Chloe grabbed her hand and held it. "I'm sorry this happened to you," she said. "I think I want you to talk to him because I'm hoping it will make you feel better. That he'll be able to say the exact thing you need to hear. I hate seeing you like this." Chloe grabbed a box from Olivia's bedside table. She peered inside. "Um, care to explain these?" she asked, holding up two custom pairs of socks.

One pair was covered with pictures of Olivia eating pizza and the other carpeted with an adorable calico cat. Olivia cried harder. "Those were a Christmas present for Zach," she stammered. "Will you get rid of them? Give them away, or you can have them."

Chloe looked at the socks and smiled sadly before placing them back in the box. "I think you should keep them."

"I don't want them—they make me think of him. Everything makes me think of him," Olivia said, and leaned into her sister, who pulled the comforter over them. Olivia's limbs felt weighed down by sandbags, her heart by something heavier. She wished she were in the bed she shared with Zach, the one that was soft, the one where every time she curled up next to him, she felt like she was floating on clouds. But no, instead she was lying on the saggy twin mattress she'd slept on until the day she left for college. Under the blanket, Meowsers rubbed his body against Olivia's bare leg.

Could her life be any more pathetic?

She heard knocking on her door. She knew it was her mom this time. She looked at Chloe, whose gaze suggested she should let their mom come in.

"I can't, Chlo."

Chloe nodded.

"Honey? It's me. You should eat. I brought you some chicken noodle soup," her mom said.

Olivia didn't respond and gave Chloe a warning look to also stay silent. She shoved her AirPods back in her ears and turned the volume up. *I don't have the flu, Mom! I have a broken heart. Thanks, in part, to you.*

Olivia couldn't decide how much blame to assign to her mom. Obviously, Troy was Fuckup Numero Uno. And Zach ranked right up there with his creepy dad. But her mom? As far as Olivia knew, June seemed unaware that Troy had plotted this. Or that Zach had been in on his dad's little plan. But regardless, her mom was still part of the problem. Her mom had almost kissed Troy at Olivia's engagement party! That almost-kiss that June had confessed in a long text message to Olivia was what had set off this catastrophic set of events. Although Chloe had pointed out to Olivia that had June *not* leaned in for that kiss, Amy wouldn't have witnessed it and Troy wouldn't have confessed to his *very upsetting* crime. So as wrong as it might have been for June to pucker up her lips for her ex, it was the reason Olivia knew the truth.

239

"I wish I didn't know any of it," she whispered to her sister now.

Chloe looked shocked.

"You seem surprised I wouldn't want to know about this disturbing father-son tag team? They aren't only in real estate together. Apparently, they stalk together too." Olivia sighed heavily.

A pained look settled on Chloe's face.

Olivia knew she sounded bitter. And deep down she understood that she had needed to find this out, as awful as it was. She was relieved she'd discovered it now instead of later, after they were married. That made Olivia's stomach tighten all over again. Even if Olivia could forgive Zach for withholding the truth, which she didn't intend to do, she couldn't wrap her head around how in the hell he'd thought it would be okay for him to marry her under false pretenses. If that had happened, if they'd said their vows and had kids and then Olivia found out? She would have had to put her law degree to good use and figure out a way to sue his lying ass.

What Olivia couldn't articulate to her sister was that she wished there had been no lie for Zach to cover up. That she could have met the love of her life the way she thought she had—organically. That she could still believe they were fated to meet on that blistering day in Positano.

Because Olivia wasn't only heartbroken; she'd been made a fool. And the trust she had for Zach was one hundred percent gone. Aside from her father, Chloe was the only one she could trust—the only one in this group of misfit toys who hadn't gone off the rails. Before Troy tried to kiss her mom, she'd been acting like a crazy person. Olivia wasn't stupid. She knew her mom and Zach's mom hadn't just been text fighting over the wedding. That they were also behind all the "mishaps." They thought they were sly, but their wedding war games were about as subtle as the Kardashians on a midday shopping spree.

Olivia closed her eyes. Now that the wedding was off, she supposed none of it mattered anymore.

* * *

June's ear was pressed against Olivia's bedroom door. She strained to hear something, anything. She thought she heard whispering and wondered if Chloe was in there. Olivia had never refused to talk to her or shut her out, literally. It was Chloe who would go toe-to-toe with her and William. Who wouldn't take no for an answer. Once she'd protesting June's refusal to stop buying animal products by wearing a Lady Gaga–inspired meat outfit at every meal until June compromised and agreed to start making two vegetarian meals per week. Chloe had only been eleven years old!

June had been surprised when Olivia announced she wanted to be a lawyer—Chloe's argumentative personality seemed much more suited to that profession. When June had said as much to William, he'd pressed his lips into a tight line. "Give Olivia a little credit, June. Maybe she isn't a squeaky wheel like Chloe, but that doesn't mean she can't get the grease." June thought about that now. Had she taken advantage of Olivia's easygoing personality when she'd over-inserted herself into the wedding planning—when she'd used the wedding, *her daughter's wedding*, to try to get back at Amy? June had felt possessed. Like the ghost of 1996 had risen from the grave and taken over June's body. That raw, sharp pain of Amy's deception had turned her into someone she didn't recognize.

And it was her daughter, not Amy, who'd ended up paying the price.

She tried again. "Olivia? I brought you something to eat." She set the soup on the floor next to Olivia's door and waited. After making sure June had gotten home safely after the engagement party, Fiona had stopped by first thing this morning, and they'd talked through what June should do. What she might say.

"Please talk to me. Believe it or not, I know what you're going through."

June wiped her eyes with the sleeve of her sweatshirt.

Troy had done it again.

He'd broken June's heart, and then he'd found a way to hurt her daughter too.

June pictured Olivia on the other side of the door, lying on her old bed, swaddled in her yellow comforter. Eyes swollen from shedding tears over the love of her life.

After June called off her wedding to Troy, she'd stayed in bed for what felt like forever. She'd protected her heart like it was a plate of glass that had been punctured. Knowing if it got hit again, it would shatter completely.

June knocked on Olivia's door one last time. She wanted to hold her daughter in her arms and tell her it was going to be okay. That she was sorry her past had become a vicious loop that Olivia was now caught in. She yearned to be the mother Eileen wasn't.

But June was worse than Eileen. Her mom had been many things when June's engagement ended—coldhearted topping the list—but she hadn't been *responsible*. She hadn't caused June's wedding to fall apart.

June waited for a long time, but Olivia never opened the door. June sat down and leaned her head against the barrier that separated them and began talking.

"I don't know if you're listening or if you have your AirPods in," June started. "I understand your pain, Olivia. I know what it feels to call off a wedding to a man you love, but due to something outside your control, you can't be with anymore." June paused and let the tears streak her face. "It feels unfair, doesn't it? You're a good person. Why is this happening to you? And did you do the right thing? If you forgive him, are you sanguine, or a fool?" June ran her finger through her hair. "The only thing I know for sure is that I'm so sorry for ruining your wedding. And I'll spend the rest of my life making it up to you."

She leaned up against the door for several minutes, but Olivia never did open it.

June needed to find a way to fix this. She pressed her thumbs into her temples. Her head was throbbing from the champagne she'd drunk last night. Reluctantly, June finally walked away from Olivia's door. She knew who she needed to call. There was only one person who could help her make this right.

* * *

Amy stared at the photos on her phone from the engagement party. Her favorite was a candid she'd taken of Olivia and Zach, heads close together, gazing at each other as if they were the only two people in the room. Why had it mattered to Amy how quickly they'd fallen in love?

She sank into the cushions of her sofa and studied the picture. Olivia's flushed cheeks, her bright eyes as she gazed up at Zach, as if they were communicating without words. Amy was quite sure she'd never looked at a man that way. Not even Troy. She'd had relationships with a few nice men since they'd divorced, and maybe she had loved one, but she'd never felt like a person had been put on earth for her. That was how Olivia and Zach were looking at each other in the photo.

It was also how June had looked at Troy last night. How Troy had looked at June. Witnessing that intimacy between June and Troy had ripped Amy's heart apart all over again. Not because she was jealous, but because it reminded her that June could forgive Troy deeply, but not her. June's absolution for Amy would have boundaries. That cut deep. What Amy had realized last night was that she'd never gotten over losing June. That the breakup of her friendship, not her divorce, had been the biggest heartbreak of her life.

When she'd thought things couldn't get any worse, Troy had called her late last night and confessed why Zach had really been in Positano.

She'd been so mad that she'd hung up on him.

She might have called him a *fucking fuckface.*

But once she'd cooled off, she'd realized she couldn't stay mad at Troy. Troy might be an idiot who never thought things through, but he was also the reason Zach and Olivia had met. And as much as everyone wished they'd met another way, they probably wouldn't have.

Amy touched Zach's face in the picture. He hadn't returned her calls or texts, and she didn't blame him. Her meltdown at the engagement party was part of the reason Troy's lie had been exposed. And she was sure Zach had heard all about it, as apparently several party guests had witnessed her exchange with Troy and June. Now Amy needed to figure out how to repair this. If anyone could do it, she could. This was what she did for a living, after all. Fixed broken shit.

Amy knew the one person she needed to call to try to make this right. The only person who could help her get her son and Olivia back together again.

She picked up on the first ring. "I was about to FaceTime you," June said, breathless. "I need to say something. I'm sorry I refused to look at baby Zach when you came to my door. That was an asshole move. You looked so damn tired. But I was so mad. That's not an excuse. I'm telling you why I was such a jerk that day. I should have let go of my anger. I'd already met William at that point. Did you know that?" June stopped, and Amy shook her head. "No, of course you didn't. How could you?" June started to cry. "If I'd married Troy, I wouldn't have met William. I wouldn't have my girls. I'm sorry, Amy. That I didn't give you a second chance. That I ruined the wedding. Everything."

Amy felt her heart open, desperate to inhale as much of this June as she could.

"I'm sorry too. I'm sorry I didn't check my answering machine when I saw the blinking red light. I'm sorry I went to meet Troy that night. I should have been with you. You were—*are*—like a sister to me. I'm sorry I betrayed you. I'm sorry I got pregnant. I'm sorry I married him after that. I'm sorry I overreacted at the engagement party. I'm sorry I ruined the wedding. And I'm really sorry I said you and Troy should have sex on the balcony! I'm so damn tired. And oh my god, I just threw up all over you."

"It's okay. I'm glad you did," June smiled through her tears. "I can't imagine how you must have felt, seeing us on the terrace. It must have hurt, and I need you to know that regardless of our past, that was not my intention."

"I know that. And I'm tired of hurting each other," Amy said, her voice thick. "I want us to be better."

"Me too."

"Let's wipe the slate clean as best we can. It won't be overnight, and there will always be"—Amy stopped and searched for the right word—"*things*." Her forehead puckered in thought. "But we can do it."

"We can," June agreed. "That's what friendship is. What sisterhood is."

There was a long pause as they both absorbed the other's words. Their agreement. The carnage of their feud had somehow cleared a path forward. And that path forward was focused on one thing: fixing the mess they'd created. But first, they both agreed they needed to get their children properly speaking to them again.

CHAPTER TWENTY-ONE

Troy hadn't been this nervous since he'd gone to his first job interview after college at Realty Executives.

On that memorable day, he had recently secured his real estate license, a new suit from Men's Wearhouse, and a haircut from Supercuts. He sauntered into the building feeling confident and energized—his new Caesar bangs making him feel handsome; if George Clooney could pull them off, so could he—until . . .

Until he realized that Brett, the person interviewing him, was a stunning *female* brunette—like *Sports Illustrated* Swimsuit Issue hot—not the old man he'd pictured when he'd talked to Brett's assistant. Since when was Brett a woman's name?

Throughout the interview, he could barely string two words together as sweat trickled down his back. Needless to say, he did not get the job.

He hoped today would go better. He *needed* today to go better. The night of the engagement party had weighed on him like a barbell against his chest. Not only had he not gotten the redo with June he'd been hoping for, but he'd hurt Amy in the process. And had a giant hand in ending his son's engagement.

He had barely slept, barely eaten since, and was desperate to fix at least one of his mistakes.

He opened the door to the bookstore, and the bells chimed. Chloe looked up at the sound. She appraised him coolly. "What are you doing here?" she asked.

"I'm here to see June?" he squeaked out, then cleared his throat before adding with more confidence, "She's expecting me."

Troy had texted her earlier, begging her to see him. To his surprise, she had written back quickly and told him to meet him at the store.

Chloe started to say something but stopped. She tilted her head toward the back. "She's in her office. And Troy?"

"Yes?"

"Try not to screw up everything this time," Chloe said, her lips tilting up slightly.

"I'll try my best." Troy headed to the back of the store, taking in the endless bookshelves along the way, remembering how June would never leave the house without a novel sticking out of her tote bag. Once Troy hadn't been able to find her at a party and finally located her in the backyard, behind a Ping-Pong table, curled up with a worn Danielle Steel paperback that Troy was sure she'd read before. A guilty smile had curled the edge of her mouth when she saw him, and Troy remembered comparing June to the other twenty-somethings there that night. Hell, comparing her to every other young person he knew. Inside the filthy house—the linoleum floors sticky from alcohol, the bathroom devoid of toilet paper—college kids were playing beer pong with dirty plastic balls, their breath thick with alcohol, their words slurred. And to be honest, that was what Troy had been doing before he realized June had disappeared. He loved that she had no shame in pulling a book from her bag and wedging herself between a raucous drinking game and a palm tree. And now, as he took in the life she'd created for herself, surrounded by the books she'd cherished for so long, he felt a sense of pride in the fact that she'd never deviated from who she was.

Troy knocked on the open door, and June looked up from a dog-eared copy of *The Alchemist*. Troy imagined it bumping around in the huge red tote sitting beside her desk.

June removed her glasses and offered him *that* smile.

It melted him the same way it had all those years ago. He flashed back to summers he'd spent with June in Mission Beach. That smile had appeared when he rubbed chocolate off her chin where it had dripped off her ice cream cone. When they Rollerbladed down the winding sidewalk along the ocean and she raced past him, looking over her shoulder and grinning. He was amazed by how, after all this time, those tiny snapshots from his memory come back with such vivid clarity. He could smell the salty air; he could see the fringe on her denim jean shorts and the hot-pink wheels on her Rollerblades.

"Hi," she said evenly. "Want to sit down?" She motioned to the plush teal chair opposite her.

"Hi," he echoed, taking her in. Her blue eyes narrowed. For the hundredth time, he wondered how she was feeling about their almost-kiss. Did she wish, like him, that it hadn't been interrupted?

She pointed to the stainless-steel coffeepot on the corner of her desk. "Want a cup?" She paused as she stared at the carafe. She looked back up to him, chewing her lower lip. "Although in full disclosure, I have no sugar. Or milk. Or oat milk? Or maybe macadamia? I hear that's a thing." She chuckled at this last part, and Troy relaxed a little.

Maybe this was going to be okay.

"What? You think I'm too good for cow milk? What am I, a psychopath?" he joked.

"Well, I know you run with a *younger* crowd," she said lightly, putting the word younger in air quotes. But Troy heard the question in her voice.

Troy leaned forward. "It's true. I've had my fair share of those newer milks—and for the record, rice milk? No, just no." He shook his head. "But you know what trying so many alternate milks has made me realize?"

June shrugged.

"That I really miss a glass of good ol' two percent." He pointed to the Mr. Coffee. "But I'm good for now, thank you." The truth was, he didn't trust his shaking hands to hold the mug. Seeing June again had unsettled him in the very best way. He hoped that his instinct to come here, to apologize, had been the right one.

She stared at him for a long moment. "Fair enough," she said, and poured the dark liquid into her own cup and took a sip.

Troy stared at her again. She was wearing a yellow sweater and jeans. She was more beautiful today than she'd been in college. The fine lines that had moved in around her eyes and mouth made Troy wish that he'd been there for the appearance of each one. That it had been his bad jokes that had made her eyes crinkle with laughter over the years. That their life had made her grin so much that her skin would eventually stretch. But he didn't articulate this. "Thanks for agreeing to see me," he said instead.

"The engagement party was obviously a complete disaster, so I was curious to find out what you have to say." She stared at him, the look on her face hard to read.

He remembered back to when they would fight. It wasn't often, but when it happened—and it was usually over some stupid thing he'd done—she would hold her face in such a way that he didn't know what she was thinking. Like now.

"I'll get straight to the point. I'm sorry for making that night about me. For cornering you on the balcony. For trying to kiss you. It was brazen and selfish and arrogant."

"Not too out of character for you, from what I remember," she said, but she was smiling. Or was that a smirk? Either way, she didn't seem to be angry.

"Touché," he conceded. "The thing is—"

"You don't need to be sorry," June interrupted. "I'd had a lot to drink. I should have stopped you well before it got that far." She gave Troy a long look.

Troy's chest clutched. "But you didn't. Stop me."

"I didn't. I was caught up in the moment. I think I was in shock that you've thought about me so much over the years."

"Haven't you thought about me?"

"I've tried not to," June said, a sad lilt in her voice. "It made things easier."

"Had we not been interrupted, would you have—"

"Kissed you back?" June pondered. "Maybe."

Troy brightened.

"But that would have not been a good idea," she added quickly.

Troy deflated.

"Oh, yes, totally. I agree," he heard himself say. But he didn't agree at all. He'd thought about that almost-kiss non-stop. In the middle of negotiation over an $8.5 million fixer in

San Marino the other day, he'd lost his train of thought imagining it—and he'd countered with a number higher than his buyer had authorized. He'd been sure he was going to lose the deal, but luckily for him, when he offered to throw in a large portion of his commission to cover it, his clients had agreed. That had been an expensive mistake, but it was worth it.

He had imagined a thousand times what would have happened if Amy hadn't walked in.

Amy, whom he hadn't spoken with since she'd hung up on him the night of the engagement party. When he'd tried to justify his actions. He could have figured out that sending Zach to Positano would have a direct impact on her, yet he hadn't thought of her once when he suggested it. One of his many fatal flaws—selfishness. He felt terrible about that, about so many things when it came to Amy. He had tried hard to make up for being such a mediocre husband by being the best ex-husband around. Telling her about off-market real estate deals, suggesting her assistant buy things for her because he knew she'd like them. Sending thoughtful gifts for her birthday. Those things were easy for Troy. What was harder was being there for other people in a real way—an emotional way.

"I want you to know, I'm going to work on my relationships—I want to be better. For Amy and Zach. But also for *you*." He let the word sit out there for a moment. There was so much more he wanted to say on that, but he knew he needed to tread lightly. So he quickly added, "Since now we'll be in-laws."

June bit her lip. "I don't know if we will become in-laws. Olivia is really upset. She has barely spoken to me about the future of her and Zach—or anything." June's gaze flitted around the room. "For now, the wedding is still off."

Troy speculated on whether Olivia was as mad at her as Zach was at him. Whether Olivia had lumped June into what Troy had done. The almost-kiss was his fault, not June's—he hoped Olivia understood that.

June continued. "In the rare windows where Olivia has given me an opening, I've tried to reason with her, but . . ." She brought her coffee cup to her lips. It hovered there for a moment. She set it back down without drinking. "She refuses to see Zach's side. And god, Troy, she reminds me so much of myself at her age. The way I cut you out. Refused to let you explain. The other night, when you wanted to talk about it, I refused."

"What I did was a lot worse than what Zach did, June. You had every right."

"I did," she agreed, and her statement hit him in the gut. Would he ever be able to forgive himself for what had happened?

"But maybe that wasn't the right way to handle it," she continued. "The problem was, I thought I knew everything. I was so damn black and white about it. I refused to see any gray. And now I look back and think, did I know anything? Bad choices are always so much more complicated than they seem, aren't they?"

"I think you knew enough," Troy said. "I got your best friend pregnant. Full stop."

June's eyes flashed at the memory. "You did. And that was awful. And I hated you both. But the real reason I wouldn't see you again after I gave the ring back, wouldn't talk to you, was because I was afraid I'd want you back. That I would be weak."

Troy absorbed that. To hear June hadn't completely given up on him back then sent a jolt through him. "It wouldn't have been weak," he said.

"It would have," June insisted. "And also selfish. But there's a part of me that's happy you tried to do the right thing with Amy and Zach. I couldn't see it then, but I do now. I'm glad you saw it through, even if it didn't work out."

"I wanted to be a good husband to her. A good dad to Zach. I hated that I lost you in the process."

Troy followed June's gaze to a framed photo of her, William, and the girls at Olivia's fifth grade graduation. They were all clearly laughing at something off camera. June's head was bent back as she laughed, and William's mouth was open as if in midsentence. No one was looking at the photographer, yet it was perfect. Troy felt a stab of jealousy that June had built a life without him.

June looked at Troy. "I truly believe some of our worst choices lead us to things we didn't know we needed. That the scar tissue from our mistakes is what makes us interesting."

"I guess I'm super interesting, then?" Troy quipped, and was rewarded by June's deep laugh.

"You may be the most interesting man in the world. Maybe more than the Dos Equis guy."

"Well, I wouldn't go that far," Troy chuckled, before turning serious once more. "I need you to know that I want to be better." Troy took a deep breath. "I was lying earlier. I don't think the almost-kiss was a mistake. In fact, I think it's the best decision I've made in a long time. And I want to show you who I can be. If you'll let me."

June took him in, her eyes scanning his. Troy felt his heart pounding. Finally, she spoke. "How about we start with all those letters you wrote over the years? I think it's time I read them. See what the fuss is all about."

* * *

June had been surprised Troy had the letters with him. She'd been wondering why he'd brought a backpack—a faded red JanSport that had seen better days. Troy pulled a beat-up box out of the bag, lifted it onto her desk, and said, "I hope this clears everything up," before smiling nervously and leaving her alone with the past twenty-six years of his innermost thoughts.

She'd locked herself in the office and asked Chloe not to disturb her. Then she'd cautiously opened the letter on top. It was in Troy's sprawling handwriting and dated June 2001.

June,

You would have loved the Victorian I showed today. It had one of those stepped gable roofs that you love so much. And the view! I could almost imagine us sitting there, taking in the sunset, with a bottle of cabernet. Do you still drink red wine?

June smiled. She still drank red wine, and white too. All the colors, in fact. And she lived in a Victorian house.

Her heart raced as she selected another letter. This one was from December 2005.

Dear June,

It's Christmas Eve. I didn't get Zach for Christmas this year, so I'm alone. My heart hurts as I think of him opening presents without me tomorrow. I stopped by earlier and gave him his gifts, a baseball glove (signed by Eric Gagne) and a bat, but it wasn't the same as Christmas morning. Do you have kids? Are you married? Are you happy? I hope so . . .

June stopped reading. Olivia would have been five, Chloe, almost three. That Christmas they'd found a Barbie jeep under the tree from Santa Claus. They'd driven around the living room and kitchen for hours, Olivia behind the wheel yelling *Go, go go*, mimicking what she'd seen June do to other drivers; Chloe giggling in the passenger seat.

She went back to the letter.

Or are you alone too? I've tried to date. I did Match.com, of all things. It was a disaster. None of them are you, June. I have a confession. I looked for you online and couldn't find anything. Where are you? It's like you disappeared. But maybe that's what you wanted, to vanish.

June dug through the box and grabbed another letter. April 1998.

Dear June,

We're getting divorced. Are you surprised to hear that? Surprised I'm telling you? It was mutual. You know how people say that, but it's not always true? With us, it is. We looked at each other as we were putting Zach down for the night and we just knew. We didn't need words. Because there had already been so many words. There was nothing left to say. We were both done. It hadn't been right between us for a long time. Maybe it never was. I work too much. She resents me for that. When I am home, I'm not a very good husband. But the bigger thing, the thing I would never tell her because it would break her heart, is that she isn't you. She was never going to be you. And as much as

I tried to tell myself you can love more than one woman and you can be meant to be with more than one person, we never fit together the way you should. The way you need to be able to to sustain a life together.

Don't get me wrong, I loved her, still love her. Will always love her. Because she's a good person. And she's the mother of my son. And she's a damn good mom too. But we can't do it anymore. It's like we're both broken. She turned on the sound machine next to his big-boy bed, and as the lullaby started playing, I grabbed her hand. We stood there for a long time watching him. I think it's going to be good for me to be alone for a while. I'm going to try to be a better dad, a better man.

June wiped a tear, imagining that scene in Zach's bedroom. June read for hours. Letter after letter told the story of Troy's life. His joys. His sadnesses. His failures. His regrets. She almost felt like she'd been there with him. June read until her eyes blurred with tears. She read until she understood. She read until her heart filled with forgiveness.

CHAPTER TWENTY-TWO

Amy opened the oven and basted the turkey. She pulled back the foil. The skin was a golden brown like Ina Garten said it should be. Amy was *not* a cook, but she'd religiously watched Ina's YouTube videos to learn how to pull off today's feast. She'd considered asking Alyssa to help her prep, but knew it would mean a lot more to Zach if she'd done the cooking herself.

If he showed up.

Her iPad dinged again. It hadn't stopped since five this morning. She had less than eight weeks until the Tournament of Roses Parade, and she was behind schedule. And Amy was never behind schedule. She barely recognized herself anymore. Since *the brunch*, Amy had been distracted. Her job had come second, sometimes *third*, to her family drama; she'd been emotional—she'd cried more times since the engagement party than she had in her entire life; but worst of all? She'd been acting like a mean girl. That had been the hardest quality for Amy to swallow; her bullish and manipulative behavior during the wedding planning was an embarrassment. She was a lot of things, but she wasn't mean. At least she hadn't thought so before June came back into her life.

And then there was the engagement party.

She'd barely slept since that night. She'd looked in the mirror every morning and nearly shrieked at her reflection—she looked old and so, so tired. She'd vacillated between being irritated as hell with Troy and also being somewhat grateful.

Why did he make this mess?

I'm so happy he made this mess. Zach met Olivia because of it.

But it means my son won't speak to me.

Amy ached over Zach's inability to convince Olivia to give him another chance. Last Amy had heard, Olivia had gathered her things from Zach's house while he was at work. He'd sent Amy a one-line text: *It's official. Olivia moved out.* When Amy responded that she was so sorry and what could she do, Zach wrote, *Invent a time machine so I can travel back and fix all of this.* Almost the same thing June had said to Troy after he and Amy cheated on her. Amy realized Zach hadn't told her because he wanted her sympathy; he'd told her because she was to blame. He'd wanted her to sit with that.

Amy had sobbed hard after that text and reached out to Olivia for what felt like the hundredth time, pleading with her to separate Troy's mistake from her son's. But her text went unanswered, like all the others.

Amy accepted her part in everything. If she hadn't gone ballistic, the engagement would still be on. The secret would still be unexposed. But, Amy thought, though she would never have admitted it to her son, maybe it had needed to be unearthed. Holding back information was not the way to start a life together.

Amy hadn't worked this hard to make something happen since she'd had to convince a reporter to hand over the cell phone video of two Rose Princesses wrestling on the ground after it was discovered one had become top friends on Snap with the other one's boyfriend.

She and Zach and Troy had spent Thanksgiving together every year. Even when the divorce was still raw, when she and Troy were the closest to hating each other they'd ever been, they had still decided it was what would be best for Zach. And maybe them too. Over the years, others would sometimes join. Once a woman Troy had dated for six months had accompanied him. Another time Zach had brought Logan and a college buddy home. The door was always open to any guests the three of them wanted to invite, but at the very least, Amy, Zach, and Troy would always be there, no matter what. That was their pact. And Amy hoped reminding them of that would get them to agree. Shortly after the engagement party, she had started a group text and sent her message.

I know things are bad between the three of us right now, but we celebrate Thanksgiving together every year—no matter what. It's our pact.

Troy immediately responded *yes!* with a heart emoji and then side-texted Amy that they needed to talk when she was ready. *Really talk*, he wrote. *I have a lot to apologize for.*

Zach had responded, *I'm supposed to eat stuffing like nothing happened? Like both of my parents didn't ruin my engagement? It wasn't enough for the two of you to destroy June's? You had to do the same thing to her daughter?*

To which Amy didn't have a good reply. She'd said she was sorry and sent a sad-face emoji, but she knew it was far from enough. Maybe nothing would ever be enough.

But Amy did elect *not* to make stuffing.

She stirred the mashed potatoes and tasted them, adding more salt and pepper and cream as Ina suggested. She added the marshmallows and cinnamon to the top of the mashed yams and slid the dish into the oven. She started cutting the French bread.

Zach was right. She and Troy had fucked up again. She'd reread the text thread for the billionth time, searching for any hidden meanings in Zach's replies. For any indication that underneath his digs, he still loved her and was planning to forgive her. The three of them had survived so many hard things—a divorce topping the list—but they couldn't get through this? She vowed to keep trying. To get her family together again under the same roof so she and Troy could show Zach how much they loved him. And prove to him that they were sorry.

Amy didn't give up. She continued to text the group thread to remind them (herself included) that they were a family—that they should be together. She sent pictures from past Thanksgivings, including her favorite, an eight-year-old Zach holding a giant drumstick in front of his mouth, poised to take a bite. Troy loved all of her comments and chimed in with his own text love language: gifs. He sent hugging pandas and kissing dogs. Dancing babies and, for reasons she still didn't understand, characters from *The Office* cheering.

But no matter the sweet words, pictures, or gifs, Zach did not respond. Amy kept hope alive by moving forward with the Thanksgiving prep anyway—ordering the antibiotic-free turkey from Whole Foods and shopping for all of the ingredients on Ina's suggested Thanksgiving feast list. Right down to the cranberries. She hadn't corrected the cashier when, after seeing Amy's overflowing cart, he had remarked that Amy must be having a big family gathering. Amy suppressed her tears as she loaded the groceries into her trunk. Silently hoping, *If you build it, they will come.*

She'd started cooking two days ago, trying to instill love into each dish the way Ina did. Hoping that through the food,

Zach would taste how much she wanted their relationship to be repaired. But she knew that was desperate thinking. She was painfully aware that it was likely going to be only her and Troy staring across the table at each other, passing the potatoes, their own awkwardness hanging in the air.

She prayed every night that Zach would show up.

She poured herself a second glass of wine and checked the clock. It was three thirty. She'd told Troy and Zach four o'clock. She looked at the corner of her living room where they placed the Christmas tree that they would get the day after Thanksgiving each year. She wondered if the area would remain empty.

At four fifteen, she poured herself another glass of cabernet. And looked at her dressed dining room table. Suddenly hating the stupid runner she'd bought. The dumb candelabras. The idiotic name cards she'd written. The minutes ticked by on her watch: 4:17, 4:18.

At 4:19, Troy texted he was on his way. He was sorry he was late. Something about a client. Amy flung her phone across the room. He wasn't the guest she wanted!

At 4:22, Alexa announced someone was at the door. Amy didn't bother to check her ring cam. She knew it was Troy.

She flung the door open.

It wasn't Troy. It was Zach. He looked like a shell of himself—his face gaunt, his pants loose around the waist. He looked awful. Amy stifled a gasp and resisted the urge to throw her arms around his neck and squeeze him—she wanted so desperately to make him all better.

"Hi," Zach finally said.

"Hi," she repeated. "I'm so happy you're here. I thought—"

"That I wasn't coming. I know. And I wasn't coming. Believe me."

"What changed?"

"Logan."

Amy nodded. He didn't need to explain. She'd known Logan since he was fourteen years old. He had always been Zach's voice of reason. Zach walked into the kitchen, and his eyes widened. The Thanksgiving spread was arranged across Amy's island.

"Did you make all this?"

Amy smiled. "I did."

"I'm impressed. Still annoyed with you, but impressed."

"Okay, I'll take that."

"Where's Dad?"

"Right here," Troy said. "Let myself in." He'd arrived shortly after Zach, holding an expensive bottle of Italian wine in one hand and nervously tugging at the collar of his gray cashmere sweater with the other. "Son," he said, and extended his hand. It hung in the air for so long that Amy was sure Zach wasn't going to shake it. But he finally did.

"Shall we eat?" Amy said, her voice three octaves too high.

They made their plates and headed to the dining room. Amy opened a bottle of 2016 Opus One cab and poured them each a glass.

"This is excellent, Aim. Didn't know you could cook!" Troy said.

"Neither did I," Amy said.

As they ate, they made stilted small talk about real estate. By the time Amy served the pumpkin pie, she'd lost hope that they'd talk about what had happened. She'd opened a second bottle of wine, hoping that would help break the tension, which was so thick she could have cut it with her electric carving knife.

"I don't think I'll ever get over her," Zach said.

Amy almost dropped her fork. Zach was opening up to them! She glanced at Troy, who gave her a look as if to say, *Let him talk.*

"I can't sleep." He motioned to his barely touched plate. "I have no appetite. I've texted, called, Snapped, everything. I went over to June's, where she lives now."

Amy's heart burned. She could feel her son's pain, as if it was radiating off his body. "What happened?"

"June opened the door and stepped out on the porch, closing it behind her, like she didn't want Olivia to know I was there. She asked me why I lied. Why Dad lied."

A heavy frown settled on Troy's mouth.

"I'm sorry, son."

"So you've said," Zach said curtly.

"What did you tell June?" Amy asked.

"I told her I was done making excuses. That I should have told Olivia the truth. That I had been a coward. That this wedding-planning experience had taught me a lot. To start speaking up when it mattered. That was why I was there at June's—to speak up. To tell Olivia she was the best thing that ever happened to me. That I would spend the rest of my life making it up to her if she'd let me. And June got teary eyed and said she'd go tell Olivia I was there."

Amy leaned forward, feeling like she was watching a sad movie she'd seen before. Knowing how it would end, but hoping the outcome would be different anyway. She'd already heard the story from June, but she wasn't going to let Zach know that.

"I was so excited. I texted Logan. Told him I thought she was going to see me. That I'd made it past her mom, so that had to mean something. But a few minutes later, June came back and shook her head. And told me I'd better go."

"I'm so sorry," Amy said.

"I cried all the way home. Cried!"

Amy and June had sat on the phone that night commiserating about their kids being unable to work things out with each other or with them. They were heartbroken. Going over things again and again. How they could have acted differently. But ultimately having to accept, yet again, that the past could not be changed.

"I'm such a mess," Zach continued. "Look at these texts I've sent V." He handed his phone to Amy.

Amy scanned them. Some were short, but others were long—like the novel-length texts Eileen sometimes sent.

I'm so sorry.

I love you.

Please give me a chance to explain.

I'll do anything to make this up to you. To get your trust back.

At the end of the chain was *Happy Thanksgiving.*

Olivia had never replied.

"Zach, she will come around. Give her time." Amy said, not sure she believed it.

"I'll wait forever," he said, and Amy's heart crumpled.

"This is my fault. I'm so sorry to both of you," Troy said.

"Why did you do it?" Zach asked.

Troy looked at Amy. She nodded. She knew he was checking with her. Could he bare his heart about June?

"I love your mom, I do. But I never stopped loving June."

Zach looked at his mom. She felt a surge of hope. She knew he was feeling protective, despite how angry he was at her.

"It's okay. I always knew in my heart that your dad never got over June. But I wouldn't talk to him about it. I wouldn't let him talk to me about it. I refused to let him go. But I knew his heart was never truly mine. I wouldn't acknowledge it, and that's a huge part of why we got divorced. Her shadow followed us everywhere. So I lost it when I saw the almost-kiss. Because I think there was also a part of me who hoped I was wrong. That his flame for her had burned out."

Zach took the last drink of his wine, his voice slurring slightly. "You guys have shit timing, you know that?"

A thin smile formed on Amy's lips.

"I need to stop being mad at you guys. But I don't know how."

"Take all the time you need," Troy said.

"I could be ancient like you guys before it happens."

"Fair enough," Amy said, taking it as a small win.

*   *   *

After she got Zach settled in the guest room, she and Troy sat in the backyard with a bottle of Blanton's. "We need to fix this," Amy said, sipping her bourbon.

"We really fucked up," Troy said.

"We need to get everyone together. You, me, June, and William, and put this broken engagement back together." Amy ran inside and grabbed her iPad. "No time like the present." She tapped it several times. "Check your email. I sent a meeting invite."

"An Outlook invite? You must mean business!" Troy teased, but a look of relief flashed over his face as he accepted the invitation.

"It's time I used my talents for good," Amy said, and her eyes glittered with hope as her iPad pinged with a response that June would be in attendance. A second ping confirmed William's RSVP.

"Let's do this," Troy said, and clinked his glass to hers. "What have we got to lose?"

CHAPTER TWENTY-THREE

We Ducked Up and Need to Fix It
Meeting Minutes
December 1st

Date and time: December 1, 7:00 P.M.
Attendees: June Abbott, William Abbott, Amy Carter,
Troy Carter
Location: Amy Carter's living room
Project: Fix Olivia and Zach's broken engagement

Transcript:

Amy: Thank you all for coming on such short notice. Please have some of this charcuterie board. You must try the Crispy Jalapeños from Trader Joe's!
June: I vote that we call the "We Ducked Up and Need to Fix It" meeting to order. Do I have a second?
Troy: I'll second.

William: Can someone fill me in on why it's *ducked up* and
not—

Troy: *Fucked up?*

William: Yes.

Amy: Autocorrect. When I tried to name our group thread,
the phone kept changing the *f* to a *d*. Just seemed easier.

Troy: And funnier.

June: It quacks me up every time!

Amy: Hang on, I'm getting a text. It's about work.

Troy: That's a shock!

Amy: Shit. It's a huge vendor canceling their float! I have to
figure out how to replace it. Can we pause the meeting?

Troy, June, and William: No!

Troy: This gives me an idea. I think I know how we can
get Zach and Olivia to speak again! Or at least the place
where we can do it.

Amy: Sorry, but I need to call Alyssa and fix this first.

Troy: Hang on. This could solve your problem too. Why
don't we use the Rose Parade to reunite Zach and Olivia?

William: I'm lost.

June: Me too.

Troy: We'll have Steven Tyler enter a float.

Amy: Steven Tyler is going to get our kids back together?

William: From Aerosmith?

Troy: No, from the Midwest!

Amy: Your old college buddy?

Troy: Yes. He can replace the company that dropped out.
I talked to him this morning. He was telling me that his
amusement park is struggling and he was asking me if
I knew anyone who might want to buy it. But he also
said he would hate to sell. If only he had some new way

to get people to notice it. He would kill for publicity he could get from the parade. If we could get him to enter a float—

Amy: Then we could use his float as the lure—

Troy: To get Zach and Olivia there—

June: To pull off some kind of romantic surprise—

Amy: To get them back together!

William: I hate to be the dark cloud raining on the parade, so to speak—

June: Look at you making a pun! I think this crazy little group is growing on you! Don't think I don't see you rolling your eyes!

William: *Anyway.* Once we get them to the parade, then what? How would we ever pull this off? Everyone has already tried calling Olivia to convince her to talk to Zach, and she refuses. Even me!

June: You?

William: Yes! The poor kid came to the hospital and begged me. Said he would do anything to get my daughter back. So I left Olivia a message asking her to call me. That I'd spoken to Zach and he had some very strong arguments for why she should hear him out. But she never called me back.

Amy: This is my department. Pulling off the impossible. If I could get the Pasadena police to drop charges when the Rose Princess from 2010 was picked up for public intoxication, then we can do this!

Troy: Amy, could Steven build a float on such short notice?

Amy: Most floats are constructed in late summer, but I could pull a few strings and get the volunteers we need to build it and decorate it during deco week, the days following Christmas and leading up to the event. People fly in from all over the world to help dress the floats, and there is always a surplus. We can use the base of the float the other company is abandoning and transform it into a float to represent Steven's amusement park. We could make a roller coaster from chrysanthemums, and the tracks could be constructed from stems and branches.

June: Fiona can help with flowers if we need them!

Amy: Thank you!

Troy: We can use Steven as the reason we need Zach at the parade. I'll tell Zach that Steven might be looking to buy a house out here. And the only window of time he has to talk is at the Rose Parade. It's an unusual request, but we get those all the time in real estate.

William: Olivia was obsessed with the parade when she was a little girl.

June: Remember how she used to set up a beach chair in the living room and act like she was watching it in person?

Amy: That's adorable!

June: I should have taken her. I never did. She's going to be in therapy for so many things because of me—

Amy: Oh, girl, we're all in the same boat! But now can be your chance to experience it with her. This is all of our chance to shorten the list of things they'll discuss with their future psychologists.

June: Olivia is just depressed enough that she might agree to go with me. Thanksgiving actually wasn't terrible. She smiled at me two different times!

Amy: Zach and I are still on shaky ground too—he didn't laugh when I surprised him with new sweatpants to replace the ones I stole.

June: Really? That was such a funny story. That you were wearing his.

Troy: You were what?

Amy: Never mind.

June: I do worry that even if I can get her to want to go with *me*, she'll say no because the parade will remind her too much of Zach.

Amy. Because of me.

June: Yes, but it's not your fault—it's where you work. I think it's worth a shot. We can tell Olivia that Zach's out of town.

Troy: What about Snap Maps?

June? Whatmaps?

Amy: Snapchat has a feature that shows everyone where you are at all times.

June: That sounds horrifying!

Troy: If Olivia looks at Zach's Snap Map, she'll realize he's at the parade.

June: She won't. She finally blocked him on all social media. Chloe told me that.

William: I checked my calendar, and I have to work on the first. But I will be there in spirit. Anything I can do leading up to the event, let me know.

June: Okay. I might need your help with Olivia.

William: Whatever you need. So let's say both kids agree to come. Then what?

Amy: June, this is your department. How do the characters get back together at the end of a romance novel?

June: I think I've got it. It's going to sound a little out there. But it just might work . . .

CHAPTER TWENTY-FOUR

January 1

When the We Ducked Up and Need to Fix It group hatched its plan to fix Olivia and Zach's broken engagement at the Rose Parade, June hadn't thought through the whole *spend New Year's Eve sleeping on a sidewalk in Pasadena* part.

As predicted, when June first broached the idea of going to the parade together, Olivia had refused. "Of all the years to suggest this, Mom! Amy works there. Zach will probably be there. There is no way I'm going anywhere near that place or his mother!"

After June said she'd heard Zach was going to be out of town, Olivia still wouldn't change her mind. That's when June and Troy, who had been texting outside the We Ducked Up group *a lot*, came up with the idea to call in reinforcements: Chloe! Chloe agreed right away, although not before she pointed out how lame the name of their operation was. She was willing to sign on because, in her words, Olivia was a disaster. She'd made some of the most depressing TikToks Chloe had ever seen. "They are so sad, Mom." June couldn't bear to see them.

After Chloe signed on, June optimistically texted Troy *Clear eyes, full hearts, can't lose*, and to her delight he responded instantly that he loved *Friday Night Lights*. Most nights, June texted or called Troy while she lay in bed, the mound of throw pillows piled high next to her, Meowsers curled at her feet. She was thankful Troy didn't want to FaceTime—the scene of a single spinster cat lady burrowed under quilts would not be sexy. They bantered about so many things, like their shared belief that skinny jeans had been invented by the devil. They discussed their favorite books. It turned out Troy liked to read, something he'd never done when they were together. He said it started when Zach got him a series of books for his birthday one year. The other night she and Troy had talked for almost an hour about a controversial novel that had been recently published.

But it took a while before June finally worked up the courage to talk to Troy about the letters.

"I read them," she said.

There was a long pause. Finally, Troy responded, "All of them?"

"Every single one. I was up until almost midnight." June recalled the final letter. The one with the note attached, scrawled in Troy's handwriting: *Read this one last*. He'd written it after the brunch, pouring out how it had felt. How his juxtaposed feelings of guilt from manipulating Zach and the joy of seeing June again made him feel off-kilter. "Thank you for sharing them with me."

"They belong to you," he said, so quietly she almost didn't hear him.

"I know, but it still felt like I was reading your diary."

"You kind of were," he said. "When I wrote them, I imagined you reading them. That made it easier to be honest with myself."

June didn't know how to label what they were doing. Was it friendship? Was it flirting? Was it more? All she knew was it felt nice. So she filed it under *Nice*.

Now, in the light of the early New Year's morning, the sun slowly rising behind the mountains, June glanced at Olivia, who was still sleeping. She watched her oldest daughter, who looked so peaceful, and wished for her that their plan worked—that by the end of today, she and Zach would be back together. Or, at the very least, speaking again. June glanced at her mother and Chloe, who were sharing an air mattress, both also still sleeping.

June had been surprised when Eileen showed up last night. Apparently, Chloe had invited her. June could feel her mouth involuntarily puckering as she realized her mother, a patchwork overnight bag slung across her body, was going to join in their girls' night. Eileen was dressed in a wool coat, scarf and hat, thick leggings, and tall UGG boots. June tugged at her own thin, worn SDSU sweatshirt and jeans that the cold air had been slicing through. "Oh, wow!" June said, trying to sound excited. But her gut tightened in anticipation of the tension they were sure to have, her mind racing with quick retorts to the recurring slights that were often thrown her way.

But Eileen's arrival had jarred Olivia out of the funk she was in. Olivia jumped up and engulfed her in a hug. "Grandma! I had no idea you'd be here—this makes my night!"

Chloe grinned. "We said this was a GNO. And she's a girl, obvi."

"BYOC, right?" Eileen said, holding up a striped beach chair. "I also prepared a batch of my legendary spiked hot chocolate!" She pulled a large thermos from her bag. "The pickleball ladies can't get enough of this stuff."

Chloe clapped. "Grandma for the win!"

Eileen turned up her nose as she glanced around the square of sidewalk June and the girls had claimed as their own. "It looks like you didn't bring much, so I'm happy to contribute. I think my air mattress will fit over there," she said as she eyed June's chair and obvious lack of a sleeping bag.

Jab number one, June thought.

When June, Olivia, and Chloe had arrived earlier, June had laughed at the people around them. She'd shaken her head and said, "Overprepared much? What, are they moving in? Battery-operated space heaters? Tents? Hand warmers? Why all the fuss? This is Southern California!" June thought she'd prepared properly. She'd brought a heavy flannel and had a cooler full of snacks and water. She was sure that would be enough.

Eileen sandwiched her chair between Olivia and June and sat down, covering herself with a thick blanket. She raised an eyebrow at June, who was shivering, but trying desperately to hide it, and expanded it to cover June's legs too. She poured the hot chocolate into four reusable cups. June shook her head when Eileen offered her one. "Save it for you and the girls. "

"Oh, for the love, June! It's freezing out here and it's only going to get worse, so you might as well warm up your insides too. And it's not like we're stranded on a desert island. We can Drizly more booze if it comes to it; surely you realize that," Eileen said, her voice dripping with condescension.

June sighed. She didn't know what Drizly was, but it was clearly some type of delivery service. June had one hundred percent not realized she could do that.

Jab number two for Eileen!

As June sipped the silky, delicious hot chocolate that instantly provided the warmth she desperately needed but would never admit, she listened as Eileen engaged the girls in conversation. June was surprised at how delicately her mom spoke to Olivia about her breakup with Zach. And she was more shocked at how quickly Olivia opened up to her grandmother, sharing how lonely she had been. How the loss of Zach was affecting her ability to concentrate in class, how she worried she might have blown one of her final exams. She admitted she was grateful to be on winter break so she could reset and come back strong—she could no longer let this dictate her life. Then she said the most surprising thing of all: that maybe everyone had been right. She'd agreed to marry him too soon, and because she was too pigheaded to listen, this was her bad karma.

June's heart ripped open when she heard that. *No, no, no,* she wanted to scream into the crowd of parade attendees. *He's a good man who made a dumb mistake, that's all. You didn't do anything wrong—this is not bad karma.* But if she'd learned one thing through all of this, it was that Olivia wasn't going to listen to June's advice, not after how royally she had screwed up. She only hoped that Operation We Ducked Up and Need to Fix It could make things right.

June stayed silent and counted the hours until the parade started at eight o'clock the next morning. As her brain began to relax, June let herself wonder why she couldn't let go of the past with her mom. Why she, unlike Olivia, couldn't bear to be vulnerable around her. As she watched Eileen listen and offer banal advice ("It will get easier!" "One step at a time!"), June's chest began to ache, thinking of how much she'd wished she could snap her fingers and erase her complicated past with her mother. That she could finally trust Eileen's intentions.

As the night grew darker, the temperature dipped with each hour. The hot chocolate and most of the food were long gone. The wait for that Drizly thing was over three hours. Same with DoorDash and Instacart and pretty much any delivery service Eileen or the girls tried on their phones. And all of the local restaurants had closed. But Eileen expertly bartered with a sidewalk neighbor. Somehow she got a fifth of peppermint schnapps in exchange for a bag of chocolate chip cookies and half a sandwich she'd packed in her patchwork bag.

When eleven o'clock struck and June finally admitted that she could no longer feel her toes, Eileen leaned over, her eyes glassy from the booze. "I have an idea. Come with me."

They left the girls and began to saunter down Colorado Boulevard. To June's surprise, Eileen looped her arm through June's. June welcomed the additional body heat. "You know, I always wanted to take you here when you were young."

"Why didn't you?" June asked.

"I guess I thought we'd get there eventually. But one year became the next, and now here I am, with my daughter's adult children. And my daughter doesn't want me here." Eileen cocked her head at June.

"Mom, it's not that. I didn't think—"

Eileen squeezed her arm. "I know. You didn't think of me. Because we aren't close."

They walked for a while in silence. Finally, June stopped next to a large camper where two space heaters sat, their grates red, hot and glowing. She inched closer to them so she could feel some of the warm air they were blasting. "You're right. We aren't close." June held her frozen hands against the heat to try to thaw them out. "I feel like I've been a disappointment to you." The confession slid out easily, oiled by the alcohol she'd consumed.

Eileen's face drew tight. "It's funny. I feel the same way—about you. That I've failed so completely as a mother that you've erased me. Watching the girls grow up and hearing them tell stories about what a wonderful mother you've been has made me realize that not only do I not know my only child, but I must have done something awful for you to not need or want me in your life." Her eyes shone and her voice cracked as she finished.

June's heart rose to her throat. "When you said all those terrible things about Troy and then he cheated on me, I think part of me thought you were happy you ended up being right."

"Oh, June. Of course I wasn't happy. Also, maybe I wasn't right? That's the thing I've learned about happiness. It's different for each person. I never should have pushed my opinion on you. I see the way you handled Olivia's quick engagement, the way you let her bask in all of the excitement when you were clearly scared shitless, and I wish I'd had the strength to do that for you. I'm sorry."

June fought off tears. "Thank you for saying that, Mom." She cupped her hands and blew in them to warm her fingers. "This may sound silly, but I think I've been waiting two decades to hear you utter those words."

"I'm a stubborn old woman, but eventually I figured it out," Eileen said, and pulled June in for a hug.

"Is this why you wanted to go for a walk?" June whispered into her ear as they embraced, tears falling onto Eileen's shoulder.

Eileen pulled away. "Yes and no," she said. "I have wanted to talk to you since Amy defended you when I gave you such a hard time about those sharks. And then I thought about how insensitive I'd been when I offered Olivia the dress I married your father in—and I did it right in front of you without think-ing. Amy sort of put me in my place about that too. In fact, you have Amy to thank for much of my newfound attitude."

June absorbed this, amazed that despite everything they'd been through Amy still had her back.

"This wedding was obviously bringing up a lot of emotions for both of us. I needed to figure out the right time to talk to you about it. So when Chloe invited me, I said yes—even though I could think of almost nothing worse than spending the night on a sidewalk."

The things we do for our kids, June thought.

"I'm sorry, June, for being so hard on you for so many years. For not *seeing* you."

"Thank you for saying that. You sound so—"

"Evolved?"

June nodded.

"Full disclosure. I've been reading those books by Glennon Doyle and Brené Brown to help me with the right words."

"Could I borrow them? Olivia and I have a long road ahead."

"Being a mother is the hardest job on the planet. You try your best, but it isn't always enough. The secret is to keep trying."

"Did Glennon tell you that?" June teased.

"That one I came up with on my own," Eileen said. "So tell me, why are we really here at the parade?"

June shared We Ducked Up's plan for Olivia and Zach.

Eileen's eyes lit up. "Brilliant. If you need a lookout person or a spy, I'm in!"

"I think all the positions have been filled, Mom, but I'll let you know if something comes up," June said. "Do you think it will work?"

"Yes! That girl is still so in love with that boy. Reminds me of another girl who was just as in love—"

June smiled sheepishly. "I might be . . . again. I haven't told anyone, and it feels so weird to say it out loud, but Troy and I have been talking a lot. And it feels right."

"Now that would be interesting if you two ended up married. Talk about full circle." Eileen laughed.

"We're in the getting-to-know-you-again stage. Plus I think that would be like we were all *too* related, if you know what I mean," June exclaimed. "But he does make me happy, and that's enough."

"That's all that matters," Eileen said. She looked over June's shoulder to the left, then to the right. "But when I suggested we take this walk, I also had another plan in mind."

"Mom, I love you and I'm happy we have a clean slate, but if you're about to say we sing 'Kumbaya' or some shit like that, it's going to be a hard no."

Eileen was amused. "Not a chance in hell. Have you met me? I'm too emotionally unavailable for that. That's the term Brené used, anyway." Eileen pulled her sweatshirt collar down to reveal her signature strand of pearls underneath. "Need I say more?"

June laughed. "Nope."

"Okay, here's what I need you to do. Stand right there and open the blanket," she commanded. June pulled apart the blanket she had draped over her shoulders for warmth and grimaced as the cold air began to make its way in. Eileen leaned over and grabbed one of the nearby space heaters and placed it against June's chest, thankfully with the hot grate pointing away from June's body. She closed the blanket over it. "Move!" she hissed. "But don't run. You'll draw attention. And maybe catch on fire," she added after.

June and Eileen sped-walked the half mile back to their slab of sidewalk as June's heart raced from the theft, and maybe also from the reconciliation with her mom. It gave her hope that she and Olivia could get back to the place they'd been before. Eileen held the space heater over her head like that guy from the *Say Anything* movie and June sat back and watched in awe, wondering what it would be like to get to know her mother, *really* know her, for the first time.

While they were gone, Olivia and Chloe had charmed some young men out of a case of White Claws. June felt as if they'd won the reward challenge on an episode of *Survivor*. As the clock struck midnight, the three generations of women toasted to new beginnings.

Now June's empty stomach grumbled as she watched her neighbors prepare a breakfast of eggs, sausage, bacon, and pancakes on their portable grill. The smell of freshly brewed coffee hung in the air, and June realized she'd do almost anything to get some. A woman in a bright-orange sweatshirt depicting one of the teams that would be playing in the college football game later that day caught June's feral stare and graciously offered her a cup of coffee. June hungrily accepted, promising to send her some books in exchange.

As Chloe, Olivia, and Eileen started to wake, June's phone buzzed. She pulled up the We Ducked Up and Need to Fix It thread and read the latest text from Amy.

He's still not here. And I must put out a fire. Troy—be on the lookout!

June chewed her nail. If Zach didn't show, their whole plan was screwed. She glanced at Olivia, who was rolling up her sleeping bag, and her heart sank. This plan had to work. June stood and stretched her arms overhead. She had kinks in muscles she hadn't known existed.

He'll be there! And I'll find him as soon as he arrives! Troy replied to the thread, then added two thumbs-up emojis.

June brightened. Troy. The eternal optimist. Exactly what they all needed right now. Blind faith. She'd forgotten that he'd had that quality until they'd reconnected. When they'd dated, sometimes it had been infuriating to June how upbeat Troy could be. But looking back now, it was earnest, hopeful. And there was nothing wrong with that.

CHAPTER TWENTY-FIVE

Amy slammed the brake on the golf cart and parked in front of the trailer where the talent resided. She read the name on the door—*Debbie Gibson, Grand Marshal*—and took a deep breath. She wasn't sure how she was going to calm Debbie down, but she hoped that knowing all the words to her 1987 hit "Foolish Beat" would help.

Amy checked her phone. Still no text or call from Zach. She liked Troy's most recent text and hoped that he was right—that their son would show up and their crazy plan would work.

*   *   *

Troy looked at his watch: 6:28 a.m. Where the hell was Zach? He was almost thirty minutes late. Troy texted him again. No reply. He called him. Straight to voice mail.

Zach hadn't been the same since Olivia had called off the engagement. He'd been mopey, distracted, and lost. Zach had missed appointments with clients, lost listings, and forgotten to send off a signed counteroffer by deadline, losing the deal. But

Troy had still done his best to be a supportive father and business partner, because Troy was the reason Zach was a lovelorn sack of shit in the first place.

Troy's phone buzzed, and his heart leapt. Zach!

He read the text—but it wasn't from his son, it was from Steven Tyler. He said his Uber was pulling up. Troy raked his hand through his hair. Should he send the safe word to the We Ducked Up and Need to Fix It thread?

Quack meant that it was time to go to plan B. He willed Zach to call him. He didn't want the reason the plan imploded to fall on his shoulders. He'd already done enough damage. He'd give Zach another five minutes.

* * *

"Dad!" Zach called out. He took in his dad's stance as he jogged toward him and blew out a series of short breaths.

Troy's back was to him. His shoulders were slightly hunched. He had one hand on his hip. And Zach knew without seeing that his dad's eyebrows were pinched together.

Zach had seen this version of Troy so often since Olivia had broken off the engagement that he had to struggle to remember his dad looking any other way. His dad. The one with a smile permanently tattooed on his lips. Zach had succeeded in sucking the life right out of him. After what Troy had done—that stupid, selfish, idiotic thing that had cost him his fiancée—Zach still felt bad for how he'd behaved. Because he'd put their real estate business in jeopardy. This morning he couldn't manage to be on time. Not after his dad told him how important this man—Steven—was to him. How crucial this deal would be for their firm.

Zach had drunk one too many bourbons before bed. In his defense, last night was New Year's Eve and he had spent it alone. Logan had invited him to a party, but he'd said no. The thought of not kissing Olivia when the clock struck midnight made him too sad. His mom's subsequent invite to watch the ball drop had only reminded him how pitiful his life was.

Then he'd slept through his alarm.

Par for the course.

Since Olivia broke up with him, Zach had struggled to put one foot in front of the other each day. All he could think about was her. He tried to push her from his thoughts, but she always worked her way in, like the sun that finds the one patch of skin where you didn't apply sunscreen.

She'd moved her things out of his house (their house?), and though he'd purged everything that reminded him of her, down to the two bobby pins he'd found in the back of the bathroom drawer, Olivia was still there.

She was in the stack of Hungry-Man frozen meals in his freezer. Every time he grabbed one for dinner, he remembered how Olivia had pulled open the drawer, wrinkled her nose at them, and said, "Hungry-Man, really? What are you, sixty-five? Do people still eat those?"

"For the record, they absolutely do," Zach had said. He remembered the way he'd picked up the Salisbury steak meal, one of his personal favorites. "When my parents got divorced, my dad would serve them on his weekends. Some of my best memories are sitting on the couch, watching USC football, and eating one of these with my dad."

Olivia's eyes had smiled as she stared at the picture on the front of the box: two steak patties, mashed potatoes, and green beans.

Then she shared a product-of-divorce food story of her own. "My dad used to take me to the hospital with him, give me a wad of dollar bills, and let me raid the vending machines. To this day, I can't *not* stop if I see one. There's something about selecting 8G and then watching that bag of Famous Amos double chocolate chip cookies drop."

"I was always a Snickers man myself."

Olivia's eyes widened. "Three Musketeers are so much better—no one wants the nuts."

Before Zach could tell her how backward her candy bar logic was or make the sexual joke that came to mind, she pushed him up against the freezer and kissed him deeply. "I love you—and if you and your Hungry-Mans are a package deal, then so be it," she'd murmured, and Zach had felt like the luckiest man in the world.

Olivia was also in his Netflix. The shows that appeared were the ones she would watch when she needed a mental break from her law classes. And he couldn't figure out how to tell the damn app he didn't give two fucks that the next season of *Emily in Paris* was out.

And last week, she was in his bedroom. Well not her, but her dress. He'd found her sundress balled up behind the bed when its strap got tangled in the Roomba his mom had insisted on buying for him. He had gotten an alert on his phone that the vacuum was stuck. He knew it was misplaced aggression, but he'd sent his mom an angry text about why he hated the stupid iRobot and was planning to give it to the Goodwill, because what was wrong with a regular upright vacuum cleaner again? He'd gently detangled the strap from the wheels and brought Olivia's sundress to his nose. He inhaled her scent, faint but still there, tears springing to his eyes as he remembered how the dress had ended up behind the bed. It had been the day she moved in. She'd been carrying a small box toward the master bath, and he'd grabbed her. They'd spent most of the day in bed, Olivia feigning disappointment that she couldn't get the medicine cabinet organized.

She also followed him to work. He'd almost broken out in tears on a listing appointment when a prospective client asked him if he was married. Zach had squeaked out a no, then swallowed down a sob and coughed loudly, but it was too late; the client had seen it. The look of pity in her eyes confirmed what he'd found out later—that she'd listed the house with their real estate rival, Kevin Howell.

That one stung and made him think he really should get out of real estate and do what he loved. Olivia would want that for him. So he'd driven up to the Hollywood Hills with his Nikon DSLR and captured the sunset. He'd felt his first stab of happiness since the breakup while in his darkroom, the orange and blue hues appearing on the prints as he soaked the film in the wetting agent. The high wore off too quickly, and he'd spent that evening sipping bourbon and scrolling through old text threads between him and Olivia. He knew if Logan or his other friends saw his messages, they would haze him for life, but he didn't care. She made him want to use the happy-face guy with hearts for eyes.

It would have been so easy to tell her the truth from the beginning. Blame it on his dad being a psycho and say that he'd manipulated Zach into doing his bidding. But he hadn't. He'd taken the path of least resistance, and it had bitten him in the ass. He'd known from the moment Olivia's eyes registered the truth, from the instant she told him it was over, from the second she'd turned on her heel, that he'd been one hundred percent wrong. That her trust in him had been destroyed. And two months later, the question remained: how did he move on from the love of his life?

Clearly, this was not a trait the men in his family were genetically predisposed to perform easily.

Troy whipped around, and Zach registered the relief on his dad's face. There was no irritation, which was surprising. Zach was almost thirty minutes late for a client and had broken the first rule of real estate: ten minutes early was on time. But Troy was smiling. Like, a huge shit-eating grin. Wow. He must really need Zach to seal this deal with his old friend.

"You're here," he said as he gave his son a bear hug. Zach wriggled out of his grasp when it became clear Troy wasn't letting go anytime soon. "This is going to be great," Troy said, and gave Zach a long look. "The opportunity, I mean. It's really going to get you back on track."

Zach felt a sliver of guilt crawl up his spine. "Dad, listen, we need to talk. About my future," he added, when Troy's face was blank.

Zach stepped closer and decided to say it all now before he lost his nerve. "I will help you with this deal today, but I don't want to sell houses anymore. I want to take pictures of them." He handed Troy a folder with some test shots he'd taken at their listing last week, the one with the vaulted ceilings and striking black-and-white marble floors.

"Photography?" Troy asked.

Zach started to say more, but a man with salt-and-pepper hair and a kind face walked up to them. "You must be Zach. I'm Steven Tyler."

"It's a real pleasure," Zach said as he held out his hand. "I'm sorry I was late."

"The pleasure is all mine," Steven said, shaking Zach's hand firmly. "And no problem at all. I only just arrived myself—parade traffic was nuts. And Troy! So good to see you, man. Who do you like for the game today?"

As his dad and Steven talked about the Rose Bowl, Zach exhaled, thankful Steven was giving him a pass and also that he'd interrupted their conversation. It was clear Zach had caught his dad off guard. But once Troy saw the business plan Zach had come up with, he would come around. They could still work together, but in a different way. Zach didn't want to live with regrets. It was now or never to chase his dream. If he couldn't have Olivia, at least he'd love his work.

A small man wearing white from head to toe and sporting a handlebar mustache walked up to them. He was gripping an iPad as if his life depended on it. He looked at Steven. *"You're Steven Tyler, right? With the amusement park float? We have a situation,"* he said, his mouth twisting beneath his stache.

The man rose on his tiptoes and whispered something into Steven's ear. Steven rubbed the back of his neck.

"Is everything okay?" Troy asked.

"One of the cast members for my float didn't show, and he's a key player. We can't do it without him." Steven rubbed his temple. "It's vital this goes perfectly. I need the visibility this parade will give my theme park. It's like the next best thing to a Super Bowl commercial! Otherwise," he said, and tugged at the collar of his button-down shirt, "I'll have to stay put in the Midwest—and maybe sell the park."

Zach felt bad for the guy. "Is there anything I can do to help?" he asked. He could go recruit someone. There were a million people lining the streets; surely some ham who wanted to get on TV would jump at this chance.

Steven's face lit up. "Really? You wouldn't mind?"

Mind what? Zach nodded as his stomach twisted.

Steven looked at the man in all white. "This guy," he said, nodding at Zach, "is going to save the day."

I am?

The man looked Zach up and down, his eyes glittering. "Well, aren't you a hero? Follow me." He walked toward a makeshift tent marked *Dressing Room.* "Let's get you suited up."

Zach followed him into the tent. His heart thundered in his chest as he watched a few dancers stretching. He was not a performer! He had two left feet, zero rhythm. In college, he'd been voted worst dancer in his fraternity. It had been funny then, but now? He also had a fear of public speaking. He'd once thrown up while giving a presentation in high school.

He looked back at his dad, hoping he'd jump in and save Zach. Didn't he remember Zach's disastrous attempt at playing the willow tree in his third-grade play? But Troy wasn't looking Zach's way. His arms were wrapped around Steven—he was giving him the same bear hug Zach had received earlier. *That's odd.* After Troy pulled away from their embrace, he high-fived Steven, then typed furiously into his phone. *Maybe Steven's business does all hinge on this.*

Zach decided he'd suck it up. Save the day. He could do this. He followed the small man to the corner of the tent, where a penguin suit was hanging on a rolling clothes rack.

Fuck.

The man handed Zach the suit and a red terry cloth headband. "It gets pretty toasty under there—especially when you're dancing."

Zach grabbed the headband and dabbed his forehead. He was already sweating.

* * *

At first, Chloe hadn't been sure about this plan to get her sister and Zach back together. It sounded like something out of a movie that would star an over-the-hill Zac Efron. Wouldn't Olivia see right through it? But Olivia had been miserable for the past two months, so Chloe figured, why the hell not? At the very least, it would make an amazing TikTok. One that couldn't be any more depressing than the ones her sister had been posting.

"Can you walk a little faster?" Chloe asked Olivia now as her phone lit up with another text message from Amy. She glanced at it. *Still stuck with Debbie Gibson. Will be there soon!* When Amy had mentioned that Debbie Gibson was the grand marshal and she and June had listened to her music in high school, Chloe had searched her up on Spotify and giggled when she thought of her teenage mom listening to "Lost in Your Eyes."

Chloe gripped Olivia's hand a little harder and tugged. "I feel like I'm pulling you!" she said to her sister, trying to keep the annoyance out of her voice. *I feel like I've been pulling you for two months.* She got that her sister was heartbroken, but it was Olivia who had broken things off and refused to give Zach another chance. Chloe was trying to be patient, but it was getting a little old.

"I don't understand why I have to power walk. Aren't we killing time before the parade?"

"Yes, but it starts soon—I don't want to miss it after everything we've gone through. We slept on the street, V!"

Olivia rubbed her eyes. "I'm aware."

A burly man in a yellow security guard shirt held his arm out as they got closer. Chloe flashed the pass Amy had slipped her a few days ago and tried to shove it back in her pocket before Olivia noticed, but she was too slow.

"What is that?" Olivia asked.

Chloe pretended not to hear her as they continued forward.

"Is that a security pass? How do you have that?" Olivia said again.

The We Ducked Up and Need to Fix It group had prepared Chloe with a cover story.

She took a deep breath. "We aren't just out for a walk—the guy I've been hanging out with gave me a pass. He was working on one of the floats and told me to come say hi. I didn't think you'd join if I told you the truth—you've been so anti-parade."

Olivia looked confused. "You're hanging out with a guy who builds floats? And you didn't think to mention this? Talk about burying the lede!"

"I didn't think you'd want to hear about a guy I like, you know, with everything going on . . ." Chloe trailed off.

Olivia screwed up her face. "I'm sorry. I've been a jerk, haven't I? If you feel like you can't tell me about a guy you like because I'm going through a breakup, then I really suck as a sister."

Chloe deflated. That wasn't how this was supposed to go. She didn't want her sister to feel bad about her not bringing up her imaginary boyfriend.

She put a hand on Olivia's arm. "You've been going through a lot and you get a pass, okay?"

Olivia's eyes watered. "Okay."

Chloe decided to go off script. She hoped the We Ducked Up group would be okay with it. "Maybe I'm not supposed to say this, but I really like Zach. And it's not too late. If you still love him."

Olivia's eyebrows squished together. "Of course I still love him. Those feelings don't disappear. But where would we go from here? Too much has happened." Olivia glanced around as if looking for answers. "I wish I could stop thinking about him, you know? I hate this. I'm wearing those stupid socks I bought him." She lifted up her pant leg to reveal the cat socks.

"Oh, V. It's worse than I thought." Chloe smiled, then added, "Socks in point, maybe you can't stop thinking about him because you're not supposed to stop thinking about him! Because you guys are meant to be. I mean, if you're telling me this guy is going to wear those, then there's a special place in the world where only the two of you would exist."

Olivia considered this. "I don't know how I could trust him again."

Chloe let out a breath. "It's not like he cheated on you. I get it; he lied. But what would you have done if Mom had made the same request to you? If the tables had been turned?"

"I don't know," Olivia said as she started to cry. She wiped her tears with the sleeve of her hoodie. "I never thought about it that way."

"You asked me how you could trust Zach again. Here's how: you just *do*. You decide that one lie *by omission* isn't going to prevent you from being with the *one person* who gets you, girl," she said, her voice rising. "If the weird-socks thing isn't enough, he also doesn't mind that you chew with your mouth open! Now that's true love, if you ask me."

"I don't chew with my mouth open," Olivia insisted.

But she did. Not all the time, but enough that it made Chloe's blood pressure rise whenever someone offered her sister a piece of gum. One day she'd watched Zach as Olivia smacked the shit out of a piece of Trident. He'd smiled at her like a puppy dog, and then he'd leaned over and kissed her on the cheek. It was at that moment that Chloe knew—he would love her sister the way she deserved.

"Clearly, you two are soul mates."

Olivia guffawed. "You're crazy," she said, but Chloe could see the wheels turning in her head.

They finally reached the Adventureland float. Men and women in white suits were running around, adding last-minute fresh flowers. Chloe flinched when she heard a woman cry out as she was burned by her hot-glue gun.

Amy peeked out from a wall of hydrangeas, tapped her watch, and held up her hand to show five minutes. Chloe acknowledged her with a smile. As if on cue, a man who must be Steven appeared, looking stressed.

"Excuse me," he said. "By any chance, are you here to work on the float?"

"No," Chloe replied. "We're looking for someone." She glanced around for her imaginary boyfriend, spotting a tall, good-looking man with a sleeve of tattoos. She'd pretend it was him.

Steven frowned. "I'm Steven. And I have a huge problem. I own Adventureland. This," he said, pointing to the enormous float behind them, "is mine. It's our first time in the Rose Parade. Can you believe it?"

Chloe blinked hard, impressed. This guy was laying it on thick.

"An actor didn't show up. Would either of you mind putting on a lion suit and jumping on the float to help? You're both the right size for the costume." He sounded desperate. Chloe wanted to applaud his performance.

"I'll pass," Olivia said immediately.

"You'd be on TV," Steven added, to sweeten the deal. "What a story this would be! Plus I'll give you a free lifetime pass to the park."

Olivia wrinkled her nose, then caught Steven's disappointed look. "I'm sorry, I would, but I'm not in a good mood. I wouldn't be much help to you. Chloe will do it, won't you?"

Chloe bounced on her toes, prepared for this. The We Ducked Up and Have to Fix It team had accurately predicted this response. It had been June who'd advised Chloe which angle to take. "Olivia," she began, "This should really be you, not me. Remember when we were kids and we'd sit in front of the TV in our beach chairs and rate the floats? How you wanted to ride on one?"

Olivia looked past Chloe to the float, remembering.

"Now's your chance!" Chloe urged. "It's been a shitty couple of months," she said, looking at Steven before adding, "Bad breakup," for context. He bobbed his head in understanding. "Why not start the year by checking off an item on your bucket list?"

Olivia glanced at the float, then her sister. Steven and Chloe locked eyes. If this didn't work, there was no plan B. It would be too late in the game to text *quack* to the group. They'd be shit out of duck.

Chloe wondered if she could physically force Olivia onto the float. She didn't want it to come to that.

"Okay," Olivia finally said, and Chloe started jumping up and down. Steven joined in. Olivia looked surprised at their excitement, so they quickly reeled it back in. Chloe gave Amy, who was still hiding behind the plant, a stealth thumbs-up. Amy held her hands toward the sky as Steven whisked Olivia to the tent.

A few minutes later, Chloe waved at her sister in the lion costume as the large float with a roller coaster track made out of flowers began to inch toward the starting line. In the very back, she spied a lonely-looking penguin, and her heart flip-flopped. One day she hoped to find someone who fit her as well as Zach fit Olivia. "Olivia, please don't screw this up," she said to herself, before walking back to watch the parade with her mom.

CHAPTER TWENTY-SIX

It was a thousand degrees inside the penguin suit, and sweat poured down Zach's face. For the record, the headband was *not helping*. He had a newfound appreciation for the costumed characters at Disneyland who worked the summers posing for pictures on the unyielding blacktop.

He half-heartedly waved to the crowd lining Colorado Boulevard as the float traveled 2.5 miles per hour down the street. He overheard the driver—wearing only swim trunks—give this stat to a reporter as he wedged himself into the tiny airless opening below the float where he would steer the contraption. He said the float weighed forty thousand pounds and couldn't travel any faster, as it was like a semitruck, unable to stop on a dime. So the drive would take at least two hours but as many as *five* to reach the end.

"How do you see out?" the reporter asked.

"Oh, I can't!" the driver bellowed, only his head visible as he descended into his cave. "I have a guy who is my eyes. Tells me where to turn, when to slow, when to speed up. Call me crazy, but this is my fifth year driving, and every time it's a miracle we make it out alive without crashing. Knock on wood!" The driver pounded his fist on the float before disappearing completely below.

The reporter's face turned sheet white, and Zach's stomach twisted. *This better be worth it.*

Zach scanned the crowd now, which seemed to be filled with one cuddling couple after another, which only made him more depressed. He should be down there with his arm wrapped around Olivia, keeping her warm while the sun made its way from behind the clouds. Or better yet, he should be in bed with her while he nursed a slight hangover from all the New Year's fun they'd had the night before. That had been the plan.

Before they broke up, he'd booked an Airbnb in Mammoth. He'd read an article about the incredibly clear mountain sky, and it sounded romantic. He loved the idea of the two of them sitting in the eight-person hot tub under the stars drinking the prosecco she loved (and he was learning to appreciate) while he pointed out Ursa Major and Minor. One of his secret talents—being able to name over twenty five constellations.

For the first time ever, Zach had wanted to get away from the pretentious crowds on New Year's Eve. In the past, he'd deliberately sought the biggest end-of-the-year party in the Hollywood Hills, wanting nothing more than to get lost in a sea of women in little black dresses and men in designer suits that fit like a second skin.

This year was going to be different because Olivia had been the one person who made him feel like a favorite jacket retrieved from that cardboard bin at the end of the school year.

Found.

Zach was staring into space when he heard a young voice scream, "Dance, penguin! Dance!"

He surveyed the crowd and followed the sound to a little boy with wild red hair splaying out from under a striped hat. He was perched on the shoulders of a tall man with a flaming beard that matched the boy's moppy curls. Must be a father and son.

Zach pointed to the child and did a quick jig, and the boy's face brightened. His goofy grin ignited a spark in Zach, and his heart sped up like a race car. Zach had been sleepwalking through his life. And this little boy with his striped hat and striking overbite had cut through his numbness and found his nerve endings, making him feel something again.

Emboldened by the boy, Zach forgot his stage fright and started to dance like no one was watching. (Not realizing 1.5 million were in the audience and another 16 million were watching on TV). A woman with a baby strapped to her chest simultaneously held up her toddler, who yelled, "More, more, more!" Zach was impressed by this Sherpa mother and jumped, kicked his legs out, and mimicked playing air guitar. The child applauded. He felt wanted, and he had to admit, *it was intoxicating.*

Zach found himself in a sixth gear usually reserved for dance parties after multiple whiskeys. He recalled a retro MTV music awards show and performed "Vogue" as if he were Madonna herself. He watered the hell out of the sprinkler, then topped it off with an awkward moonwalk that was much harder than he anticipated, because penguin feet. The crowd didn't seem to notice. The cheering was so loud he might as well have been Michael Jackson. When the float paused again, he was ready with the running man, which he felt was an oldie but goodie.

He followed up with a classic, the Carlton, and was rewarded by screams from several women his mom's age. But it was the children for whom he was performing, fueled by and addicted to their delight. Their innocence.

The morning sun's heat finally arrived, and his body was soaked with sweat beneath the costume. But he didn't mind, because seeing these cuddling couples and families had inspired him—as soon as he got off this float and took a shower, he was going to find Olivia and get her back.

He was not taking no for an answer.

Maybe he'd bring the penguin costume.

If he had to, he'd dance a thousand Carltons, run a hundred running mans, moonwalk a million miles if it meant he could spend the rest of his life with her. A toddler wearing a parka over her princess gown gave Zach a thumbs-up, and it felt like a sign. He saluted her and took a stab at the electric slide.

* * *

"We need you over there *by him*," a woman with black-rimmed eyeglasses and a headset hollered to Olivia from behind the wheel of one of the makeshift roller coaster cars. Olivia still couldn't figure out how they made the tires from dyed roses. The woman pointed to a penguin performing a really jacked-up version of the sprinkler. At least she thought it was the sprinkler. Could it be the snake? "That penguin is a hit!" she added, sounding surprised. "But enough with his solo show, he needs a partner."

"But does he really?" Olivia questioned. Because she wasn't sure the penguin wanted to share the spotlight. Was being a costume character his career? She studied the mangled fur on the chest of her lion ensemble. This thing had clearly been worn more times than she wanted to think about.

The penguin was now pretending to lasso something. Did he do this at children's birthday parties? He was a natural with the under-ten demographic, although she might have suggested some updated dance moves, not the ones from her parents' generation.

Olivia wondered if her mom or dad had ever jumped on a dance floor with a crowd doing the Chicken Dance. The thought made her smile.

She'd treated June terribly. She'd heard her mom's tearful speech through her bedroom door and wanted to open it so badly. But she couldn't. She was too hurt and needed to sort through who she was truly mad at. For a while she'd blamed her mom for losing Zach. If her mom hadn't known Troy, then Troy wouldn't have wanted to track her down. Then, if her mom hadn't almost kissed Troy, he wouldn't have told the secret of how Zach and Olivia *really* met. For weeks Olivia had shifted the blame from one person to the next, never quite sure who to convict. She finally had to face it: things hadn't worked out because of the two people Olivia hadn't wanted to think about. Olivia and Zach. They'd broken up because of their own choices. They had no one to point the finger at but themselves.

"Go on! He's starting to beatbox!" The woman shooed her. "We don't have all day!"

Don't we have, like, four hours? Olivia begrudgingly made her way to the boogying penguin and stood awkwardly next to his rounded white belly. She bent her knees gently to the beat of "Please Don't Stop the Music" and convinced herself it passed for dancing.

She felt a tap on her shoulder. It was the penguin, who shook his enormous head at her pathetic knee bends. He bowed his bill and offered his wing to her. The crowd cheered, and Olivia discovered a smile on her lips. She wrapped her paw around the penguin's flipper. He shuffled his webbed feet, and she shook her hind legs. She grabbed her tail and swung. He turned around and twerked. They were like "Da Club" meets fourth-grade square dance class. She started to laugh. Which made her want to cry, because she hadn't heard that sound come from her own mouth in . . . she didn't know how long. This penguin sure knew how to have a good time.

She tried not to think about how Zach would have loved this story. How much she would have enjoyed telling it. He'd pepper her with questions, inserting jokes in all the right places. Probably align with the penguin in his dance move choices.

Olivia remembered Chloe's earlier words: that the only requirement for forgiveness was the willingness to forgive. She understood the only person standing in the way of her happiness was herself. Maybe she was willing to let the waves erase the line she'd drawn in the sand.

Olivia thought about her mom again. The anger June had held like a death grip for so long. The stubbornness that had kept her from being able to forgive Amy and Troy. Olivia had seen the way June's eyes bored into theirs at brunch, like she wanted to hug them and slap them at the same time. Maybe June's journey was supposed to take two and a half decades. Maybe she hadn't been ready for Troy until now.

Olivia knew her mom had been talking to Troy a lot. Since she'd been at home again, she'd heard her mom say his name and listened to her laughter through the walls. It was a different laugh than she had with Fiona, or really anyone else. It was a flirtatious laugh—a laugh that held hope and excitement. A laugh like Olivia had with Zach.

Olivia had been pissed at first that her mom was talking to Troy. It felt like a betrayal. But she also admired her mom's ability to forgive, something she hadn't yet found the courage to do. All she knew was she didn't want to wait two decades before she got the chance with Zach again. As Olivia hip checked the penguin to "This Is How We Do It," she realized that she didn't want to cut people out of her life who were legitimately sorry. Who had made mistakes and learned from them. She didn't want to wait twenty-six years to realize she could have been more forgiving back when. And as soon as she said good-bye to the penguin and his fly ass moves, the first thing she'd do was call Zach.

She hoped it wasn't too late.

As the float slowed to a stop near Green Street, she and the penguin had really hit their groove. Their moves had become more coordinated, and it was clear they were a crowd favorite. The woman with the headset called out that they were trending on Twitter: #lionandpenguinohmy. And there were already over a million views of a TikTok that two kindergarteners had made impersonating them. Olivia couldn't wait to tell Chloe.

The woman motioned for Olivia and the penguin to remove the heads of their costumes so she could take a photo for Instagram. The penguin shrugged at Olivia. Or she thought he shrugged. It was hard to tell. Then he pulled at his yellow beak.

Olivia blinked several times, trying to make sense of what she was seeing. Zach? Zach was the penguin? She didn't understand. He was sweaty and looked slightly thinner, but it was him in that bird costume. She ripped off her lion head. They stared at each other.

"Zach?" Olivia said, as his name caught in her throat. Had she somehow manifested him? "How did you know—"

"I didn't," he said, wiping sweat off his forehead with the back of his flipper. He looked past Olivia with a knowing smile.

"But I think I know who did." He gently tugged her paw and rotated her to face the crowd. Through her lion fur, his touch made Olivia's stomach release a thousand butterflies.

She spotted her mom, Chloe, Troy, Amy, and Eileen standing together, their arms linked like a sports team. They looked satisfied. And hopeful. And a little bit scared. Olivia was all those things too. She made eye contact with each of them. She locked eyes with Troy the longest. She handed him a broad smile, before she turned back to face Zach.

"I'm sorry," he blurted. "I never should have—"

"I know," Olivia said, placing her finger on his lips. Those full, beautiful lips. God how she'd missed them. "You shouldn't have. But you did, and I lost my shit. And then I was stubborn and angry and so mad. But at the core, I was miserable without you. I realized that isn't the life I want. I want you. I want us. We make a good team—dancers or otherwise." She laughed. "So what do you say?" She took a step closer, their bulging bellies bumping. Her heart was bouncing around in her chest. She looked down and studied the black fingernails on her paw. "Should we give it another chance? That is, unless you have plans to go on a kiddie birthday tour to satisfy all your new fans?"

She felt like that girl on the boat in Positano. Scared she'd said too much, but hoping it was exactly the right amount.

Zach stared at her for what felt like forever. Finally, he spoke. "I think this penguin is ready to retire. Plus, I'm pretty sure I threw out my back on Green Street."

Tears welled up behind Olivia's eyelids.

"You're the only fan I need anyway," he said, cupping Olivia's chin and bringing his lips to hers as the masses below screamed their approval. Olivia thought she heard a cowbell?

An air horn? Someone yelled, "Get a room," and Olivia couldn't have agreed more. They really should.

As Zach kissed her, she felt herself melting into him, the reconnection of their shared synapses shooting off like fireworks. It was as if his kiss was performing CPR on her soul, bringing it back to life after being dormant since the engagement party. She was his and he was hers. The way it was meant to be.

CHAPTER TWENTY-SEVEN

February 14

June wiped her eyes as she watched Olivia carefully place the veil on her head. "You look beautiful," she said, sniffling as she helped pin it to her hair.

Thank God for waterproof mascara.

"Zach is a lucky man."

Olivia's eyes danced. She smoothed the front of her wedding dress and studied her reflection in the full-length mirror. "I think I'm the lucky one."

"I never thought these words would come out of my mouth, but you're both pretty lucky that Troy leaned into his stalker side." There was a beat when Olivia didn't respond, so June added, "Too soon?" and wondered if her joke had fallen flat—if it had, in fact, been too soon. But then the first giggle from Olivia came, and they laughed so hard their eyes watered.

"Mom! Stop! I'm going to ruin my makeup!"

June would walk into that ceremony with foundation rivers running down her face if it meant they had *this* again. That she and Olivia had arrived at a place where the past really was in the past.

June's limbs felt light. The week after the parade, while changing the display in her bookstore window, she'd come across that book again—the one with the smug blonde doctor on the cover: *New Year, New You! How to Forget the Past So You Can Have a Future.* She'd opened it to the first page, predicting it would be silly—that she'd read one word and toss it in the bargain book bin. But she read it from cover to cover while sitting in one of the beanbags in the children's book section. Chloe had peered at her from behind the counter but knew better than to say one single word.

Olivia was texting someone. June wondered if it was Zach—if they were sending each other their last thoughts before walking down the aisle. June swirled with pride at the woman her daughter had become. Olivia was stronger and more self-assured. June could hear it in how she used her voice now, no longer afraid to speak up about what she wanted. Yesterday, Olivia had told Fiona that she did *not* want to toss the bouquet of gerbera daisies Fiona had crafted for her—that it was *a boomer thing.* Fiona and June had traded a smile.

June was confident that Olivia was making the right choice in marrying Zach. June was very fond of him—he had the whole *make your mother-in-law feel good* thing down pat. He'd been coming by the bookstore on Monday mornings, when June lugged the heavy boxes out from storage to the new-release section. Zach did it for her now. He'd also taken pictures for the bookstore's new website and—June couldn't believe she'd agreed to it—TikTok account. This had also won over Chloe, who had screamed that June had finally come out of the Dark Ages. Troy had been in the bookstore that day and had jumped on the bandwagon. "When we Google June Abbott," he said, "we'll be able to find her now—she won't be buried under some CEO!"

As June got to know Zach better, it was uncanny how much of his dad she could see in him. Zach's positive outlook, his strong work ethic. The way he clearly wanted to please Olivia. Earlier, June had swallowed her tears when Olivia peeled back the delicate paper of Zach's wedding gift to her—a signed first edition of *Summer Sisters* by Judy Blume, her all-time favorite. Olivia had pressed it to her heart and closed her eyes. "It's perfect," she whispered.

This morning, Olivia had excitedly sent Zach's gift—custom socks with her face on them. And a cat June had never seen, but apparently his name was Bart? Olivia has assured June that Zach would love them and wouldn't mind that they were *gently used*.

June felt an arm loop through hers and looked over. It was her mom. She leaned into Eileen as they watched Olivia give herself another once-over before the ceremony started. Olivia tugged at the veil and met June's eyes in the mirror.

Olivia's veil had been made using material from Eileen's wedding gown. June touched the fabric pinned inside her dress, next to her heart, also from her mom's gown. She glanced at Chloe, who had walked into the room carrying Olivia's pristine white high-tops, which she would be wearing with her dress. Chloe's headband was also made from her grandmother's gown.

Eileen had insisted they each have a swatch. For herself, she'd had a flower made that she was wearing as a brooch. "It will reconnect us," Eileen had insisted, giving June's hand a small squeeze when she told the women. Her mom's gesture had felt apropos—*out with the old and in with the new*. And June was more than ready for this new chapter with Eileen. June had caught Amy's eye as her mom handed them each a piece of her gown at the rehearsal dinner, and she'd flashed her friend a smile that she hoped carried the weight of the thank-you that was in her heart.

* * *

Chloe adjusted her headband as she looked at her family. Today, hers would expand. She was gaining a brother! She was still getting used to the idea that she had to share her sister. It had always been the two of them. But as she watched Olivia, a nervous smile lifted the corners of her lips as she clutched her bouquet and prepared to walk down the aisle, Chloe knew Zach was the right man to join their orbit. Plus it was fun having an internet-famous couple in the family. After the parade, Olivia and Zach had been interviewed by several morning talk shows about their lion-and-penguin dance going viral online. No one could get enough of the crazy family story that went along with it. Chloe had gotten T-shirts made for everyone to wear at their joint bachelor and bachelorette party, with a picture on the front of Zach and Olivia in their costumes and a caption that read, *We'd be LION if we said we weren't FLIPPIN meant for each other.*

Chloe looked out the window of the bridal suite and spied her date, Conner, in the backyard, chatting up Fiona, who was finishing covering the aisle in rose petals. Conner was still as handsome as when she'd spotted him at the Rose Parade and decided he was the imaginary boyfriend she'd been looking for. Strangely, it had been him who'd called after her as she headed back to watch the parade; later he'd told her he hadn't really needed directions to the nearest restroom. He was sweet and she adored him, but she wasn't in any rush to get serious. But as she grabbed the train of Olivia's gown, she couldn't help but imagine where life might take them.

*   *   *

In the next room, Troy adjusted Zach's tie, and Amy felt a burst of love for the two men who had shaped her life. She smoothed her emerald dress. (June had opted for a marigold stunner and insisted Amy wear the green. That it really was her color.) She wondered what June was thinking as she helped Olivia get ready to become a wife. For Amy, it felt surreal to send her son off to be someone else's person. And not anyone's person. *June's daughter's.*

Earlier, she'd asked Zach if they could take a walk on the beach. She wanted to acknowledge that she knew he belonged to someone else now, and although it would be hard to let go of him, she could see how happy he was with Olivia. "It's time for me to cut the cord," she'd joked, "again," and teared up.

Zach had said, "Second time's a charm," and hugged her hard. They'd stood there, the only sound the waves lapping at the sand. As two birds flew overhead, their bodies circling each other, Amy decided this had all been worth it, because it meant she had gained Olivia as a daughter. And reclaimed June as a friend.

But *friend* was a label she and June had agreed they needed to earn. They'd shared a bottle of champagne the other night as they finalized the seating chart and mused that their newfound relationship would be like a marriage—for it to succeed, they would have to put in the work. The first time around, they'd blown it. But Amy and June 2.0 had decided they were more than ready for this challenge. They'd made it their goal to share their fiftieth birthdays together next year, like they'd planned to do when they were in college. June also shared that she and her mom had found a fresh start as well. That she'd been surprised by how soft her mom was with her when they'd talked at the Rose Parade. How open she'd been to fixing their relationship. Amy smiled to herself, hoping that what she'd said to Eileen had made the tiniest impact on that. It made her happy to know she'd done something to help June.

They were a little drunk when Troy's name came up.

"I wanted to ask you something," June said, chewing her lower lip. "I'd like your blessing. To see where things go with Troy."

"My blessing?" Amy nearly choked on her Vueve Clicquot.

"I wouldn't feel right if you weren't okay with it. He's the father of your son. He's—"

"Yours. You can have him, anti-snoring chin strap and all!" Amy laughed.

June's mouth had fallen open. "No, don't tell me that!" Then she thought for a moment. "I want you to know that it's you and me, all the way. I lost sight of that last time. And I won't do that again."

Amy grabbed June's hand. "I won't let you."

* * *

Olivia slid her arm through William's as he forced himself to step forward down the aisle of rose petals that were splayed in a neat path across Eileen's backyard. It was harder to give Olivia away than he'd thought. Now he understood why they called it that. It did feel as if he was about to hand off the most important person in his life. He fought off the lump in his throat as Zach stepped forward and shook his hand, his eyes shining at the beauty of his soon-to-be wife.

William felt a lightness in his chest. After spending more time with Zach after the Rose Parade—playing several rounds of golf with Zach where he was able to properly vet his future son-in-law—he was genuinely happy to welcome him into the family.

* * *

The officiant welcomed everyone to the wedding of Olivia Abbott and Zach Carter. Troy nodded in understanding at Zach's best man, Logan, who was already dabbing his wet eyes. Troy's were full of tears too. He had a pocketful of tissues ready because he knew he was going to lose it.

Troy watched the photographer crouching down to get the best angles of Olivia and Zach and thought of Zach's major career change—from selling real estate to photographing it. But Troy had to admit, Zach had talent. To be supportive, he'd hired him to take pictures on a few listings and had been shocked at the way Zach had found the essence of the houses with his lens. The angles and perspectives he captured in the homes made them seem almost if they were alive. The response to both listing ads had been tremendous, and the clients had been thrilled.

Troy told himself that he and Zach were still partners, in a way. But now Zach was free to live his life without regrets. And as Troy knew all too well, regret would eventually topple your life if you gave it too much oxygen.

Troy turned his attention to June as Zach and Olivia said their vows. She was crying freely, and Troy thought that she'd never looked more beautiful. Troy knew he'd been far from a perfect man. But he made his own silent vow to be everything that June deserved, if she'd have him.

ACKNOWLEDGMENTS

In the summer of 2020, we hit an all-time career low. After wallowing in an extensive pity party, we finally decided to share the rejection we'd experienced. To those of you who listened to our podcast, We Fight So You Don't Have To, reached out to us on social media, sent us texts, emailed, and called, thank you. Thank you for listening. For supporting. For connecting. We would not be here right now without you.

How do we properly thank the person who embraced us with open arms while our career was careening into the ditch? Our agent Holly Root believed in our talent. She championed this novel. She never gave up on us even when we seriously considered giving up on ourselves. (We would ask her: *Is this it? Are we over?*)

We inquired recently why she decided to represent us, and she said we were a puzzle she wanted to solve. She knew it wasn't going to be easy and that's what she liked about it. How badass is that? Thank you, Holly, for your patience as we struggled to find our voice and for your unwavering belief in this book. In us.

Elisabeth Weed, we will forever be grateful to you for your graciousness in connecting us with Holly. You said she was the perfect agent for us, and you were right.

Speaking of Hollys who gave us another shot, thank you to our editor Holly Ingraham. Your thoughtful notes and insight made this novel what it is today.

Huge props to publisher Matt Martz and the entire Alcove team. Madeline Rathle and Dulce Botello in marketing and publicity and Rebecca Nelson in production. To our copyeditor Rachel Keith, thank you for shielding us from so many bad grammar choices! And to cover designer Heather VenHuizen, you nailed it.

Tiffany Yates Martin, there are no stronger or better words to use here than *thank you*. You know why.

To Julie Slavinsky at Warwick's, yet another person who continued to believe in us when she didn't have to. When she could have focused on much bigger and more successful authors. Thank you!

So much gratitude to Reese Dannenfeldt for helping us get inside the minds of twenty-year-olds!

Much adoration to our many author friends who had endless shit-talking sessions with us when the future looked pretty darn bleak. We love you! This novel is dedicated to you, and every author out there. Lifting each other up is the only way we'll succeed.

Huge thanks to Marisa Gothie and Nichole Thery-Williams for loving this novel so much that you wrote the book club questions for it! We heart you both.

To our readers who kept asking when the next book was coming and patiently accepted our super vague responses— thank you. YOU are the reason *Forever Hold Your Peace* exists.

And last but never least: Mike and Matt. It's been one hell of a roller coaster ride these past few years. Thanks for buckling in.

Dear Reader,

I knew *Forever Hold Your Peace* would be the perfect book club read, and I offered to write the questions along with my friend Nicholle. I was thrilled when Liz and Lisa agreed.

I am a true believer in a book finding you at the right time. When I was able to read *Forever Hold Your Peace*, I needed a book that would make me fall in love, smile, and believe in second chances. This book did all three. I read it and laughed at the quirks of the characters, rooted for Zach and Olivia, hoped for a reconciliation between Amy and June, and swooned at the new book boyfriend I found in Troy. *Forever Hold Your Peace* explores so many different concepts that affect all of us: friendships, forgiveness, first loves, family. These are characters you will root for and with whom you will want to form your own relationships.

Nicholle and I had the opportunity and privilege of meeting Liz and Lisa in 2017 at our first book expo. Both ladies were friendly, sweet, and incredibly funny. We walked away from the meeting knowing that we wanted our friendship to be like theirs—something that could withstand anything. Since then we have both read all their books and listened to their podcast. Their friendship with each other and the way they interact with their readers is nothing short of amazing. All their novels show the depths of friendship and how it can change you. In *Forever Hold Your Peace*, the personalities of the authors came through and made the novel feel so real.

Forever Hold Your Peace is a novel that allows you to escape and become completely immersed in the hilarity, drama, and passion these characters go through. It is the perfect beach read, and I will be recommending it to everyone this summer.

—Marisa Gothie
Bookends and Friends Book Club
IG: @marisagbooks
FB: Authors are our Rock Stars

QUESTIONS

- The title *Forever Hold Your Peace* can be interpreted in many ways. For example, it is the phrase mentioned at weddings, the characters have secrets that they have held, and a peace has been garnered between June and Amy. Discuss the title.
- The novel explores different types of relationships and how they shape the characters. What did you think of the mother-son relationship between Amy and Zach? What about the father-son dynamic between Troy and Zach?
- *Forever Hold Your Peace* is a multigenerational novel and explores the dynamic between mothers and daughters. How did Eileen and June's relationship affect the way June interacted with Olivia? How did their relationship influence other decisions June made or reactions she had?
- Troy places a lot of pressure on Zach to follow in his career path. Zach has a dream of being a photographer but keeps it secret. How do you think the secrets of Troy's past influence his need to have Zach be like him? How are the secrets the men have reflected in each other? What do you think

about the final agreement they made to blend these two needs?

- There's more to the story of how Zach and Olivia came to be in Positano at the same time. Do you think that Zach should have been honest with Olivia about how they met and who helped facilitate their meeting? Would you have had the same reaction as Olivia when you found out the truth?

- Amy and June had a very close friendship and then a falling-out. Have you ever experienced this type of friendship? Would you have forgiven Amy?

- June owns a bookstore. Would you want to own your own bookstore? If so, what would the name be? Would you have a theme?

- Olivia and Zach both are excited about getting married, but June and Amy use the opportunity to plan the wedding to keep their feud going. How do you feel about the planning? Should Olivia have stood up for herself more? Have you ever been involved in wedding planning and met a "bridezilla"? Of the two weddings, which do you think fit the characters' personality more?

- June and Troy go on a quest to find a "quirky" gift—the toy sharks. Have you ever been forced or enticed to search for a specific item? What was it?

- Do you believe in love at first sight?

- Do you believe in second chances?

- How did the scheme to reunite Zach and Olivia show the personalities of the other characters?

- Do you have any traditions on New Year's, like watching the Rose Parade? Have you ever seen the Rose Parade? Have you ever slept outside for an event or to get tickets for something?

- If the authors were to expand on these characters, would you want to read a prequel about Amy-June-Troy? Would you want to read a sequel to find out what happened to the characters?
- If this novel was made into a movie or a TV show, who would you cast? What songs would you include in the soundtrack?